WEAPONIZED EBOLA

Steel cylinders, six feet in length, four around, the Angels of Islam were, essentially, small drones, much like the CIA's Predator. With rocket fuel to launch them, either from an apartment rooftop or a neighborhood ballpark, the terrorists meant to send them soaring over American cities, cutting loose an airborne contagion in aerosol form—Ebola—bioengineered, four to five times more lethal than even Ebola Zaire, which was already proved in case histories as fatal nine times out of ten.

No cure. No hope. No chance.

According to what Hal Brognola had learned, once this strain of Ebola rained over a major population center, the virus required no incubation period. It could sweep around the entire planet in six weeks.

Armageddon. The end of humankind.

Other titles in this series:

STONY MAN II
STONY MAN III
STONY MAN IV
STONY MAN V
STONY MAN VI
STONY MAN VII
STONY MAN VIII
#9 STRIKEPOINT
#10 SECRET ARSENAL
#11 TARGET AMERICA
#12 BLIND EAGLE
#13 WARHEAD
#14 DEADLY AGENT
#15 BLOOD DEBT
#16 DEEP ALERT
#17 VORTEX
#18 STINGER
#19 NUCLEAR NIGHTMARE
#20 TERMS OF SURVIVAL
#21 SATAN'S THRUST
#22 SUNFLASH
#23 THE PERISHING GAME
#24 BIRD OF PREY
#25 SKYLANCE
#26 FLASHBACK
#27 ASIAN STORM
#28 BLOOD STAR
#29 EYE OF THE RUBY
#30 VIRTUAL PERIL
#31 NIGHT OF THE JAGUAR
#32 LAW OF LAST RESORT
#33 PUNITIVE MEASURES
#34 REPRISAL
#35 MESSAGE TO AMERICA
#36 STRANGLEHOLD
#37 TRIPLE STRIKE
#38 ENEMY WITHIN
#39 BREACH OF TRUST
#40 BETRAYAL
#41 SILENT INVADER
#42 EDGE OF NIGHT
#43 ZERO HOUR
#44 THIRST FOR POWER
#45 STAR VENTURE
#46 HOSTILE INSTINCT
#47 COMMAND FORCE
#48 CONFLICT IMPERATIVE
#49 DRAGON FIRE
#50 JUDGMENT IN BLOOD
#51 DOOMSDAY DIRECTIVE
#52 TACTICAL RESPONSE
#53 COUNTDOWN TO TERROR
#54 VECTOR THREE
#55 EXTREME MEASURES
#56 STATE OF AGGRESSION
#57 SKY KILLERS
#58 CONDITION HOSTILE
#59 PRELUDE TO WAR
#60 DEFENSIVE ACTION
#61 ROGUE STATE
#62 DEEP RAMPAGE
#63 FREEDOM WATCH
#64 ROOTS OF TERROR
#65 THE THIRD PROTOCOL
#66 AXIS OF CONFLICT

DON PENDLETON'S

STONY

AMERICA'S ULTRA-COVERT INTELLIGENCE AGENCY

MAN®

ECHOES OF WAR

the TERROR file Book 2

A GOLD EAGLE BOOK FROM
WORLDWIDE®

TORONTO • NEW YORK • LONDON
AMSTERDAM • PARIS • SYDNEY • HAMBURG
STOCKHOLM • ATHENS • TOKYO • MILAN
MADRID • WARSAW • BUDAPEST • AUCKLAND

First edition October 2003

ISBN 0-373-61951-0

ECHOES OF WAR

Special thanks and acknowledgment to
Dan Schmidt for his contribution to this work.

Printed in U.S.A.

ECHOES OF WAR

CHAPTER ONE

Captain Ruiz Ortega of the *federales* was sorely tempted to speak his mind on race, religion and politics as he mentally reviewed some of the uglier bigoted, jingoistic spews of vitriolic poison he'd heard from both sides of his so-called guests. They considered his country a bleeding ulcer of crime and corruption, for one thing, forever spilling out more mixed-blood peasant savages lorded over by obscenely wealthy pigs who were little more than godless blights on the world as they wallowed in the droppings of their ill-gotten gains. They talked about his countrymen as pagans who claimed to believe in the God of Roman Catholicism, but their ignorance found them paying lip service to a deity while fleeing across the border in hope, which was really envy of the heathens they craved to be like, clamoring for all the pleasures and trappings of the hell-bound to the north. They…

Well, that was some of the kinder and gentler talk he'd caught when wandering into one of their meetings or overhearing one of their phone conversations, the foreigners always speaking in English as if he were the invisible uniform of authority, or meant to be a silent, seething audience of one lackey.

Weighing the moment, he decided it was perhaps too much tequila blabbing back at him. The words of other foolish men were merely stinging pride at the moment, when he knew he should focus all of his energy on potential action, the trouble, in flesh and blood, that was out there in the night, circling, coming on. He told himself to let it be, chalking up their ignorance and contempt of his culture to pure arrogance, misguided machismo, while he waited for the other half of the foreign visitors to make their appearance at this bloodsuckers' hour. Considering the volatile and lethal devil's brew of foreign nationals about to gather under the roof of Cantina Zapulcha, coupled with the fact he had a roaring tequila buzz in his skull, along with the deadly seriousness of this rendezvous, he thought it best to skip hurling his own incendiary opinions out in the open, at least for now.

Maybe later.

If, that was, the meeting between the Arab terrorists and the North Korean special forces operatives didn't erupt into some shoot-out that might put the entire town—an outlaw haven of narco-traffickers, bandidos, killers, rapists and other sordid assortment of *contrabandistas* and brigands—on the map, thereby finding the entire Mexican army swarming the place to either join in the killing spree or clean up the mess while taking the usual bribe to see no evil.

Only one of several problems, since there was, he knew, the not so small matter of an informant—recently found out as a DEA pigeon as his call to some yankee cutout had been monitored—out there, en route, even as he drank and waited for the show here to begin, to meet with gringo operatives in the desert. For that unforeseen matter he had just hired on the spot and marched out a team of local cutthroats to eliminate that particular headache before it blew up into a migraine no amount of tequila could quash. If this so-named El Condor, however, was in fact racing to meet with DEA agents...

Unfortunately, to say the least, the night wasn't shaping up the way he had envisioned, smooth sailing, all parties mollified, back to business as usual.

Not good. None of it.

He let any thoughts of gloom and doom and unnecessary expenditures of payoffs slip away for the moment, content to stand at the bar and pour another three or four fingers of tequila. He squeezed a fat slab of lime over what he considered his magic elixir, the salve on wounded pride, his bolster for courage in the event he needed to pull his 9 mm Browning pistol, join his platoon of soldiers, all of them brandishing gringo assault rifles. To a man they were braced to dive into any firefight that would surely become a free-for-all, if only in the sheer interests of survival.

Arabs, he snorted to himself.

There were eleven of them to his deep two o'clock; forged passports and visas declaring they were Spanish nationals—as in Spain—but Ortega knew better, since he'd played no small hand in dealing out the bogus credentials for this new breed of wanna-be conquistadors. They were terrorists, plain and simple, a hodgepodge conglomerate of Kuwaitis, Saudis, Iranians, Yemenis, all of whom, swarthy and dark haired, could have easily passed for Latino, which, he knew, was part of the ruse.

Infiltration. Disguise.

They had been smuggled into Mexico by some French gangster's freighter out of Marseilles. They had come ashore on the coast of Vera Cruz, part of a plan long since hammered out by a major drug cartel that owned anything and anybody in the country worth owning, the terrorists doling out great sums of money like twenty-first-century conquerors to build the foundation for some grand scheme of jihad. That they were bent on rolling their juggernaut of murder and mayhem north of the border made it palatable, like the bittersweet taste of tequila burning down his throat. As long as their intention was to kill entire unsuspecting masses of gringos, that was fine—no, in truth, he corrected himself, that was about as good as it could get.

And there it was, he thought. His own hatred of gringos had equalled, perhaps nearly surpassed, his love of their terror money. There were, however, he considered, certain glaring differences between the gringos and these Muslim fanatics and the inscrutable Asians.

Arrogance, for one, at least in terms of its source, its seething belief in its own volition ready to become action that would launch them to victory and glory.

The gringos came down here in their Learjets or crossed the border in brand-new SUVs, scuba diving, huffing up vast quantities of cocaine in Acapulco or Cancun, or getting drunk and lusting for brown-skinned Mexican women in the border towns. He could at least understand the arrogance of having too much and not knowing where to draw the line while flaunting their wealth in the gaunt and dirty faces of peasants they held in utter contempt and disrespect. But the Arabs were slightly different in what he perceived as their own contemptuous regard of his country, forever talking to him as if he were just one of those filthy peasants meant to serve, a bootlicker in uniform, unworthy, clueless as a non-Muslim to some cause they believed was divinely inspired. No, their money wasn't meant to buy pleasure, sate their every want and whim. To some extent that was confusing, even frightening, since what use was money when a man couldn't buy what he could see, touch or taste? The Arabs here had purpose, reason, drive, their cash meant to insure they were sheltered, secure in the knowledge they could implement their bloody goal without interference from the authorities, all of whom were for sale. A vacation for the Arabs was about as far away in their minds as earth from Pluto. They were in his country in preparation to strike a massive blow against the gringos, or, as they referred to the Americans, the infidels.

And the Asians? Who knew how they thought, though Ortega had seen enough of them to know they, too, had a definite and insidious reason to land in Mexico. They were there to set up their various safehouses where they could carry out an ongoing operation, which was still pretty much unknown to him, although he had some nagging suspicions where it was all headed.

Thus a definitive moment of truth was mere minutes away from seeing the light.

The floating rumor out of Mexico City, was that the North Koreans were coming to inquire as to why they had been paid in counterfeit currency for what Ortega had heard were new and sinister weapons. Precisely what the ordnance was he didn't know, only that it was something that had bridged a Rubicon to supertech mass destruction.

And there was yet another problem he might have to confront. Right then, the last shipment of pesos, about thirty steamer trunks full of currency, was being analyzed. If his own money, unfortunately already converted into useful, valued currencies and dispersed through various offshore accounts, turned up bogus, there would be hell to pay.

How it would go down here, he didn't know, but he, in fact, damn well cared. Which was why he'd formed a strategy on the ride in from his outpost to the south. Half of his soldiers had taken up different positions around the sprawling cantina. His remaining troops were stationed as backup—or snipers, depending on how the action unfolded—in the hotel directly across the street. In the event of some explosive retaliation by either side, Ortega had given his soldiers standing orders to defend themselves from harm.

All of the Arabs, he knew, were armed with a mixed assortment of assault rifles, machine guns, pistols under topcoats, the lot of them crammed around tables at the far corner, smoking, sipping coffee, looking surly. Another problem for Ortega to consider was the rabble still gathered in this rathole, which was little more than a 24/7 drunken orgy for all manner of local and drifting outlaw scum. To a man, they were all involved in some form of criminal activity, all of these dirty, disheveled, grim-faced patrons toting pistols or huge sheathed knives. They were still lounging about the bar even at that ungodly hour of the night, carousing, laughing, bartering for one of a dozen or so whores for a quickie romp upstairs. It seemed an unlikely place for such a dangerous meeting between two potential warring factions to go down, but Ortega had arranged for the rendezvous to happen here on purpose. If nothing else, say bloodletting erupted, it would be easy enough to sweep the bodies into the desert and dump them in a mass grave, or simply let the sun and the scavengers consume the flesh in due course. And since everyone here had something to hide, there would be no loose flapping of tongues if, say, the DEA ventured in, or one of his own, outranking him and holding hands with the gringos, rode into Ciudad Zapulcha. If that happened, there would be an investigation, some truths better left in the dark spilling light on the doorstep of his Coahuila command center.

He was checking his watch, aware the North Korean called Ying had already alerted him he was ten minutes away, when he heard the rumble of powerful engines out on the street. A glimpse in the mirror behind the bar revealed that the Arab contingent had come alive with new intensity, cigarettes stabbed out, bodies going rigid.

Watch his ass, keep his eyes peeled, was all Ruiz Ortega could think to tell himself. A moment later, he turned his head, staring through the dust-slick, bug-spattered plate glass window where light still spilled from the adobe blocks across the street. The glass was going back up to his lips when he froze, blinking. If he hadn't seen them with his own eyes, he would have believed himself thoroughly intoxicated to the point of hallucinating. At least fifteen North Koreans had disgorged from GMC SUVs. It wasn't so much the array of assault rifles and subguns they wielded that drew his eye; rather, it was the sports coats, open to reveal flaming Aloha shirts, thousand-dollar silk slacks, Italian loafers and dark sunglasses.

Ortega thought he should pinch himself. He wondered if perhaps he hadn't nodded off, only to wake up on a beach in Acapulco. These were the best of the North Korean special forces? They looked more like overdressed gangsters on holiday, profiling for the envious masses of wanna-bes, ogling females.

They might have marched through the door, single file, decked out as if it were just another day at the beach, he decided, but Ortega had seen enough bad people in his day to know when a man had come to take human life. As they piled in, then held their ground as a herd inside the door, staring toward the Arabs, Ruiz poured himself another drink. He noticed his hand was shaking.

BEING A FORMER Los Angeles police detective, Carl Lyons believed he knew a little something about character.

Or, at least, bad characters.

Character, in his mind, had one defining quality, which was integrity, and that always involved telling the truth, no exceptions.

In a perfect world—or in this case a perfect stakeout, which was going to lead to the ever elusive perfect hit—the Stony Man warrior and leader of Able Team would have longed to have faced down just one tough problem this time out.

Fat chance.

Both the moment, he thought, and the DEA informant called El Condor, had swelled up several major, problematic hemorrhoids.

Lyons stood on the ridgeline, M-16/M-203 combo in his fists. He peered into the darkness at the shadow just below. The informant claimed he'd been uncovered as a snitch, stating a few hardasses were coming to clean all of their clocks. The moment passed, but Lyons wished to hell he could clearly read the face, peer into the eyes, judge the man's character—or lack thereof, with cop instincts. The voice had sounded right enough, as far as he could tell, no waver in tone, no hesitation, just a cold statement of the facts. Body language? Forget about it. In his experience as a cop, almost without exception, snitches and rats knew how to play both ends against the middle, always looking out for number one. Acting, and lying, was first nature to them.

Lyons glanced at Hermann "Gadgets" Schwarz on his flank. His Able Team comrade was likewise loaded down in full combat regalia, holding a matching assault rifle combo.

Problem number one leaped to the ex-LA cop's mind. The two of them were on their own for the time being. The outlaw town that was Ciudad Zapulcha was off in the distance, but it was lit up enough for Lyons to have counted off any number of armed problems meandering around. Mack Bolan, the man also known as the Executioner, and the third commando of Able Team, Rosario Blancanales, were off in the desert, rounding up a major drug trafficker who had been aiding and abetting a terror scourge called al-Amin, for either some rough justice or some rough Q and A.

By now, if all had gone well, and so far on this mission very little had, Bolan and Blancanales should have either bagged Hernando Cordero or razed his hacienda, leaving the drug dealer little more than a bloodied carcass in the ruins as buzzard chow. Lyons hoped they were on the way. His tac radio was ready on his hip for good news for a change from Bolan, since Striker had ordered radio silence unless he called first. What he knew about this outlaw town southwest of the border of Laredo was all bad news. North Korean operatives, enraged about getting shafted with counterfeit money in exchange for weapons of mass destruction, the likes of which even rattled Lyons to the bone, were on their way to have a chat with a small army of al-Amin thugs. There was no way of knowing enemy numbers, but Lyons had to figure they were outgunned forty, maybe fifty or more to one.

Schwarz broached the subject of problem number two, growling, "If this is a setup, amigo..."

"No. It is not."

"How do you know you've been made?" Lyons asked.

"A feeling."

"A feeling," Lyons repeated. "You can't do better than that?"

"Clicking noises on my phone, and a device on my computer that warns me if my e-mail has been monitored. Shadow men hanging around the lobby of my hotel only minutes ago, and they look at me without looking. I have done this long enough. I have survived as a DEA cutout to know when I have been compromised. To be compromised in these parts is a death sentence."

"No shit," Lyons said.

The Able Team commander spotted problems three and four. Two dark silhouettes, SUVs, he believed, were wheeling around the south end of the town, hitting the uneven desert floor at a hard jounce, headed their way. Lights were out on the vehicles, so he couldn't count heads, but Lyons didn't think they were coming out there to buy them a drink.

"Mr. S.," he told Schwarz, using the handle Gadgets had introduced himself as to El Condor, "you drive." A quick search over his shoulder, and Lyons made out the distant black humps of hills to the north. This was hard desert country, plenty of gullies, arroyos, brush, boulders and high ridges, hopefully decent hiding points where they might be able to unleash an ambush.

"Okay, you," he barked at El Condor, "you come with us! Our ride, sit up front. You armed?"

"A Bowie knife."

"You do exactly what you're told. *¿Comprende?*"

"*Sí.*"

"You so much as twitch for that blade," Lyons told him, "I'll shove it up your ass, rip out your guts and feed them to you as you check out of this world. I'm in a bad mood. In fact, I've been a bad mood for days."

"I understand. I am with you. I have no choice but to cooperate."

"We'll see," Schwarz said. "I take it you have a plan, Mr. L.?"

Lyons grabbed El Condor by the arm and shoved him toward their Hummer. "I'll lay it out while you drive."

CHAPTER TWO

Mexico, he thought, was a culture of survival.

Or so Aurelio Orontos had often heard many of his thirty-two cousins, six brothers and four sisters often complain in Utacaz, his village of birth on the Yucatán peninsula. They might have taken some degree of angry pride in being a walking testament to that perverse outlook on life in Mexico, but many of those family members had long ago been consumed by the ravages of poverty. He used to think he should simply be grateful that he was still free, and breathing, as they had succumbed, one by one, to the harsh realities of being desperately poor. Whether disease, starvation or rotting away in a prison, convicted mostly of crimes that were little more than a means to an end to feed themselves or their children, it made little difference in the final judgment of cruel fate. Dead was dead. And the poor were everywhere in Mexico, forever multiplying like a festering sore on the landscape, and he knew they would always be a blight on this culture of survival. It was almost as if, he often thought, God was angry with the country, shunning them in favor of the rich gringos to the north. He wanted no part of being less than dirt poor ever again, and God had long since ceased to exist in both his heart and mind.

He wanted money, a better life, and he would never find it, he had long ago determined, swathed in the rags and mired in the filth of his village. So he had gone in search of something, anything that would allow him to be a man among men, never having to worry how he would feed himself again, grabbing whatever booty he had seized during his brief career as a "revolutionary," vacating the village, gone forever.

That seemed another lifetime, living minute to minute, killing, raping, robbing, just so he could feed himself, or purchase a bottle of tequila to drown the pain and drudgery of an existence barely fit for a mongrel. Those days were, thankfully, as dead and gone as those he had victimized to fill his pockets with a few dollars. At the ripe old age of twenty-two he was long since sick and tired of merely still surviving, enduring. In a land where a few grew rich and powerful at the expense of the many, Orontos wanted to live, like one of the cocaine kings he craved to emulate. All of them, in particular Hernando Cordero, the newest lord among drug lords, had all the finest material things in the world.

Money, power and pleasure. What else, he thought,

was there to live for? Crime did pay. So why not help himself to a slice of the pie while he was still young and ambitious, before it shrank to nothing while others took what they wanted first, leaving him with the crumbs?

Five hundred dollars U.S., though, the skimpy wad the captain had given each of them to hunt down the informant and kill whomever he was going to meet, wouldn't put him in the category of the elite criminal entrepreneur, but he hoped this would be the first rung up the ladder to the top, an ascent to his own vision of heaven on Earth. At least, if he did the deed here, taking back the severed head of this El Condor to the captain, he could show himself worthy of a chance for bigger and better challenges.

Such as muling drugs, guns and illegals through one of the many tunnels he'd heard were dug by Cordero along the border into Texas.

Inroads, he thought, a way to climb out of the gutter of being still nothing more than a bandit or assassin.

"Faster, Cuchillo! You're losing them!"

Sitting in the shotgun seat of the Jeep Cherokee, he gnashed his teeth as Cuchillo jounced them through a rut in the desert floor. Headlights wavered over the lead SUV, another pack of four, purchased by the captain, a sorry lot of bandits and whoremongers that left him wondering if they had what it took to do the job. His cousin Mendito, who had made the hard journey north with him in search of a better life, was pulling away, but they were still three hundred yards or more behind their quarry.

Orontos gripped his Thompson submachine gun, eager to use it to advance himself up the ladder. He scowled over his shoulder, his nose stung by tequila fumes and the stink of marijuana smoke. Taqueraz and Paco, one of them giggling, both stoned, were more concerned with passing the bottle and joint between themselves, as if they needed chemical courage to face the night and its dangers.

"Focus! Put the garbage away! Now, or I let you out!"

They grunted at each other, Orontos watching them, thinking these small-time smugglers of illegals might turn their pump shotguns on him, too intoxicated to separate reason from some savage impulse to rebel with misdirected violence. Another drag and a pull on the bottle, then Paco flicked the joint out the window. The only clear head among this entire pack of cutthroats, Orontos knew someone—like him—had to take charge.

Orontos faced front, urging more speed out of their wheelman, Cuchillo muttering something he couldn't make out, the vehicle shimmying as they slammed through some ditch in the land carved out by Mother Nature.

They lost sight of the Hummer as it vanished over the lip of a rise. Chains of black hills loomed in the distance, one of many gullies and arroyos swallowing their prey in the rugged belly of this desert beast. Then Cuchillo showed he had a keen grasp of the obvious.

"They are going to hide in the Choalla gorge! They are luring us in. I think they mean to ambush us!"

Orontos shook his head, his lips pulling tight in a sneer. "Fall back of Mendito. Ride in very slow. Stop when I tell you."

They were over the rise, going down, Cuchillo easing off the gas. Orontos believed there were only three of them, catching sight of the trio of shadows as they piled into the Hummer, hauling hard and fast to the north next, pulling them deeper into the desert. But what was to say, he thought, there wasn't an entire army of gunmen waiting in the Choalla? If that was the case, he figured his cousin and friends would draw fire first. That could work to his advantage, after all, as he did a little math, multiplying seven by five hundred, no problem if he had to pilfer the dead and add to some walking-around money. It had been tough, to say the least, to walk away from a good time with Layla back at the cantina. It still galled him to have given up the night of pleasure, but this was business, a vision of a better tomorrow sure to come if he succeeded here. With money in his pocket, he was sure a fair degree of fame, or notoriety, at worst, would follow. Soon he would have all the women he could pleasure. He only hoped this hunting party wasn't too whacked out on booze and dope, reflexes all but soured....

He would see if they were up to the task, as ambitious as he was, and soon enough.

They were in the gorge when he spotted the lone shadow ahead. His arms were up, as the figure stood just far enough outside the shroud of headlights from the Hummer, Orontos feeling some sixth sense for danger flaring.

"Stop here!"

Cuchillo hit the brakes, Orontos watching as Mendito and his crew piled out of their SUV when it happened.

He wasn't sure from which direction the missile flew, but as Orontos watched, the SUV was lost inside a blinding saffron flash of fire, and he knew several things had just become as clear as the four bodies sailing away in all directions.

They were outmatched, outgunned, ambushed to hell, and he feared he might never taste the sweet fruit of success he so lusted for.

Orontos bailed out the door, hit the ground running and dived out of instinct just as another thunderclap rocked the night.

IN MEXICO, Hermann Schwarz knew, when a man accused of a crime stood before justice, he was judged to be guilty until proved innocent. That went double for the bad hombres hitting the gorge right then, he determined, two SUVs crammed with gunmen, vehicles spewing dust spools as they rocketed toward El Condor.

A simple execution, bypassing any standard of legal haggling or a string of lengthy appeals, was up and coming for their pursuers.

Case closed.

M-16/M-203 leading his advance up the gully, NVD goggles in place to guide him through the dark, Schwarz quickly reviewed the ambush as put to them by Carl "Ironman" Lyons. Whether or not the DEA snitch was true in his claim of cooperation, Schwarz knew the coming attack would prove him out, one way or another. El Condor had been given a Beretta 92-F, just in case the plan went awry and he was left to defend himself. The DEA cutout was a stationary shadow—or target—down there near the Hummer, meant to draw in the combatants, confusing them by his solitude, or so the scheme went, until they could drop a double 40 mm whammy. For now, it would be all he and Lyons could do to correct the treacherous moment, set it straight—as in a body count—and proceed back to the outlaw town.

And then? He couldn't say, since from the start of this mission it had been little more than a blood-and-hellfire trail. How many dead had they left behind since boarding the French freighter *Napoleon* off the coast of Miami? Twenty, thirty, a hundred enemy numbers? Far too many to tally accurately. All of them had been racing on pure adrenaline since the drones were seized. First they'd decimated a trucking warehouse run by al-Amin terrorists out in Everglades country, then moved up the Gulf Coast, putting the torch to another terror waystation in New Orleans. Next in line was Houston, where a hit team of North Korean operatives had beaten them to the kill. They had stumbled into a wholesale slaughter by the Asians, who targeted Arabs using a charity as a front to funnel murder money for what was really the rabble remnants of al-Qaeda and Taliban thugs who had managed to flee Afghanistan, regroup, and form a new and more sinister organization to carry on the jihad. Now they were down in Mexico, backed up by a joint DEA-Mexican drug task force, looking to lop off the head of an unholy alliance between drug cartels, al-Amin troops and North Koreans, who, allegedly, had sold weaponized Ebola to the terrorists but who had been paid in counterfeit currency and...

Schwarz told himself it was best to deal with the moment, engage his thoughts, expend all his energy one battle at a time. He had no intention of becoming another statistic on this campaign.

Schwarz's com link crackled with Lyons's voice. "Gadgets, tell me you're in position and ready to rock and roll on these *bandidos.*"

Lyons was across the gorge, the north side, Schwarz knew, poised to snap shut the other half of the scissors assault. He dropped into a narrow depression, hoping it was free of anything poisonous that might dig fangs into his legs, when he saw the lead SUV sliding to a stop near El Condor. Schwarz, gauging the range to roughly forty yards below, keyed his com link. "Ready whenever you are."

"I'll take the homeboys in the lead. Count off three clicks, then let it rip."

Quickly he shed his night vision gear, the thought of getting blinded by the first blast out of the gate another bad thought among many. "Roger."

"Start counting. Over."

His four marks were disgorging on his two-count when Lyons blew up the night, obliterating the first SUV, decimating the four figures with the blast, scattering wreckage and body parts. Schwarz tapped the trigger on his M-203. The missile zigged on, trailing smoke and flame, then impacted, a direct hit on the starboard side of the second SUV. Even still, he counted two survivors picking themselves up, having cleared the brunt force of ground zero on a sprint. There would be cobwebs for them to clear, as they staggered to their feet, so Schwarz reckoned to end it before they pulled it together and lurched for cover in the gully.

ORONTOS CLAMBERED to his feet, would have sworn he heard the chiming of a thousand or so church bells in his skull. The night was on fire, up and down the gorge he saw flames shooting everywhere, wreckage winging all around. Suddenly he didn't feel so ambitious, much less even remotely confident he could survive.

The truth was, he felt his bowels quaking, a startled cry bleating past his lips as he reeled forward, searching for cover, his weapon. He was scouring the darkness, his scalp burning as he became aware he was cut with deep gashes, blood stinging into his eyes, when he made out the shadow of Paco beside him. One second Paco was standing, his mouth open as if he wanted to shout a warning. The next instant there was a dark spray erupting from his skull, and still more biting liquid hit him in the eyes.

Orontos tripped over the body, slapping at the burning wetness on his face. He heard bullets whistle past his ear, instinctively knew only Paco's sudden demise had spared him. The chatter of weapons fire, the whine of bullets striking stone began to clear his head, adrenaline taking over. It seemed an hour later, but he scrabbled around, found his machine gun, a miracle of sorts unto itself, considering a few seconds ago he wasn't even sure what country he was in. Vision began to return as he fisted blood out of his eyes, and he was certain his attacker was high up the rocks, a shadow near a cluster of boulders. Only one man? There might be hope yet. The gully he found himself in appeared to cut a parallel course beside the faceless enemy. If he could stay low, climb quick and fast enough, outflank the opposition…

He was looking back to where the first blast had erupted, unable to discern if any of the others were left to stand and fight, when something dug into his lower leg, a sharp pain shooting clear up into his groin. Orontos screamed, not so much out of pain, as terror. The burning lance, again and again, and Orontos began pumping his legs, flailing his path uphill, aware of the horror he had stumbled into.

They were everywhere, he saw, writhing black shapes, sliding out of the cracks, lunging and tearing into his legs. Orontos shrieked, hopping around, firing his machine gun at the mass of serpents. He wanted to curse the injustice, weep over everything he wanted in life but knew he would now never have. It was just a fleeting impulse, the need for salvation, the terror that all was not only lost in this world but also in the next, consuming him. He was sure he heard the words coming out—Hail Mary—then he felt something else tearing into his body. Only these blows were punching him higher up, as he felt bullets coring through his chest, impact kicking him back into the snake's den.

SCHWARZ KNEW exactly what the enemy had traipsed into, the thought that if he had moved up that particular gully instead…

There was no time to ponder his good fortune, even though he wanted this fight nailed down so he could clear out for firelit turf where he could see things that crawled in the night.

He had just dropped the first of the two survivors when he'd lost sight of the other gunman, a short hosing of autofire chasing his enemy to cover. Aware the shooter was coming his way, Schwarz was just about to move out and intercept him when the shadow howled, lurching up, arms flapping, the machine gun blazing away at his source of horror and pain.

A quick stitching of autofire across the hardman's chest, and Schwarz flung him back, ending it for the hapless victim before his system was shut down by serpent's toxin.

A search of the gorge, and Schwarz spotted El Condor capping off a series of rounds, the Beretta jumping around in his two-fisted grip as he plugged what appeared the last hardman standing down there.

"Gadgets! Come in!"

Schwarz stood, scanning the bowl around him, his heart pounding. It was one thing to shoot down an armed opponent he could see. What unnerved him was the thought of ending up like...

Schwarz responded when Lyons barked his name again. "Yeah!"

"Striker just called! He's moving in now, so don't start blasting away."

"Why the hell would I do that?"

"You tell me! It took you ten seconds to answer

when I can see you're still in one piece from over here!''

''I'm coming down!''

It took him a full and nervous three minutes by his mental calculations, but Schwarz reached level ground, unmolested by snakes. By then he saw the Hummer pulling up behind El Condor, coming in from the east. Schwarz was walking ahead, toeing strewed bodies along the way to make sure they wouldn't rise again, when Bolan and Blancanales stepped out.

''Problems?'' he heard the Executioner inquire as Lyons stepped out of the shadows and into the firelight.

''Nothing we couldn't handle.''

Classic Ironman, Schwarz thought, and felt a nervous grin tug at his lips.

''What was your problem up there?'' Lyons growled.

''Snakes,'' Schwarz answered. ''Nothing I couldn't handle.''

CHAPTER THREE

Irqhan Rabiz had been ready to confront the North Koreans since word first reached him they had landed in Mexico City. He knew their problem, and he was fully ready to solve it for them, or else.

Fighting and killing infidels in the name of God was nothing new to the Saudi. This night, if violence erupted, he would treat the North Koreans no differently than he had so-called Afghan freedom fighters, those American mercenary lackeys he had sniped or blasted off the mountains with mortars on the way out of Afghanistan.

Such was the way of a holy warrior, he thought. Traitors to Islam would feel the wrath of God every bit as much, if not worse, than non-Muslim heathens.

He was on his feet, keeping the Uzi subgun on the table but his hands wrapped around the Israeli weapon, as the one-time benefactors of the jihad marched, slowly and clearly full of their presence, into the saloon. They acted more like arrogant American movie stars on public display than the cold-blooded killers they were reported to be, but the face of cool, calm and collected, he knew, was their inscrutable way of telling them all one basic fact.

They believed themselves in charge of the moment, ready to explode into action on a whim, in control of the life or death of every single man or woman under that roof.

Or so they thought.

Rabiz had other ideas. And they didn't involve pandering, sucking up or currying favor, although he considered himself something of an actor, ready to fall into character, depending on what the moment called for.

It was no accident he was called the Chameleon.

As previously ordered, half of his own force stood, sidled away from the table, maintaining their grips on various pistols and subguns, their stares focused on what Rabiz told them was a clear and present menace to their mission. Standing orders were shoot to kill if the Asians left them no choice, and that included noncombatants who might get in their way. Collateral damage was always acceptable, since the death of any infidel served God.

Likewise, as if on cue, six, then seven of the flamboyantly overdressed Asian operatives fanned out around the bar, hemming in the contingent of corrupt *federales.* Their lackey, Captain Ortega, he noted, went rigid, then did what he always did best, which was pour himself another drink. They held weapons low by their sides, Rabiz watching the slight figure who took point and led a group of seven toward his table. He assumed the North Korean in the flower-and-flamingo shirt was the cutout called Ying. An enigmatic smile froze on those lips, head bobbing, shaded stare working around the room, taking it all in, assessing strategy, Rabiz assumed. How the Asian could see behind those black RayBan sunglasses made Rabiz wonder if he were showing off what they perceived as some power of supernatural eyesight, or attempting to ratchet up the heat of intimidation.

Whichever, Rabiz wasn't biting. He was quite prepared to die here in this dusty, dirty cantina in the middle of the desert.

He waited, glancing at the weapons, returning the smile, the head-bobbing routine, twin bulges beneath Ying's white sports coat warning him the North Korean messenger had more on his mind than verbal negotiation. Rabiz suddenly felt a great weight settle on his shoulders as, against his will, his mind reflected on past events. How it had all come to this was a mistake born fairly out of desperation. When the infidels began churning up Afghanistan with their smart bombs and laser-guided bunker busters, a contingency plan to exfiltrate hundreds of al-Qaeda and Taliban warriors out of the country had gone into action.

The sheikh, if he was even still alive, had been blessed by God with a vision of the future, and long before Rabiz had the first inkling he would become one of the chosen. The sheikh had laid the foundation, with help from Russian and French criminals and his link to the North Korean program of high-tech weapons of mass destruction, to carry on the jihad, even in the event of his martyrdom. A major operative, groomed years back, had been named, literally, the Successor. To attempt to elude murder or capture at the hands of the infidels, top fighters had been smuggled out of Afghanistan. Whether they slipped the infidel noose through Pakistan, Iran, Tajikistan or Chechnya made no difference. As long as the bulk of them, armed with money, names of contacts and a mental list of various missions, remained free, the jihad would see glory.

His own journey had taken him into Iran, where he had been shipped out on an oil tanker bound for France, another merchant mariner with all the right credentials to pass scrutiny if American Navy SEALs boarded the vessel. From there, with forged paperwork, and a brief layover in Spain, his own cell was flown and boated, a few warriors at a time, to Mexico, where a larger organization was already in place. Backed by prior financing, sleeper operatives all over the world finally coming awake, a new organization, al-Amin, had arisen out of the ashes of al-Qaeda and the Taliban.

But there had been problems in recent days, some of which had been anticipated, others with solutions he believed best left to the will of God. For instance, the shipment of the North Korean drones had been seized by the Americans. Word from cutouts in America was that some covert war had been launched against various al-Amin fronts. Money was being seized, operatives slaughtered from Miami to Houston by a nameless, faceless enemy. There were more drones, ready to be shipped into Mexico, he understood, then smuggled by tunnels dug by the drug lord, Cordero, but Rabiz knew he needed to focus solely on the moment. That counterfeit money was being produced, and had purchased the original shipment of drones from the North Koreans, was news to him. He knew there was a plan in motion—now aborted—to continue payoffs in bogus cash to their Mexican benefactors. The phony-money angle wasn't his personal business, but his orders were to address it now, attempt to mollify the North Koreans, somehow see if he couldn't rectify the situation.

"I am Colonel Ying. And neither myself, nor the general, prefer not to stay in this worthless country any longer than necessary."

"I am prepared to talk. I am prepared to renegotiate and correct our misunderstanding," Rabiz said, watching as the smile vanished from Ying's expression, then returned.

More head bobbing, then Ying turned, snapped his fingers at the burly Spanish bartender and gestured toward the jukebox.

Rabiz heard his heart thunder in his ears. The problem with the North Koreans was they did and said one thing when they meant something else entirely. In his brief experience dealing with them, he knew they were always looking to the future, a way in which to keep and hold the upper hand.

"You! Music!"

"It takes money, amigo! Yours."

Rabiz heard the colonel rattle off a stream in his native tongue, then one of his operatives swiftly marched to the bar and slapped down some currency.

"American rock and roll, if you people down here have any," Ying barked. "Play it loud. Play many."

"Yes, we people have that. You want loud, I have just the songs for you."

Some of the laughter had died among the seedy whoremongers, Rabiz noticed, the local riffraff engaged in all manner of illegal activities darting glances their way, some of them with hands draped over hip-holstered side arms. The tension level had risen a few heated notches, understandably so, he thought, as some of the patrons led whores by the arm away from tables, up the stairs.

Out of the combat zone.

"Please," Ying said, gesturing for Rabiz to sit. "You wish to talk, we talk."

The first chords of heavy metal flayed the air, Ying barked an order at one of his underlings. A chair was pulled from another table and slid in front of the Arab contingent. Rabiz waited, Ying sitting first, the smile gone, then the Saudi nodded for his group to reclaim their seats.

"Yes," Ying began, "there has been a most unfortunate occurrence, a misunderstanding, as you put it, between us. The trouble is, several of our operatives, carrying your counterfeit money, have been arrested by the FBI. Will they talk? Will they open doors for the Americans and lead them straight to my superiors? Who knows? My orders are clear, and I intend to carry them out."

Rabiz wanted to believe he could read between the lines, certain an implied threat was left hanging, but he clung to hope they could work it out. "I have been instructed to arrange another payment. You will be amply compensated for any and all—"

Ying waved a hand. "You need the motherboard, the critical component that will guide your drones from our satellite. Yes, I know what you are thinking. That perhaps your own scientists will find a way to steer them by radio remote. That will take time to develop, something neither of us has. I understand your organization is being hunted by some American covert force. Perhaps they are even on the way as we speak."

"There has been some trouble, granted...."

"But nothing you cannot take care of?"

"Do we deal again, or not?"

"I think if you try to contact a certain man who

ran United Front, this charity that laundered your organization's money, you may have your answer.''

Rabiz felt his chest knot with tension. The North Korean was talking but saying little, hurling out riddles. But he was speaking of the charity front in the past tense.

''I see,'' Ying said. ''You are unaware of what has happened in Houston.''

''I only know that several of our operations in America have been hit.''

''But you are strong down here in this cesspool of a land? You are telling me you can continue your terror dreams with or without your American operatives?''

Rabiz chose his next words carefully, a sinking and sick feeling in his gut already telling him how this meeting would end. ''And with or without me the operation will succeed.''

''Jihad,'' Ying said, nodding. He pulled out a slip of paper, set it on the table. ''If you wish to have the motherboard, there is our new price, and where you can find that which you so desire.''

Rabiz glanced at the paper, Ying rising, backing up a few steps.

''Go on, look at it.''

He reached out and took the paper, pulling it back, glimpsed the North Koreans spreading out. He opened the slip of paper, hand inching for his Uzi, looked down—and saw blank white staring him back.

"Nothing," Ying snarled. "That is what we are prepared to offer, and that is what you are about to be."

The North Korean was digging inside his jacket when Rabiz heard the first rounds of subgun fire blister across the saloon. He wasn't sure if his men or the North Koreans had shot first, but any hope of renegotiation was lost.

Snapping up his Uzi, Rabiz threw up the table, a thick wooden shield that blocked the first few rounds capped off by Ying.

THE BIG SHOW had started without them.

The sounds of weapons fire rattled from the cantina, echoing across the desert plateau. As Mack Bolan bailed from the Hummer, M-16/M-203 combo in hand, he put together a quick plan of attack, hauling Hernando Cordero out behind him. The drug lord was a major catch, a gold mine of intelligence the Executioner had intended to plumb, but now another dilemma faced the Stony Man warriors. Another battle dumped any Q and A on the shelf. There seemed no option, Bolan thought, but to wade into the pitched battle, help the enemy savage each other. From the start of the campaign it had been run and gun anyway, seizing whatever intel they could as each al-Amin stronghold was blitzed and burned.

"Sounds like the North Koreans and their al-Amin pals agreed to disagree," Lyons said, stepping away from his own Hummer, assault rifle/grenade launcher in hand, the massive SPAS-12 autoshotgun slung across his shoulder.

"Any ideas, Striker?" Blancanales asked.

"Only one," Bolan told the Able Team warriors. "Pol, you and me hit the back side of the cantina. You two make your way for the front side, come in from the east."

"I'm assuming all hands are fair game?" Schwarz said.

"I'm not worried about netting any more prisoners," Bolan said. "If it's armed and walking, take it out."

"And this one?" Lyons asked, nodding at Cordero. The drug lord was cuffed, shivering in his robe in the brisk night air.

El Condor volunteered guard duty. "I will watch him."

Bolan gave that all of one second's consideration. The informant came to them with high marks from the DEA. And from what he'd seen back at the gorge, the man shooting up one of the enemy, Bolan figured he could count on El Condor to still be there, if and when the four of them returned.

"Do it," the Executioner told El Condor. A hundred-yard or so hike to the cantina, Bolan figured, and with any luck they could roll in, decimate whatever enemy forces were still standing.

Silently, the Executioner led Able Team into the night, toward what he was certain was a slaughter.

CHAPTER FOUR

Ruiz Ortega reacted in the only manner he thought prudent, considering his stature, those offshore accounts meant to pave the golden road for retirement in the Bahamas. As the massacre erupted without warning, he was up and diving over the bar. The captain had seen it coming, even with a brain fogged by half a bottle of tequila, reflexes muddled to the point where his body was a sack of jelly. It wasn't hard, picking up the angry vibrations between the Arabs and the North Koreans, expressions set in stone all around, body language full of menace. Their lips were moving, but he was unable to hear what they were saying but knew they weren't comparing notes about choice vacation spots on the Yucatán.

And then the shooting started, but he had a plan already sketched out, in the blurry shadow of thought.

It was hard to tell who fired first, which side scored the opening kill, but Ortega knew he was somewhere smack middle in the line of fire, milliseconds ago flanked by North Koreans at the bar, those Asian shooters throwing up subguns and blazing away, directing fire down the bar front, his ears nearly shaved off by scorching muzzle-flashes.

Ortega flopped across the bar, dousing himself in the face with flying tequila as he dropped on the other side, landing in a heavy crunch on top of shattered glass. The Browning was out—no point in allowing himself to get murdered without at least putting up a show of resistance—his legs somehow lifting him, then carrying him down the bar as weapons fire chattered on. Now what?

Crouching, he looked up, one of his soldiers staring down from across the bar, a near childlike expression of hysteria on his face. Rodriguez, he believed the young man's name was, his arms flapping, his mouth open as if he were about to demand answers for which Ortega didn't have the first damn clue.

Other than that, it was every man for himself.

What was that peculiar look on the kid's face all about? he wondered. Accusation? Terror? It didn't matter in the next and final analysis, as Ortega saw the head above him erupt like rotten grapefruit bashed by a tire iron, half the skull cleaved off, blood and brains sailing overhead. He was a little too slow, all that tequila talking back now, ducking away, then took the gore shower in the face, cursing, aware he had to do something, anything....

But what?

All he could think of was to save his own skin

somehow, find a way to vacate the shooting gallery, visions of the Bahamas clinging somewhere in the back of his thoughts, but the fear factor somehow was hurling mist over the dreams of a better tomorrow.

Where to, and how to get there? The front door? No good, since his men across the street would see him rushing away from the fight, a frightened dog kicked in the rear, not the first shot fired by himself in anger.

Out the back, then, scurry through the chaos, use tables, pillars, whores as human shields to absorb any errant rounds. He figured he could ally himself with the winning side. There was a good chance none of his troops would make it out of the cantina, live to tell the tale to their friends in the hotel that their fearless leader was nowhere to be found when the shooting started. He didn't view his own skulking retreat as cowardice.

Far from it.

This was Mexico, and he was a federal policeman, which meant his word about anything might as well have been written in stone, handed down by God himself, if subordinates knew what was good for them. How many hardened criminals had he personally arrested, tortured over the years? Dozens? How many doors had he kicked in, the second or third or maybe fourth man through, gunning down entire nests of bandits? Four, five?

The question of courage, to stand and fight or crawl

away and not fight, was moot. This was a straight-on, last-man-standing butcher's deal. Let the terrorists and their North Korean counterparts kill each other. Good riddance. Explanations, rationalizations and all manner of justifications could come later, if and when he had to report this slaughter to both his own superior and the North Korean general he had met one time, in the shadows, taken money from to aid and assist the other side—as he had the Arabs.

The next looming obstacle, he found, was Guavio, the huge bartender blocking the immediate way out near the end of the bar. Whether he was simply caught up in the madness of the moment, enraged that he had been ordered around to drop money into the jukebox and play gringo rock and roll...

Well, Guavio was thundering out the 12-gauge sonic booms, his own bellowing competing with the infernal racket blasting from the jukebox, a tribal beat and grinding heavy metal that seemed as loud as the hellish din of weapons fire.

Ortega was considering the situation, his Browning drawing a bead on Guavio, when that particular problem was solved for him. One instant Guavio was upright, pounding out the wrath of the pump shotgun; the next heartbeat he was jerking and dancing around, branded all over his torso with gouting holes of crimson. The impact from dozens of rounds combined with the pull of gravity to carry Guavio into the bar mirror. Glass rained as the man slid down the liquor rack, bringing with him tumbling rows of tequila.

Grimacing, ears burning with the din of battle, howling of men in their final moments, Ortega crawled to the end of the bar. He hauled himself through the puddle of blood and tequila, looking back to check his rear.

It was clear of shooters—better yet, there were no watching eyes of his own soldiers.

Lifting himself to his knees, flinching as a wild round tattooed the toppled stool beside him, he took in the chaos. They were firing away at each other, point-blank in some pockets. North Koreans and Arabs blazed on, chopping each other up with bursts that abruptly ended as combatants zeroed in from other points of engagement. A few of the more stalwart patrons were now jumping into the act, hurling up tables, handguns booming before autofire began ripping up their roosts, gruesome facelifts sealing their fate.

Now or never, Ortega decided, sighting on the closest hallway that led out the back. It was a six- or seven-foot dash to a nearby pillar, where he could get his bearings for a second, then proceed with the final short race for the hall.

Ortega got up and ran.

THE TABLE MIGHT HAVE saved Rabiz from getting shot up by Ying's opening barrage, but it wouldn't hold off any extended bombardment. Already chunks near his face were getting blasted off, wood splinters slashing his jaw, hot lead snapping past his ears. For some reason, the shooting turned away from his flimsy concealment, just like that. Abdullah was out in the open, screaming "God is great," sweeping the Italian Spectre subgun around, his eyes wild. It looked promising for all of two seconds, Abdullah going for broke, then he was falling, convulsing behind a crimson shroud, his weapon thrust ceilingward and spitting out a few more rounds before he thudded up beside Rabiz.

A look around the corner, Uzi in hand, and Rabiz snatched up the discarded subgun. Two weapons were better than one. Rabiz suddenly decided he wanted to live to fight, carry on the jihad another day. What good was his death for God now? He was one of the chosen, wasn't he? Surely it was God's will he somehow made it out of there to carry the torch for jihad.

But how to escape? The entire cantina was a hornet's nest of flying lead.

They were firing all over the room, side to side, front to back, bodies on both warring sides spinning as they were riddled with countless bullets. The *federales* were going down likewise, and the North Koreans had gone berserk, shooting anything in sight, blasting the lawmen up and down the bar where they sat, stood or tried to run. Where was Ying?

There!

The colonel was somersaulting over the bar, triggering two large pistols in an acrobatic roll that would have done an Olympic gymnast proud. Other North Koreans were firing on the backpedal, sliding toward the front, blocking any exit for combatants or otherwise. Collateral damage was in the process of spilling to the north and west, where whores lurched into the lines of fire, scruffy patrons joining the action only to get doused by waves of autofire. Along the balcony, Rabiz saw some of the other rabble popping out of their own little love nests, weapons ready.

That was the answer, he determined, watching as another whore went down, the top of her head sheared away by a short burst of subgun fire. Snatch a whore for armor, then bolt out the back door.

He lurched up and came out shooting, a double subgun fusillade from the hip that turned two white sports coats to crimson rags. Return fire sought him out, but he was charging to his right, bullets whistling past his scalp, three of his soldiers howling out the war cries of jihad, marching straight for the bar, into their martyrdom.

It was only a glimpse, as he flashed grim sights on a whore cringing under a table, but Rabiz found the *federale* captain beating him to the retreat.

And Ortega, judging the mad dash for the hallway, was clearly not interested in any attempts in saving whatever lives of his own men that he could.

Rabiz knew he might not make it out of there, and

if he did, what then? In the interests of saving face, he shouted at three of his men, hunkered behind a table and churning up the bar with subguns, to form a running wall.

The whore was crying something about her six children, but Rabiz wasn't interested if she was going to leave behind six or sixty orphans. A handful of hair, and he wrenched her out into the open, locked an arm around her throat.

And just in time.

He flinched as she screamed, jerked like a mad puppet in his grasp, blood splashing his face. It was difficult, holding her upright, but adrenaline pumped extra strength into his arms. He fired one-handed around her limp form, hosing the length of the bar with his Uzi. Hamid was tumbling ahead, Rabiz concerned he might drop directly in his path, force him to alter his course, expose himself to NK fire. Whether it was rage, the will of God or whatever, Hamid held on, dancing back, bullets tearing into his chest, the barrage pinning him to the wall.

And out of the way.

There was temporary cover on the other side of the hall, but a *federale* came flying over a table, a vaulting blur in the way. Uniform drenched in blood, the Mexican staggered to his feet, called out the name of his captain.

It sounded like a plea for salvation, the man crying out to be spared the wrath of this hell, but the soldier found only instant and unforgiving death as a new storm of bullets slammed into his back.

"CAPTAIN ORTEGA!"

The homestretch was in sight at the end of the hall, one flimsy wooden door barring the way to freedom.

Heart racing, screams and gunfire rattling in his wake, Ortega made out a familiar voice, would have sworn it belonged to one of his men. He couldn't be sure, considering the pandemonium.

He was about to look back when a door to his right and dead ahead flew open. A large Indian he knew by the name of Tazicqua, a cocaine mule for Hernando Cordero, lumbered into his path. Maybe it was some form of telepathy, the Indian reading his thoughts, intentions to flee and leave his men stranded to die there while he charged off into the night that made him look so fierce and poised to kill. Maybe it was the fact that he could read the terror in Ortega's eyes, thinking him a coward, deserving only of death. Or maybe it was the prior grudge he held when Ortega recalled having stiffed him on a few ounces of white powder when the Indian was tapped on cash, cocaine so diluted it would have taken half the bag just to catch a decent buzz. Whichever it was, the desired moment of payback had arrived, and it was rising in the form of a nasty double-barreled shotgun, the sight of black bikini briefs hugging his massive, muscular frame somehow comical, considering the hell that raged in the cantina.

Ortega shot him twice in the face, on the fly, a double peal of thunder erupting toward the ceiling, bringing down a shower of dust and plaster. Another fifteen, no, ten feet and he was on the way, his feverish hope that paradise in the Bahamas wasn't lost when he heard his name hollered again.

Turning, he discovered the shouter was Lieutenant Alvarez. Somehow the young officer had cleared the slaughterzone, diving over a table, a temporary buffer to the crazed shooters dancing to their death knell on the saloon floor. He was rising, the strangest expression—was that loathing or imploring?—on his face when he took whatever he was thinking of his commanding officer to the grave.

Ortega winced at the sound more than the sight, one, maybe more of the shooters out there stitching Alvarez up the back, skull bursting first, then mists of red taking to the air as the spewing corpse was kicked down the hall.

Ortega urged greater speed out of his legs, more terrified than ever he would catch a bullet in the back, so close…

So far.

It was a blur, the door in his face suddenly, as he bulled into the thin barrier, wood giving way to his flying bulk. He was falling through open space, no bullets tearing into his back, when he thought he glimpsed two shadows off to the side. No way now, clear and free of the killing, would he be stopped. He leaped to his feet, Browning coming up, when he knew, instinctively, it was over. Or was it?

They rolled out of the night, gringos, he believed, although one of them, his face framed in a soft sheen of light cutting through the opening he'd blasted out, looked Hispanic. For some reason, they checked their fire, big assault rifles in their hands, some sort of grenade launcher fixed to the weapons. He considered reasoning with them, since they hadn't gunned him down, when he realized the Browning was sweeping up in his hand, locking on. He heard his mind scream it was all a huge mistake, then the Hispanic-looking man was lifting the ominous assault rifle.

Ortega shouted, "Wait!"

Or thought he did, since his scream was swept away by the stutter of autofire.

CHAPTER FIVE

Juan Salvadore was thinking how sad, how painful life in his desperate, impoverished country was for the vast majority—the poor—when he felt a wave of bitter anger threaten to tumble over him. He wasn't sure what was bringing on the round of superheated emotion, but he had some ideas.

Some clues as to the source of his mounting anger were good, some bad, some downright ugly and sinister.

The mystery commandos claimed some of the fire in a corner of his heart, but they were the good part of the equation to his troubled thoughts. They had gone off to the cantina, brave men, foreigners, gringos, no less, there on his soil, doing what he wished he could do. Suddenly, he craved to be part of the raging battle, if nothing else but for justice, or, he corrected himself, killing in vengeance, aware some ghosts would never rest, as the memory of her and the son he would never know came howling from somewhere in the deepest, darkest cavern of recall.

Instead of acting on his burning hunger for sudden revenge—though he had volunteered to stand guard—he was left behind, sitting outside their Hummers, alone in the cold and the silence of the desert night.

Of course, he wasn't entirely alone, nor was it entirely quiet out there on the ridge. Nor were the bastards inside the cantina directly responsible for the horror of the past, though they were something of symbolic demons of the scourge that had ripped his own life to bloody shreds, the distant yesterdays having changed him forever, setting him on a course from which there was no turning back.

And the man also known as El Condor felt his wrath stirring even more at the mere sight of the same sort of cannibal that was eating the heart, soul and guts out of his country.

Drug dealers.

Like vultures never sated, he thought, or a virus that spawned and infected as it raged unchecked through the host bodies of weaker or greedy or desperate men, they gobbled up any hope that Mexico could turn some corner away from crime, corruption and poverty. With the drug lords' undying appetite for more money, more power, with their unquenchable thirst to murder, bribe and take, Mexico, he feared was doomed to remain mired in every conceivable ill, flaw and folly known to man. Narcotraffickers, he knew, ran his country with iron fists, with ready cash or blazing gun, the rule of the land, the law of the jungle that was Mexico. And as long as they were in charge, padding the bank accounts of politicians, lawmen and soldiers with their riches seized at the misery of others, there would never be any hope that a noble and decent government and military could step up, steer the masses of mostly God-fearing people into the promise of good jobs, education, food, decent shelter. In his mind, dealers were the worst sort of criminal, their souls every bit as black and savage as the bandits who preyed on peasant families attempting to slip across the border in search of a better life in America, far away from the myriad and seemingly unsolveable ills of Mexico.

He heard the autofire in the distance, thought he saw the commandos melting into the shadows near the cantina, gone to slay the very same kind of demons that haunted him from the past.

He came from a poor farming village to the west, a town so long forgotten, so washed in blood, he couldn't recall its name unless he chose think that hard about a squalid place that wasn't even considered good enough to put on the map. How many of his cousins and brothers had he seen fall prey to the wicked scheming of drug dealers who rode into town, in search of couriers, mules for their poison, promising some nirvana on Earth to men who worried where the next meal for their families would come from? Or how they would even merely put shoes on the feet of their children. Too many dead to count.

He had warned them, time and again, as they returned with cash in their pockets, rushing for the first bottle of tequila they could get their hands on, that there was always a price to pay when the Devil bestowed on them the promise of the world.

And the price tag came heavier than the town expected.

The DEA had rolled in one day, planting informants, gleaning intelligence, and he had allowed principle, the basic tenets of his religion—good versus evil—to walk him into their arms. He had a young wife, a child on the way to consider. He had been a dirt-poor farmer, and it seemed far cleaner to accept the money of the righteous in the war against the drug dealers than fall into bed with the Devil.

The war against the narco-traffickers, in short, he remembered, had eventually turned cousin against cousin, brother against brother. One by one they were arrested by the DEA. Or abducted in the middle of the night, along with their families, marched out into the desert, shot in the head before they could help the DEA in their war against the evil that had lured them in.

He shuddered next, the misty vision in his mind's eye of…

The rage came out of nowhere, an all-consuming fire.

He felt the hot tears, welling up behind his eyes, thought he heard himself call her name.

"Conchita."

"What did you say?"

It took what felt like an hour before the vision of her gutted body faded from his mind, along with the sight of the small, naked, bloody unborn...

"Be quiet." He looked at the shadow perched on the passenger seat. He noticed he was trembling, the pistol up, aimed at the king in this world, the latest scourge that kept on swallowing up Mexico.

"My friend, listen to me carefully. You know who I am."

"Yes, I know who you are. I know also what you are."

"Then you know I am a very rich man. I can also be very generous."

"Really."

He was curious and decided to bait the moment. If nothing else, he'd watch the man squirm, try to buy his way to freedom, so he could return to consuming what little hope was left of Mexico.

"Are you listening to me?"

"Go on."

"Take off these cuffs. I know a place close, drive me there, I have associates...."

"Men with guns? An army?"

"Yes, yes. There are only four of them. It will be no problem to return and kill these gringos. Help me do that, and I will reward you."

"How much?"

"You name your price."

It felt as if he were moving in slow motion, slogging through the vestiges of a bad dream, on the edge of coming awake. Before he was aware of what he was doing, the pistol was up and out, the muzzle planted between Cordero's eyes.

"You are making a terrible mistake."

"The mistake was made long ago, and by scum very much like yourself. Here is my price, drug lord. You tell me you have the power to change my life?"

The man hesitated, eyes searching his face. "You know I do. For better or for worse. You have a choice."

"So you say. Tell me. Do you have the power to bring back the dead?"

Another pause, Cordero peering through the shadows. "What sort of question is that? Are you mad? Are you drunk?"

"I am neither. But you answered your own question. Since you cannot raise the dead, I have no use for your power."

The moment passed, Salvadore restraining himself from pulling the trigger. He stepped back, Cordero grunting, defiance in the sound, a muttered oath he barely heard, since it was lost to the sounds of men—good and evil—killing one another in the distance.

"My strange friend, with his bizarre sense of humor," Cordero said. "You just made the wrong choice."

"If you only knew the truth, you would not sit there and say that. I daresay," he muttered to himself, turning away, "you might beg me for your life."

RABIZ WASN'T sure he cared for the way in which Abu Salim was looking at him. Was that contempt in those eyes? he wondered, slapping the whore, who was clutching a sheet to her filthy nakedness, to the bed. Was that a look of accusation? Questioning his courage? Wondering why he was abandoning their brothers-in-jihad to do the fighting and the dying out in the saloon?

Right then he had other, far weightier concerns than addressing Salim's particular disturbance. Such as getting out of town, in one piece, link up with one of the other two cells to the south. It had been a fluke, making the hall, no bullets eating him up, when the cowardly captain had gone out the door, a human rocket, only to stand and get shot down by what Rabiz was certain were reinforcements on the way to join the fighting. A quick step over the whoremonger Ortega had shot, into the room, shutting the door behind, and Rabiz was now moving for the curtained window. Beyond stretched an alley, but more questions than answers cropped up now that he was in flight, bailing. Was another batch of NK gunmen waiting outside? How many? Or was the cavalry, DEA or more *federales,* riding now into the slaughterzone? Did he break for the desert? Or attempt to slip into his vehicle out front?

He decided next to leave his fate in God's hands.

Pulling back the curtain, he would have sworn he just saw shadows surging past, heading toward the main street. He looked back at the whore, considered shooting her, just in case someone barged in and she pointed the way to his escape route. Not the best of ideas, he decided, since whoever was about to charge in from the back might hear the Uzi stutter. No point allowing a hunting party to latch on to him when he'd made it this far.

One more look at Salim, aware he would have to rationalize all of this at some point, and he opened the window. Poking his head outside, he found the desert clear of any onrushing armed combatants. Still, the idea of blundering all over the desert in the dead of night…

The motor pool, then.

He was out the window, hitting the dirt alley, when he scoped two armed shadows hitting the corner at the far end. Across the alley was a broken row of adobe structures. He decided to slip into the darkness, find an angle adjacent to the motor pool, wait it out, watch whatever was going to happen out front. Somewhere in all of this sprawling squalor he would find a way out, plenty of vehicles scattered to commandeer.

Rabiz raced across the alley, melting into a dark

crevice between two buildings. Silently, he prayed to God to guide him safely through the night, take him far away from this madness. The jihad was more important than hanging around to commit suicide. His death now, he believed, would only disappoint both the sheikh and the Successor.

CHAPTER SIX

The plan, Carl Lyons knew, was for Bolan and Blancanales to move in from the back, hit the hardforce from the blind side, drive them, running and mauled, out the front door. And right into their waiting guns.

A vise of death, a ring of fire.

Lyons didn't have any problem with that, since every terrorist or North Korean operative killed now was one they wouldn't have to deal with down the road. And where this particular highway to hell would lead them after Ciudad Zapulcha, was a lunatic's speculation.

It was incredible, if he chose to think long and hard about how, when and where this campaign of rolling slaughter started.

Miami. R and R. Sun—well, sunburn and poisoning in his sorry case, he briefly recalled—fun, booze and girls. A swank strip club, he bitterly remembered, where the hedonistic foray came to a bloody screeching halt as Lyons hit the wall's edge of the alley, taking in the extensive motor pool. There were at least ten vehicles in all, which meant the number of shooters going at it inside was somewhere around the quarter-century mark. He needed to get his mind fixed on the butcher's chore at hand, he knew, but Miami was still seething somewhere in the back of his mind.

It seemed like only minutes ago, since they had been running on adrenaline for at least a thousand or so miles, racking up a body count of epic proportions in his estimate, from Miami to this snake pit in the middle of the Mexican desert, but Lyons still had lingering visions of Gigi—Shania Twain's clone—in his head. All that damn punk kid bartender with the haircut from Mars had to do, he thought, was keep his mouth shut, serve him another drink or three...

Instead of being a stand-up act, the squirrelly sack had marshaled up the security cavalry, a major brawl following that saw himself and his two Able Team pals tossed into Dade County lockup on a list of charges long enough to dangle a double-digit stretch in prison. And Gigi? The SOB magistrate, no doubt chewing on what little authority he had left after Brognola had gone to bat and gotten them released, all charges dropped, had conveniently lost Gigi's number. Why was he still bugged about that?

He knew.

They—or he—had embarrassed themselves, threatened to expose their deep cover as commandos for the ultracovert Stony Man Farm.

"Carl? You with me?"

A quick search of the main dirt drag revealed shadows hunkered up and down the street in alleys, behind crumbling adobe walls, malingering around ratty pickups. Lyons had to wonder who was who, what was what. The ungodly racket had drawn every cutthroat in the area outside. There was no mistaking subguns and shotguns in the hands of shadows holding their ground close to the flickering glows of kerosene lanterns.

Lyons scowled at Schwarz. "What the hell are you talking about?"

Schwarz claimed a firepoint at the rear of a GMC. Lyons took the front, on a knee, M-16 aimed for the front doors of the cantina.

"I don't know—you tell me. If I didn't know better, I'd think you'd left your heart in Miami."

"You're right. You don't know any better."

And that was as far as the exchange went.

Lyons saw two NKs bursting out the door, decked out as if they were, in fact, in south Florida, instead of going the distance in a grimy scorpion hole in the desert.

It took a full second, as a blanket of autofire hit their cover, glass slashing off Lyons's scalp, before he realized a small army had opened up on them from a three-story building across the street.

THE EXECUTIONER LED Blancanales down the hall, combat senses torqued to overdrive. Pol's immediate task was to cover their backs. There was no telling who might come charging out any number of doors, looking to mix it up, winging more lead into a pitched battle that looked to Bolan as if it was on the verge of winding down.

Reaching the edge of the hall, Bolan began picking targets, clipped two swarthy types off their feet with bursts up their spines. The problem was, an armed figure loomed to his right next, halfway down the steps, a sawed-off riot gun up and ready to blast Bolan in two. A snappy pivot, and the soldier shot from the hip, a bloody figure eight tattooed on his target's chest, knocking him down but not before a sonic boom of 12-gauge buckshot tore out the ceiling over the Executioner's head.

A few heartbeats, taking in the action, and Bolan found at least twelve hardmen still going at it. For the most part, the enemy's back was turned to them, Blancanales taking up a firepoint behind a wooden beam, directly across from Bolan.

The Executioner saw the North Koreans, figured eight in all, going for the front door, nailing a few al-Amin thugs on the way out. A 40 mm hellbomb down the chute of his M-203, and the Executioner sighted on the NK group spilling out into the street.

He hit the launcher's trigger, intent on helping them flee the firezone in bits and pieces.

"WHO THE HELL are those guys?"

Lyons couldn't say, but he damn well cared. At

first count it looked like eight, maybe ten muzzle-flashes were lighting up the windows, streams of sub-gun fire pinning them down beside the GMC, blowing out windows, ruptured tire hissing.

"Gadgets!" he hollered, ducking as another but longer wave of bullets slashed the GMC, a rolling drumbeat that could see them both shot to hell if they didn't do something quick. "Help me put a grenade down their throats. I don't care how you do it, just get it done!"

"Aye, aye!"

He knew Gadgets would do something, anything, even if that meant exposing himself for a heartbeat to their wild salvo. Up and sighting on the middle window where at least four bright flashes were wedged together, pounding out the autofire, Lyons sent the 40 mm round flying. It impacted just below the sill, punching out a massive smoking hole. Two more explosions rocked the street next, one more fireball blossoming in another window, but it was the bodies sailing out of the cantina on a smoky cloud that caught Lyons's eye.

A two-man death squad, he knew, had made the scene.

Survivors, six in all, began scraping themselves up, staggering for the vehicles at the far end of the motor pool.

"I think we cleared out the problem across the way, Carl!"

Schwarz, he saw, glancing over his shoulder, was right on his six.

"Then let's keep on rocking!"

And Lyons surged ahead, pounding out a long barrage of autofire.

COLONEL KUP YING didn't like the idea he had been sent out on what was little more than a suicide mission. He had been told what and how to do it, the meeting—like some psychic vision scripted by his superior—outlined for him by General Duk Jung in the teeming squalor of Mexico City. Right down to the blank note, the message he delivered to Rabiz, up until he had unleathered the twin Berettas, the general, grinning over brandy, telling him essentially his life and those of his men meant nothing to him. But since he could tell his job here was nearly done, he gave the immediate future some brief consideration, part of which was to bail, live to fight another day. All of them to a fighter, the dead included, had performed with tenacity, under relentless fire from the Arabs, giving more than they got. Later, their own federal and political contacts could make this carnage and any repercussions vanish. He hated to leave behind his dead soldiers, but there was no choice. Still, it bothered him when tough, brave young soldiers were marched out to give up their lives to cover up mistakes.

Taking phony money from the Arab terrorists, for example, cash delivered to cutouts, a sizable percentage of which was returned to Pyongyang to vanish into Kim Jong's coffers so he could keep on swilling cognac and watching Rambo movies and…

There wasn't time right then to mentally kick around the buffoons and scoundrels who ran his country. Later, when he made his way back to North Korea, there would be a day of reckoning for those he deemed clearly unworthy to run his country, his own stature as an officer who led from the trenches and succeeded in stomping out the al-Amin snakes elevated to true godlike dimensions. With his reputation as a warrior god assured, he would command a loyal following, soldiers and operatives who would help him take out Kim Jong Il, and thus show the Americans what an axis of evil could really do.

Rabiz, devious jackal, had beat him to the punch, hurling up a table, fleeing moments later down a hallway. Gone, but hardly forgotten.

There was still wet work left to do in Mexico, more terror cells to hunt down.

Again, later.

Right now survival took precedence.

There were two late arrivals, blasting in from the back end of the saloon, Americans, he thought. The trouble was they were armed with grenade launchers, and the crunching din out front warned Ying the worst was perhaps yet to come.

It did.

He was nearly out the door, wedged inside a protective circle of his shooters, backpedaling and firing at the few terrorists left, when the wall seemed to blow up nearly in his face. As luck had it, Ying saw the missile flying for them and bulled his way through two or three of his shooters. He was flying next, unsure whether the shock wave or his own feet had launched him clear of most of the devastating effects of the blast.

It took an agonizing few moments, his senses reeling, but he found his legs, began to stagger toward his GMC. It took another few chimes in his skull before he heard the autofire, then something that sounded like cannon peals erupting down the motor pool.

He sensed the coming danger, Beretta up and swinging toward a big figure extending a huge shotgun. Ying nearly toppled, his aim wavering off the mark. If he could make the GMC, or at least find cover…

He wasn't sure what happened next, but he felt something ripping through his upper arm, felt a slick shower bathe the side of his face. The excruciating pain came next, his brain attempting to frame a question as to why his left hand wasn't squeezing the Beretta's trigger when he felt the burning acid of bile reaching up his throat. Horror settled into his thoughts, aware of what he would find. Slowly, as the autofire blew through his men, that huge autoshotgun eviscerating what were little more than stick figures in sight misting over, Ying looked down at the ragged gristle where his arm used to be.

CARL LYONS CONSIDERED himself an all-or-nothing kind of guy, whether at work or play, and that was exactly the sort of proposition he was faced with here. He kept marching ahead, the SPAS-12 taking over, delivering rolling doom to the North Koreans. The guy with the missing arm was no longer a threat, a geyser of red hitting the air, sure to bleed out as shock set in.

Scratch that guy.

They tried to run for cover behind a GMC, but Lyons put a burst through the windshield. Screaming now, two NKs were grabbing at their eyes where glass had blinded them to everything but their own deaths, hopping up, in full view, figurative bull's-eyes painted on their chests from where Lyons marched.

One, two sonic booms and Lyons flung them away from cover that never came, gaping holes in chests large enough to wedge a basketball in.

Schwarz, he glimpsed, checking the area of slaughter, swept over a moaner and pinned him to the dirt with a quick burst up the spine.

All done.

Inside, Lyons heard the steady chatter of autofire. He motioned for Schwarz to take cover beside the hole one of their teammates had blasted out. Schwarz nodded, Lyons checking their six across the street. The problem in the hotel, whatever it was, seemed solved. Even still, he would watch all those armed stationary shadows.

This whole town, he knew, was bad news, and it would be grim relief to put this hellhole behind him.

WITH ANY LUCK Rabiz figured the smoker with the shotgun would never know what hit him.

The Arab had found his ride, cutting a course for the far southern edge of the town, a block away from the fighting. The Mexican was lounging on the tail end of his black pickup, a sickly sweet whiff of the smoke telling Rabiz he was puffing away on marijuana, enjoying the sounds of men fighting and dying, as a weird smile was frozen on his lips. Rabiz, crouched beneath a stone wall, had ordered Abu Salim to make his way down on the truck from the other end. He was to look inside, see if keys were in the ignition.

Rabiz waited, the pot-smoker giggling over something, unaware of the shadow behind as Salim poked his head through the open window. The thumbs-up came, and Rabiz rose. He went for a head shot, scoring brains, blanking out the high as the sombrero flew away with half the Mexican's skull. Over the wall, and Salim was already behind the wheel. Grabbing the passenger seat, Rabiz heard the engine cough, sputter. He was cursing this wretched country where nothing and no one but criminals worked when the engine finally grumbled to life.

The truck lurched ahead, Salim giving it some gas. They were gone, and they were still alive.

It looked like God, he thought, was on their side.

THE LAST THREE of the terrorists went down under sustained bursts from Bolan and Blancanales, flinging them in separate directions, bodies corkscrewing before they collapsed to the ground. A short, heavy silence followed, but Bolan heard the nervous footsteps up top, someone cracking home a fresh clip into a weapon, cocked and locked. The Executioner likewise fed a fresh magazine to his assault rifle, crouched beneath the landing, taking in the carnage.

"Hey, down there! Listen to me, whoever you are. I lost friends here tonight. Good men, business partners it will take time and *mucho dinero* to replace! Someone has to pay for my time and aggravation. Since you appear the only survivors, I suggest you carefully consider your options. Money or lead. Your choice."

Bolan found the two shadows in the thinning smoke cloud, made out the faces of Lyons and Blancanales. That they had cleared the front was a definite plus, all enemy numbers dead and accounted for.

Now this nonsense, Bolan thought. Some bandit or drug dealer holding up the exit.

The unseen problem began shouting his demands again. Bolan used the moment to patch through to Lyons on his com link, whispering, ''How many, Carl?''

''Four. Right against the rail, six feet to your right.''

''Let's do it.''

''Answer me now!''

A nod at Blancanales, and Bolan led the surge into the main room. Their M-16s up and stammering, Lyons and Schwarz poured it on, three streams of autofire converging with Bolan's burst on the targets above. The foursome up top returned brief fire, but they were already dancing, howling, cursing as the rail vanished in a storm of wood shards. They held on for a heartbeat, trying to readjust their aim, but the Executioner and Able Team had them scythed to bloody rags, pitching out of sight.

The Executioner backed up, searching the hall, the doors up top, another magazine cracked home into his M-16. No more takers looking to make a fast buck off the carnage.

''Let's quickly walk through it, see if one of them's still breathing and might shed some light on this mess,'' Bolan told Able Team.

''At first look,'' Schwarz said, following Lyons toward Bolan, ''I'd say it's a wrap here, Mack.''

''You never know,'' Bolan said. ''We'll go out the back, but keep your eyes peeled.''

CHAPTER SEVEN

Weaponized Ebola.

"God in Heaven," Hal Brognola muttered. "Where will it end? How?"

Now he was talking to himself. Understandable, he supposed, given the facts as he knew them. But exactly who was he expecting answers from? Was he imploring for some supernatural guidance to get them all through this crisis? Right then, he wasn't sure of much, other than the nightmare reality staring them all down. The longer he sat, mulling over the horror of it all, the immediate future of the world, with all its dire ramifications if they failed, if the terrorists succeeded in dispensing...

If...

There were days, far too many lately, when Brognola feared where the human race was headed, that the apocalypse may be as close as tomorrow, the push of a madman's finger on a nuke button, say, or a few ADMs smuggled into the U.S, set off in downtown Washington, New York, Chicago. He damn near wished what they were dealing with were that simple, and clean.

Nuclear holocaust, despite the horror, was quick, painless, he had to imagine, if victims were vaporized at ground zero. Well, the evil scheme they all now faced was beyond anything in their collective previous experience. It had left him, for one, he admitted to himself, shaken to the core of his soul.

And the crisis that the cyberteam and operatives of Stony Man were dealing with was so horrific, threatening not only Western civilization but could well launch a plague of Armageddon-esque dimensions across the entire planet, Brognola hadn't been able to sleep since the six drones had been seized by Mack Bolan, Able Team and a joint Justice-DEA task force as a freighter belonging to a French gangster was set to dock at the port of Miami, dump them off into the hands of a sleeper operative now in the custody of the Justice Department. And when the contents of the drones were analyzed by the CIA, NSA, CDC and experts at Fort Detrick? He had blanched.

Ebola.

He rubbed raw eyes that hadn't seen sleep since God knew when. When he tried to drift off, a catnap at best, visions of a black plague filled his mind's eye, jolting him fully awake, shivering, his brow mottled with cold sweat. He would envision an endless landscape of dead and dying Americans, bleeding from every orifice. He would see them shrieking in agony, begging to die, in fact, if only to end their hellish misery. They toppled in the streets, shopping malls, restaurants, in their homes, children falling dead in their schoolrooms, the black vomit of hemorrhage spewing from their mouths. They cried out to God for deliverance, they...

Alone in the War Room of Stony Man Farm in the Shenandoah Valley of Virginia, the man from the Justice Department gnawed on his unlit cigar, staring at the wall monitor that framed the source of a dread he hadn't known in some time, if ever. They were tagged the Angels of Islam by fanatic Muslims of al-Amin, an organization that was composed of whatever al-Qaeda and Taliban fighters had made it out of Afghanistan and sleeper Arab operatives around the world who had been stirred to wrath. Steel cylinders, six feet in length, four around, they were essentially small aerial drones, much like the CIA's Predator. With rocket fuel to launch them, either from an apartment rooftop or a neighborhood ball park, the terrorists meant to send them soaring over American cities, cut loose an airborne contagion in aerosol form—Ebola—bioengineered, four to five times more lethal than even Ebola Zaire, which was already proved in case histories as fatal nine times out of ten. This hybrid strain was, according to the best and brightest microbiologists from the Centers for Disease Control, one hundred percent fatal. No cure. No hope.

No chance.

According to what he'd learned, once this strain of Ebola hypothetically rained over a major population center, no incubation period for the virus was necessary. It could sweep around the entire planet in six weeks.

Armageddon. The end of mankind.

They looked like giant silver insects to the big Fed, what with steel wings that, he had learned, were meant to receive signals from either radio remote control on the ground, or sail across the sky on guidance from GPS from outer space, which told him some rogue nation had a satellite it wasn't supposed to. They had sophisticated battery packs and computers, a propulsion system that was comparable, but on a miniature scale, to a jet engine, laser guided, the whole nine yards to keep them up, flying and murdering. As well, their casings were mined with C-4, which meant should one of them be shot down by a fighter jet in the interests of homeland security, the lethal shower would still fall to Earth.

The al-Amin bastards had covered all bases.

The mere notion he suspected more of these weapons of mass destruction were out there—either smuggled into the United States already or were being manufactured by some state sponsor of terrorism—had rendered his nerves all but shot to hell. His eyes burning, stomach churning with tension no amount of antacid tablets seemed capable of soothing, he sipped coffee that tasted like battery acid and popped two Rolaids.

But what was he to do? he wondered. Throw his hands up? Despair? Hand the job over to somebody else? He was only human, after all, mere flesh and bone, prone to exhaustion, fear, anxiety. What to do then?

He knew. And the word *quit* wasn't, never had been part of his vocabulary. Not to mention the easy way only happened in scripted Hollywood fantasy.

Untold and countless innocent lives, unsuspecting of the horror he knew was poised to strike America, depended on what he did or didn't do. That went double for the Stony Man warriors out there in the trenches.

HUMINT—or human intelligence—had unearthed what had to be the most insidious terrorist plot to date in recent years. Three separate crisis points were getting the grim attention of the Stony Man teams. Unfortunately, he thought, the call was made to split up the five commandos of Phoenix Force, given the facts, the numbers of enemy operatives and ongoing operations flaring up from Russia to Mexico. Even Stony Man had its limitations, at least in terms of operatives it could field. He wished to God he knew something, though, what the hell was happening in real time. This was no time for patience, sitting in limbo.

Bolan and Able Team had cut a blazing swathe through al-Amin operations from Miami, through

New Orleans, Houston, had demolished everything from terrorist warehouses to a Muslim charity front, tallying up a fat body count in the process. This was war, declared on America by her enemies, and Brognola could well understand and appreciate the fact no one was interested in taking the other guys captive for detainment in Gitmo. Now they were entrenched and rolling against a drug cartel south of the border that was linked to terrorists. No word for hours on that front.

Then there was Gary Manning and T. J. Hawkins. Peeled off from Phoenix, they were in Marseilles, walking targets, or so the battle scheme went, attempting to create a gang war between the two top and rival criminal organizations in France, having sold themselves as up-and-coming entrepreneurs in the sale of weapons of mass destruction. Silence out of France.

David McCarter, the leader of Phoenix Force, Calvin James and Rafael Encizo had, though, called in to report Chechnya was a bitter wrap.

Meaning more problems, little solved over there other than a decent body count of terrorists.

The door to the War Room opened. Brognola looked up as Barbara Price walked in with a folder he hoped contained some good news for a change. Price was the Farm's mission controller. Under normal circumstances, the stunning honey blonde, Brognola knew, would have been a welcome sight for his sore, tired eyes.

Price claimed a seat beside Brognola, looked at his haggard expression and said, "You look like you could use some sleep, Hal."

"I can't. I mean, every time I try...all I see are millions of dead bodies."

She looked away, grim, nodding.

"Anyway," Brognola said, toughening up, "what do you have?"

"I just received a report from a source of mine at the NSA. There was a massive explosion in Marseilles, and I'm afraid to think why we haven't heard from Gary or T.J. It doesn't look good, Hal."

When she lapsed into tight silence, Brognola scowled. "Come on, Barbara, don't make me sweat it out any more than I already am. Are they or aren't they?"

"We can't verify it, of course, but an apartment building was literally vaporized by a blast...well, it was under surveillance, or supposedly so, by the CIA. It was an al-Amin safehouse, directly across an alley from René Puchain's nightclub. First reports indicate the nightclub was demolished."

Brognola felt the cigar nearly slip out of his mouth.

"Before I came here, I called in a marker of mine over at the CIA. They have operatives in the area," Price said. "They're there now."

Brognola felt his stomach roll over. He knew the

day had to come when one, even, God forbid, several of the Stony Man warriors would pay the ultimate price. Wage war was what they did. Every war saw casualties, and there was never any guarantee their own people would live to return to the Farm. It was a cold, grim fact of their world. He sat in silence, staring at nothing. Still he would cling to hope. It wasn't confirmed....

"As soon as you know something—"

"You'll be the first to know," Price said. "Okay. We're waiting to hear back from David."

"DNA analysis?"

"Right. They're back at Fort Pavel in Georgia. The way David tells it, there was nothing left of the Chechen village when they pulled out with the Russians and their CIA counterparts but a bunch of rubble, wreckage and corpses, most of which were blown to so many unrecognizable pieces during the initial air strike. No point in getting a body count since—and David sounded a tad irate—the Russians were executing civilians suspected of being terrorists before they left. They found a sizable cache of weapons in the al-Amin–Chechen rebel stronghold, but nothing of real intelligence value."

"Back to square one. If, that is, it turns out the missing body parts they bagged didn't belong to Nawir Wahjihab."

"We'll know if it is the so-called Sword of Islam soon enough."

"Sword of Islam," Brognola grumbled. "Angels of Islam. I'm thinking Wahjihab is somewhere else, Barbara. There could be six to twenty countries where he's either got ringers walking around or he's disguised himself, plastic surgery every other week..."

"I understand. All we can do is keep our people hunting, in the game, while we do what we do. Okay, we've discussed the possibility that a clandestine lab may be manufacturing more of these drones. The key to finding it, if that's the case, is to get a line on the five missing Russian microbiologists."

"Sold like cattle by the Petre Kykov Family."

"We believe so. Suggestion. We cut David, Cal and Rafe loose on the Kykov gang."

Brognola nodded. "Do it. As long as they're over there in that neck of the woods...and until we..."

He let it trail off, knowing it was wasted energy to get sidetracked lamenting on what they hadn't confirmed.

"Something else, Hal. This has been confirmed by the NSA, the CIA and NASA. North Korea recently put what Pyongyang has called 'an experimental satellite' into space."

"Well, we already know the North Koreans are bedfellows with the Russian Mob and al-Amin terrorists. There you have it. The link. The drones. Kim Jong can squawk all he wants about their country getting stamped as part of the axis of evil. Now they've maybe got a satellite by which, as we've hashed over, could be capable of guiding these Ebola-packed drones from space."

"If that turns out to be true, Hal, our side may have no choice but...well, but to shoot it down."

"Worry about that later. Politics and bad press is for the other guys to sweat over. Okay. Any word from Striker?"

"Not yet."

"Give it a little more time, then I want a sitrep from all three teams." He looked away from Price then, considering all the grim news dumped in his lap, what he had to do in the coming hours came to mind. "I'm going to have to chopper back to D.C. by the end of the day's business. A source of mine—what I can only refer to as a shadow cutout whose name I don't even know, or who he even works for—contacted me. He claims he has something big to hand over. I'm going to check it out. But stay in touch."

"Will do."

The briefing over, Brognola felt Price work a concerned eye over him.

"If you laid off that poison Bear passes off as coffee," Price said, referring to Aaron "the Bear" Kurtzman, who headed up the cyberteam, "you might be able to get some rest."

Brognola returned a smile he really didn't feel. "I'll keep that in mind, Barb."

When she left the War Room, Brognola felt the heat of anxiety rise inside again. Sleep. He wished if only he could. Something warned him the coming twenty-four hours would prove make or break.

Do or die.

God help them all, he thought, the human race included if…

He shoved the ominous thought aside. It was time to rise to the occasion, do whatever he could to see their side won this, no matter what or how they did it, and left the enemies of America this time out bloodied and trampled in the poison of their evil.

Before it was too late.

Marseilles, France

GARY MANNING WASN'T sure if he was alive or dead, or even really where he was. The big Canadian had never given much thought to what may or may not await human beings on the other side, much less contemplated the concepts of heaven and hell, but he felt strangely disembodied, floating up, up and away.

Or was it his imagination? Was he dead? Was this heaven? Hell?

He thought he chuckled—or was that a groan? He couldn't be sure his eyes were even open, but it looked like an impenetrable cloud of smoke was either drifting above him—or was it coming down to take him away?

But the smoke burned his eyes, tearing them. A sign of life?

Somewhere in the throbbing pain in his skull he heard his voice, attempting to piece together what had happened, calling out to him to remember, growing in urgency, even anger and desperation. The gangster, Douchet, no. Puchout? No. Puchain, that was the French gangster. Some deal they had attempted to strike up, only were ambushed in the streets of...

Where the hell was he? "They"? Somebody else with him?

France, somewhere. Paris? No. It was a dirty, teeming, big ugly city...by the water? Notorious for crime, smuggling? Think, dammit!

Mars...Marseilles.

That was it. Some rival had marched him—somebody else, a buddy?—back to this Puchain. Then, through the mist, he saw himself and his comrade, side by side, grinding up a bunch of greasy thugs with assault rifles, then marching into a shooting gallery, explosions rocking a big room that he wanted to recall as fancy, lavish. A war was under way, Frenchmen against swarthy types...Mideast?

Yes, that was it, he thought. They had been Arabs. Terrorists.

He stared up at the smoke, eyes stinging even more, but he didn't want to close them, wondering why he was afraid but relieved. Was this heaven or was it hell? Figure the day had to come sometime. Danger, yes, it was coming back. It had been a way of life, in fact. What had he been? What was he?

Some sort of commando, he believed. He lay there, immobilized, trying to feel his body, staring up at the roiling cloud, waiting to hear a voice of thunder and wrath. He saw it then. A figure, looked European, German perhaps, someone—a terrorist—they had come to France to hunt. Or had they? A shadow in the night, a figure darting through the smoke, running from the raging battle? The face of the gangster, then, this Puchain, uttering a name...

Wahjihab.

It was strange, thinking that if he was in fact dead and there was a God waiting to judge his life on its merits or lack thereof, he racked his brain to recall how good or how bad his life had been. To do what? Concoct any number of plausible excuses and rationalizations? What did he have to be afraid of? Funny, he thought, why it would happen that way, wondering about himself, though aware he had been a brave, even noble man in life, fighting evil, he believed, knowing that if a few good men didn't do something...

Principles? A value system?

"Gary?"

The voice sounded familiar. A sound next, like feet crunching over glass, or snapping wood. The smoke began to choke his lungs, the pain shooting through his body, jolting nerves, stirring a fire.

The pain, that was good, he knew on instinct. He was still alive.

He felt something jabbing in his side, a weight on his stomach. He coughed, heard his name called out again, this time with more urgency, closer now. He dug his hands through wood and glass, jabbed by needles, more pain now reviving his senses.

He was Gary Manning. And he was a commando. He worked for Stony Man Farm—that was it. And his buddy was still alive, despite the massive explosion that had blown down the night club.

"J.T.?"

"That's T.J. Thomas Jackson Hawkins."

Right. He looked up at the face, more familiar now, even though it was wreathed in smoke. There was an assault rifle in T.J.'s hand, the free one reaching down to help him stand.

"Grab your weapon, Gary. We need to blow this dump."

He heard the sirens, a shrill wail, coming from some great distance. The stink, the smoke was welling nausea in his gut. "What the hell happened?"

"We nearly got blown to kingdom come, that's what."

Manning found the M-16/M-203 combo wedged in a mound of wood shards.

"If we had been standing on the other side," Hawkins told him, "if you hadn't shouted a warning and we hadn't dived over the bar, we'd be buried with the rest of the dead out there."

Weapon free, Manning took his comrade's hand,

shimmied to his feet. "Man, oh, man, I don't feel so hot." He touched his scalp, gashed in spots, blood running down the side of his face. He looked at his friend and fellow warrior of Phoenix Force. Hawkins was peering at him, concerned, a trickle of red running down the side of his face. Features smudged by smoke, it was hard to tell how many dings and cuts he had.

"You going to be all right, Gary?"

"Yeah. You?"

"Better than you seem right now. Let's boogey. Some fresh air might clear out the cobwebs."

Sounded like a plan, Manning thought, as Hawkins indicated what appeared the quickest and clearest path out through the wasteland of rubble.

As bad as he felt, the strange thoughts he had, Gary Manning was damn glad both of them were still alive. For now, that seemed more than enough.

CHAPTER EIGHT

The fear factor was the least of it. After the successful conclusion to any operation, which both furthered jihad and gave praise to God, carving terror through the surviving infidel populace was a given, a mere token gift to their enemies from the holy-war package, silently telling them there was more to come. For instance, the Jews of so-called Israel, he thought, had been living in dread for years, as they should, altering lifestyles, fairly tiptoeing through the routine of their days, terrified of even sipping espresso in a Tel Aviv café, throwing a wedding party or dancing the night away in a disco. These days, he thought, their own homes, opulent enclaves with all the creature comforts denied the Arabs of the West Bank and Gaza, were little short of small fortresses where they cringed and hid behind the guns and tanks of their soldiers. He knew soon enough that would change, once he funneled more money, more guns, more explosives into that country. In time, the holy warriors of what would someday be Palestine would even attack their homes, hurl themselves at their very doorsteps, show them they weren't even safe under their roof at night. And the Europeans? he considered. Well, they had grown somewhat hardened to the violent facts of life in their various countries, going about their daily and sinful business of chasing money and pleasure, not jumping at the sight of Arabs over their shoulders, their cities not the armed camps like Israel. Past, present and future bombings and mass shootings of crowds, and the Islamic world could fairly proclaim they were the work of any number of criminal organizations, from the IRA to the Basque separatists to the Sicilian or Italian Mafia.

It was the total and complete destruction of America he concerned himself with, visions of tens of millions of dead infidels in their city streets sweetening his dreams each and every night. The most insidious killer virus known to man would sweep like wildfire from New York to Los Angeles in the time it might take to cover the distance by jet. The mere fact that Americans endured their days now in a state of paranoia and anxiety wasn't enough. The sons and daughters of Satan, he thought, could well afford to dump billions of their blood dollars into beefing up all manner of security, airports, train stations and such, armed high-tech cocoons what with their X-ray machines, strip searches, bomb-sniffing dogs, locked cockpit doors on their jets, air marshals and so forth.

There was always a way, where there was enough

money, to circumvent their security, always some small chink in what they believed was their armor that could be cracked wider, fully exposing them as naked and defenseless against the wrath and judgement of God coming down on them by Islamic peoples they oppressed. How smart, how prepared, how concerned—how "good"—could they possibly be, he wondered, when their own INS reissued visas six months after the pilots of God had been martyred?

No, Nawir Wahjihab considered leaving survivors cowering in fear of the next strike as little more than dessert after a big meal.

It was the body count that mattered most in the eyes of God.

The explosion he touched off by radio remote had been a glorious thing to behold, though any amount of destruction never seemed enough. Five hundred pounds of C-4, dirtied by radioactive waste, no less, had reduced at least half of the block on la Canebière, he'd seen, to rubble. There was little more now, due east of Vieux Port, than rising funnels of black smoke, climbing in puffed billows, so huge they blotted out portions of the brightening sky of a new day. The inevitable sirens shortly followed, those weird little police cars the French used, cracker boxes squealing onto the scene, the fire trucks likewise forced to halt far up the street, as he'd stolen a few minutes, viewing the disaster area from the steps beyond the industrial dock. It seemed like an hour to him, but in reality it was only minutes as the twisted wreckage of parked cars hurtled into sky, then pounded down, slabs of stone and sheared wood pelting spectators, sending them scurrying in terror.

It pained him that he had lost more than twenty warriors back there, both in the former safehouse and during the shoot-out with the gangster and his thugs. The apartment building, next to the gangster's lair, had been their safehouse for months. It was a shame to lose it—all but gone now, the building having been primed to become little more than a smoking radioactive crater—since he would be forced to put this country behind for a year, maybe more, at least. Operations in the European theater would carry on elsewhere, not a problem really, in hindsight. Germany, or Holland perhaps. Maybe England, where there was a huge Arab population, mosques nearly as common as their churches.

He climbed the stone steps and began to weave a hasty course through the first of several mazes where wood-and-stone structures were still dotted with yesterday's wash, window after window lined with strung clothing. It would be good to make the safehouse here once again, where he would be back among his brothers in jihad.

There was both good and bad news to report, but they expected as much.

Yes, it angered him to think of what he was forced to do here, Marseilles out of the scheme as a haven, the gangster who had helped him smuggle the first shipment of the Angels of Islam…

A failure? Or a simple inconvenience? Or was it revenge? Covering his tracks? It was true that the shipment of the drones had been seized by the American authorities before they could be delivered to his operative in Miami. Word had reached him via sat phone and e-mail in Morocco that their operations were now under some commando-type assault. He wasn't sure precisely how much damage had been done to their operations in America, but, worst case, there was the Mexican connection if they were shut down in the United States.

He had come here, following a short ride in his yacht from Morocco, in light of that disastrous news, halfheartedly believing he could continue to do business with Puchain, but knowing the seizure of the drones would point directly to the gangster. Thus endangering himself, if the Frenchman had been grabbed by the American law or intelligence forces, began talking if only in a vain attempt to save his own empire.

Wahjihab had gone into the nightclub, declaring war on the gangster, his soldiers going down, martyrs all, while he ran out, making sure he lived to carry on the jihad another day. He didn't view his sudden flight and escape from harm and certain death as cowardice. Far from it. He had been chosen by the sheikh himself, pronounced as the Successor before the

American vultures began swooping down, raining their smart and laser-guided bombs, the barbarians to this day believing they had dismantled future operations against them. It was simply God's will that he stayed alive until the Angels of Islam could soar over American cities. It might prove a tough sell, just the same, when he reached the safehouse and was forced to explain why he was still alive when so many great and holy warriors had gone to Paradise, not even a scratch on his plastic-surgery-altered features. Perhaps, or so he wanted to believe, the others would simply accept his role as Successor, keep the faith that he was a divine instrument of God, to be protected at all costs, even revered. That whatever he chose to do or not do was God's will being carried out through him.

That if he died, all hope for the most glorious of all attacks against their enemies, would go to Paradise with him.

Faces watched him from balconies, but he kept his head bent, aside from brief glances at his surroundings, averting their stares. It was reassuring that he was heavily armed. Say a gendarme suddenly blocked his path, wishing to question him, but he was comforted, more or less, by the weight of the Uzi slung across his shoulder, the explosives wrapped around his torso, both subgun and mass killing power concealed beneath his topcoat. There was a way out, already planned before he docked, and he silently prayed for safe passage out of Marseilles. Two countries, where cells were already established, would be temporary way stations, hopping points back to where the facility had long since been established.

There were—and he smiled to himself—more Angels of Islam under development right then.

Nawir Wahjihab knew he only had to stay alive if the dream was to come true.

HIS HEAD WAS CLEARING, as Hawkins had stated it would once they broke out of the rubble and began beating a hard exit from the ruins of Puchain's club. The air was hardly fresh, stale and reeking, he thought, of chemicals and smoke, but it helped to put distance to the choking black palls. Even still, Manning was groggy, his limbs not quite functioning in the well-oiled manner of what he recalled as a body hardened by athletic prowess. Recall, though, was back, every dirty shred of awareness of what their blood mission here in Marseilles was all about.

Somehow they'd gotten lucky, spared the brunt of the tenacious force of a blast he knew was no doubt set off by the al-Amin operatives. Covering their tracks, or Wahjihab—if that's who he'd seen fleeing the club—bringing down the block? Why? Revenge? What?

At the moment, Manning knew they had other, weightier considerations than getting immediate answers to questions best left on the backburner.

The black van slowly rolling down the alley didn't do much, in terms of relieving any anxiety, but it got the adrenaline pumping, flushing out more sludge, if nothing else.

Dawn had broken over Marseilles, Manning noted, but the sky was black in large patches, the smoke of utter destruction rising behind them as they made their way south through a twisting maze of narrow streets. Shadows of Marseilles citizenry, jolted out of bed by the blast, scurried everywhere, voices shouting to one another in a babble of foreign tongues. Sirens wailed in the distance but the immediate plan, as Hawkins had reminded him, was to get back—head east next, then move north—and have a short chat with Vincent Rousiloux.

Very brief, since they intended to kill Rousiloux and whatever thugs he had left standing.

The number-two gangster in the city was still on their hit list, and Manning knew there was unfinished business where the odious rat man was concerned.

They concealed their M-16s best they could, tucked under their trench coats. Any up close look by French authorities wouldn't pass them off as part of the frightened herd surging all over the city, but Manning had to believe the gendarmes had more pressing matters right then.

Manning was tempted to look over his shoulder at the van, but Hawkins said, "Don't look, Gary. If we can swing around the next corner..."

It appeared as if by magic, or on cue, and the trap became clear to Manning in the next instant. A clone of the black van raced around the corner, nearly clipping three pedestrians on its streaking flight toward them. Hawkins cursed, Manning about to break out the assault rifle but the van sluiced to a halt, sliding at an angle to block any hard charge past it. Instinct warned Manning to hold off breaking out the M-16. If they were gendarmes, FBI, Interpol…

Manning wheeled in time to find the trailing van lurch to a halt on their rear. A dark figure burst out the passenger door, told them, "CIA. Don't do anything stupid with those weapons! You want to get out of this city, you want to finish whatever it is you started, you'll get in and hear me out."

Manning and Hawkins exchanged a look, then the big Canadian told the CIA man, "You've got five minutes on our clock. This better be real, and it better be good. We're not in the mood for bullshit games."

"It's real enough, and it's not good."

VINCENT ROUSILOUX knew he was dreaming, even though the visions swimming through his head were so real, so alive.

It was sweet, and he wished he could stay there forever, floating in a place where life was all bliss and eternal pleasure. It was happening like this, more often lately, as he passed out, soaked to the gills in whiskey, the dreams in living color like watching a film. But the dreams were fading as an annoying hand roughly shook his shoulder.

"Vincent! Vincent, wake up!"

He shuddered awake in a pool of sweat. It took a few moments before he realized where he was, slumped over in the booth at his club. Back to reality, but what was happening? Why did his soldier sound in a panic? He groaned, suffering the pain of a monster hangover. He felt the drool running from a corner of his mouth, then coughed, craving a cigarette, flicked at the rat's nest of curly hair hanging down to his thin shoulders.

Two of his men stood beside his table. He touched a burning cheek, anger building as the knowledge filtered through the mud in his skull that one of his men had slapped him awake. "What?"

"There was an explosion. An entire apartment building, the one next to Puchain's. Gone. So is Puchain's club. No word from our people. I assume the worst. The authorities, they are everywhere. Should they come here, should they find the bodies of our people...."

He waved him off. Something had gone terribly wrong, and the gist of what he heard was that either the explosion might be linked to him... Or what? Would some of Puchain's hitters have survived? Blame him? Come storming into his place, blasting away? He couldn't think straight—he needed a stiff drink first, then figured that could wait. Instinct warned him it was best to get out of Marseilles until this mystery was sorted out.

"How many men do I have here?"

"Eight."

"We leave," he said. "Take as many weapons as we have."

"Where?"

"Madame Duvraux's, of course!" he snapped. He couldn't remember if her villa was in Cassis or Aubagne, but his soldiers would know. Her sprawling cathouse was as good a place as any, a safe haven where he could hole up until he understood the full ramifications of what they were dealing with. He detested the fat, gruesome redhead, who reminded him all the time of the mother who originally got him into the prostitution racket, but she was a business partner and for a few dollars shoved into the cleavage of ample bosom she would hide them. Then there was the American and the Canadian to consider, strangers who had come to him with a scheme to kill Puchain....

Maybe they were the cause of this mysterious disaster. Maybe they were still alive.

Rousiloux strangled down the bile and held out an arm. "Help me stand up, damn you!"

CHAPTER NINE

Gary Manning nearly went ballistic when he found their war bags in the spook van. Somehow he kept his cool, but fought to keep a civil tongue in his head. Whatever was going on here, it wouldn't help their mission to start locking horns with the CIA. It never paid, in his experience, to trade punches with what was still considered the world over America's top—or most notorious—intelligence agency, Uncle Sam's next best thing to God, or the Devil, depending on which yesterday's Company bedfellow was today's number-one bad guy.

"I'm Lachlin," the dark, goateed spook in the shotgun seat said, then nodded at the driver. "Parker. And that's Fisk back there."

Opening the bags and checking their Uzis, Berettas, the multiround projectile launcher, the loads on the clips, counting grenades, Hawkins and Manning then stole a second to glance up at the bald, mustachioed figure in black, hunched over the control consoles of the com center on wheels. At first glance, Manning noted GPS screens, tracking sensors of some area of the city marked by red blipping lights. Fisk wore a headset and twisted and turned the dials to what the big Canadian guessed was a police band monitor.

"Nothing's been touched."

That remained to be seen, Manning knew. It had been risky, stashing their weapons and sat link in the room of a hotel that was one cut above a den of thieves, drug addicts, whores, scum of the city lurking or traipsing all over the place, but it would have drawn more attention to them if they wandered all over the city with bags loaded with weapons that no amount of explaining to French authorities would send them on their merry commando way. Hindsight now, but Manning had been given a code he could tap into the sat link, a special alarm chip inserted by Hermann "Gadgets" Schwarz, which would warn them if the system was compromised.

Shucking off their topcoats, the two Stony Man warriors began strapping on combat vests, harnesses, webbing. Whatever the Company's game, Manning knew the two of them had their own plans.

"And you two are...?"

"Mann."

"Hawke. Special agents of the United States Justice Department."

Lachlin grunted. "Uh-huh. And I'm Gandhi."

"You care to tell us what the hell this is all about?" Manning growled.

"Al-Amin still has a cell in the city," Lachlin said.

"Let's start with the obvious first," Manning said. "Our bags. And why you just happened onto that mess back there."

"We had you under surveillance. What you did, pal, you blew about a year-long investigation into Puchain and his connection to al-Amin. We were ready to drop the net on Puchain, the al-Amin operatives, the whole goddamn enchilada before you two cowboys came blasting into the picture. So you can lose the attitude. The only parade rained on is ours. Someone—a lady by the name of Barbara Price I used to know from the NSA—called in a marker on me. She told me to comb that rubble and see if you two were still on the planet."

The Farm's mission controller, Manning knew, which meant they knew about the blast. In short order, Manning would have to touch base with Stony Man, if nothing else than to put to rest any fears of their potential demise.

"We've got another cell of al-Amin butchers north of the city proper," Lachlin went on. "We're going after them. So I'd rather you two not muck up any more of a multimillion-dollar operation with your wild-man routine."

"Wahjihab," Hawkins said. "We understand this big Sword of Islam is in town."

"This the guy?" Fisk asked, producing a black-

and-white picture, which Manning took and inspected.

"We didn't exactly have time to introduce ourselves," Hawkins said. "Tough to do when the place was blowing up all around us. But, yeah, that's the guy we think we saw running out of the club when it hit the fan."

"If you knew he was here," Manning said, "why didn't you just grab him?"

"We would have," Lachlin growled. "We were going to do just that before the fireworks started and they took out what looks like damn near a whole city block. What I'm saying, no, what I'm telling you two is if you went to stay in the game, you'll do things my way the rest of the time you're here in Marseilles."

"Or?" Manning posed.

"Or you're out. Or maybe the gendarmes or Interpol would like to have a lengthy discussion with you two—and by the way, the French aren't real big on foreign gunslingers, badge or not, coming here, wasting their citizens, even if they are criminal scumbags."

"We're going after Vincent Rousiloux," Hawkins said.

"Forget him, he's small-time."

"Not to us," Manning said. "With Puchain out of the picture, that little ferret might just step up to the plate, wanting to pick up where his dead buddy left off with al-Amin."

"We've already considered that possibility," Lachlin said. "I've got a team on the pimp now."

"So, I gather he's a little more to you than a small fish in the pond?" Hawkins said.

"In or out?"

Manning looked at Hawkins as both men claimed a chair. In what was being tagged by the media as the new war on terrorism, it was inevitable, the big Canadian supposed, that sooner rather than later they would cross paths—or swords—with any number of intelligence or law-enforcement agencies.

"What the hell, huh?" Manning said. "Sounds like you'd make our lives miserable anyway. But understand this. We're not here to gather intelligence, arrest anybody and hold their hands on a Herc ride back to Cuba. And we want to put old Vince down for good."

"I can live with that."

"We'll see," Manning said. "So, what's the big plan here?"

IT WASN'T QUITE the reception Wahjihab expected. He had envisioned a moment of personal glory where there was warm hugs all around, plenty of pats on the back, the ten remaining fighters of al-Amin in Marseilles bowing and scraping, praising his efforts all over the living-room floor.

Obligatory embraces, perfunctory greetings instead,

and Wahjihab waited until the leader of this cell, Hamid al-Zuraq, stepped up, clasped him on the shoulders, a quick hug. Was that a shove? Wahjihab wondered, as the Saudi drew back. Was that contempt in his eyes? If he was thinking him a coward, he would be wise, Wahjihab thought, to hold his tongue.

"It is done, brothers," he announced to the group. "The French gangster is dead, but so are the others. You are the last of the cell in this country. They died, brave warriors. Our mark was left on the city, praise God."

Was that a sneer on al-Zuraq's lips?

Wahjihab decided it was time, once again, to shore up their resolve, remind them this was war, that casualties would happen, that the whole was greater than any individual life. Except his own, which he decided it best to skip mentioning.

"They gave their lives for God. They are in Paradise. Do not weep for them. Their families, like yours, will be well provided for," he said, reminding them of the fund set up for them in Saudi Arabia. "In the event I was followed, or you have been discovered, you are to remain—"

The impertinent al-Zuraq interrupted, brusque. "The CIA has already found us."

"What?"

"While our brothers were dying in the city, we have observed a black van, parked down the street. Our thermal imaging turned up three occupants, all of them armed. We intercepted a cell communication to a team in the city that is on the way. Americans. I suppose, after your speech, you would like to leave here while we cover for you?''

Wahjihab felt the tension rising around him, stares boring into him, leaving him to wonder if they were mirrors of the arrogance he found in al-Zuraq's eyes. What was the thin veil of hostility all about? Did they not understand their own role? Could they not accept the fact he had been personally chosen by the sheikh to live at all costs until the Angels of Islam flew over America? Even in the name of jihad, he supposed it was asking nearly the impossible for these men to sacrifice their lives. And for him, one man, so he could leave the country, safe, on his way to make history, to reclaim the glory of Islam for all of them.

''Go with God, brothers,'' Wahjihab told the group, then took al-Zuraq by the arm, led him into the kitchen alcove. ''I trust you have the directions you were ordered to provide.''

The Saudi stared at Wahjihab, then pulled a piece of paper. ''Go out the side door. Down the hill, past the cathedral, about a quarter mile then, the way is marked to Pont du Mour on that paper. Khalid is waiting in a white Volvo to drive you to a helicopter that will fly you to a boat waiting off the coast.''

Wahjihab looked at the paper, memorized the directions, the list of names and numbers he would need wherever he landed next. "I sense there is something you wish to say to me."

Al-Zuraq seemed to think about something, then finally said, "It is not important. It is as you said. This is jihad. All of us, at some point, will be called upon to make a sacrifice."

The Saudi was judging him, Wahjihab was sure, speaking but not saying what he really wanted. It was no time to debate the issue of who was more important in the larger scheme. It was time to go, before the CIA, it sounded, crashed through the doors.

"Show me the way out of here."

THE CIA'S BIG PLAN was about as simple and straightforward as it could get.

Rush and blast.

Scaling the rocky incline for the two-story house above, M-16/M-203 combo in hand, Manning factored in the pluses and minuses, figured the two of them—now unofficially part of the Company Strike Force Scorpion—stood a fifty-fifty chance to remain standing once the smoke cleared. The enemy head count was unknown. Could be ten, could be as many as twenty, Lachlin had informed them during the hour-plus drive north of the city proper. Problem number one. Strike Force Scorpion was made up of all of six blacksuited Company shooters with MP-5s, grenades for any big-bang entrance or room-clearing chore in their combat vests. For the Company's part, its operatives would launch a full frontal assault, while Manning and Lachlin, com links in place, keyed in to the CIA hitters, waiting on Lachlin to give the go, blasted their way inside from the back. A lockjaw of flying lead, nothing fancy. Wahjihab had just been made going into the safehouse by the stakeout team down the block.

The biggest concern Manning had was the booby-trap factor. Say the al-Amin cell had piled up a couple hundred pounds of C-4? Say there were mines ringing the compound, whether the courtyard or the rough terrain leading up the backside? Say…

Lachlin had shrugged it off. Apparently, two of his ops had mini-bomb detectors, but even if they picked up a whiff of plastique on the way in…

Manning missed it on his first pass, crouched and hauling himself from tree to tree, but Hawkins whispered, "Gary."

Turning, the big Canadian saw the ex-Army Ranger pointing at the minicam, buried in some thorny brush. They were made.

Manning was about to key his com link and tell Lachlin as much when the shooting started.

They appeared on the balcony, already tuned into their advance, winging out the autofire. Manning felt the hot lead nearly scalp him, as he dived beneath the lip of a jagged precipice that, he was grateful, was simply part of the rugged, hilly landscape.

HAMID AL-ZURAQ BURNED with anger and resentment. Too many good warriors in Marseilles had already given too much for one man. He had his orders, straight from other top lieutenants, mullahs and imams and such, and he would see them through. Still he didn't like it. This Wahjihab had been chosen, though, by Osama himself, or so the story went, as the Successor to strike what al-Zuraq had heard would be the greatest blow of all time against the hated Americans. The problematic question he had about the Omani was if the man had heart and guts enough to even succeed in delivering any more Angels of Islam. Say there was some ultimate moment of truth, where Wahjihab had to personally launch the winged avengers while facing down the guns of American operatives? Would he throw his hands up, offer himself as a puppet mouthpiece to the infidels? Would he go the distance?

Did he truly believe? Or was he just a pretender?

Many questions were left to be answered, but the future had arrived for al-Zuraq and his men, and he knew he wouldn't live long enough to find out if Wahjihab would succeed. It was time to fight, stand their ground as long as possible, die and claim their rightful place in Paradise. It galled him, just the same, the son of a poor street vendor, a former soldier in the Royal Saudi Army, that he had accepted Wahjihab's money in the first place, aware now he would never see his family again, make certain they were provided for as the Omani had vowed they would be.

Yes, like many Saudis, he hated the imperialist Americans, wishing only they would pack up and leave his country. Like many Saudis, he could see through their greed, their military aid, their armed presence nothing more than a devious ruse so they could keep their hands on the valves of the pumps of black gold. Al-Zuraq believed in jihad, though, too long seething that something had to be done to restore Islam to its former glory, or, at worst, save his own country from the oppressive interference by the Americans. And the Successor had come to him with the semblance of a plan, enlisted his services. He had three wives and twelve children to consider. So he had taken the money.

He found five of his soldiers, lining up at the row of windows, AKs, Uzis and RPG-7s ready to blow the invaders into hell. The monitors in the study had already picked up six black-clad figures out front, two in the back. The safehouse was perched on a hill, far enough away from local residents of what he guessed passed as a French suburb, but isolated enough so that any approaching invaders could be singled out by their tracking devices.

He glanced at the small duffel at the edge of the divan. Inside, twenty pounds of C-4 was primed and ready to blow at the touch of his finger on the radio remote. He dropped the detonator box in the pocket of his windbreaker, cradled his AK-47. Not yet.

They were vaulting the low retaining wall, breaking off in two-man teams, angling for their motor pool when al-Zuraq gave the order to shoot at will.

Down the line windows were blasted out by the first volley from his warriors, al-Zuraq catching the rattle of autofire from upstairs as the others cut loose on the back-door invaders.

CHAPTER TEN

Working with the CIA, if that's what T. J. Hawkins even chose to consider it, was never high up on his list of things to do. In fact, it didn't even make the B list. Spooks, in his experience, had their own agenda, careers to think about advancing, jerking off other agencies with lies and half-truths, while they seemed to tap-dance a high-wire act between "diplomatic missions" and their own gallivanting around Third World countries, espousing their own glory in roles as military advisers to ragtag bands of rebels. Some operatives even jumped the Stars and Stripes ship, went for themselves, looking to land ashore on Easy Street by forming alliances with drug cartels, gun runners, even terrorist organizations. Sure, there were exceptions to every rule, he knew, but the warriors of Stony Man had gotten suckered by the CIA before, and more than once. Present case in point?

Lachlin, or whatever the hell his real name was, had pulled off the burglar act in their hotel room, probably rifled through their bags, maybe considered bugging their sat link so as to discover the identity of whom they pledged allegiance to.

The good news was that Gary Manning was back on-line, the hellacious jarring he'd taken apparently worn off, though Hawkins was still concerned the big Canadian might have a lingering concussion. The bad news was that three, maybe four terrorists had nearly caught them with their pants down, blazing away and...

Hawkins nearly missed it, fear and adrenaline fusing as he spotted the warhead poking between the curtains of the balcony. Cover fire for the rocket man nearly won the morning for the bad guys, Hawkins glimpsing Manning rolling away from the blanket of lead chopping up the hillside, punching divots in the landscape. Braving the lead storm, Hawkins hit the trigger of his M-16, a long full-auto burst that hit the rocket man square in the chest. He was a shadow stick figure, tumbling out of sight, loosing the warhead in death spasms.

But Hawkins saw he got the job done, better than expected.

The warhead slammed into the top edge of the window, a blossoming fireball that decimated half the upper floor.

And abruptly silencing all guns up top.

"Mann! Hawke! One of you come in!"

Hawkins was up, listening as Manning patched through. "Yeah!"

"Are you in yet?"

"We're on the way now!" Manning answered.

"Get inside, then hold a position near the back until I give the clear!"

"What? Why?"

"I've got a surprise for these bastards coming in now," Lachlin said. "A Huey with a fat Gatling package to grind these bastards into yesterday's beef kebab! Ought to eat up half the house!"

"Thanks for the heads-up!" Manning snarled.

"You're welcome."

Did the asshole just chuckle? Hawkins wondered.

"Any more surprises, Lachlin?"

"Not at the moment."

Hawkins heard Manning curse as the CIA agent signed off.

"You believe this?"

"Indeed I do," Hawkins said, falling in beside the big Canadian, his eyes and the muzzle of his assault rifle fixed on the smoking hole, the back bay window and French doors. "Welcome to the wonderful world of spookdom."

THE BATTLE WAS LOST before they even fired off the first few rounds or triggered an RPG. As his AK-47 pounded out a burst, tattooing the minivan, al-Zuraq saw the black gunship rise up out of nowhere and soar in from the east. It was a big-winged leviathan, tinted cockpit glass hiding the flight crew, but there was no mistaking the Gatling gun, spinning and smoking out what he knew would be the first few hundred rounds in a storm that would blow in the front wall, a razoring wall of lead that would decapitate and eviscerate all of them. He wheeled, going low, attempted to run from the hurricane of steel-jacketed monsters blasting in the windows, but he felt the hot knifing tear across his legs. His howl of agony was lost in the screams of his soldiers getting diced to crimson ribbons, flung all over the living room.

He had one final chance to take as many infidels with him as possible. Perhaps even the explosion would send rubble flying and tearing into the chopper's rotors, or even bring it down in the fireball.

He was down, on his belly, but not out, the screams fading now, bodies thudding off the far wall. They would burst inside, any second now…

He reached into his coat pocket.

MANNING DIVED to the kitchen floor, beside Hawkins. The Gatling storm went on for what the big Canadian reckoned was a full minute or more. Too much time to stay put, and he could be sure it was definite overkill, not much more of the terrorists left out there but slick puddles of goo. Holes the size of basketballs were punched through the kitchen wall, plaster, smoke, glass raining over the outstretched forms of the Stony Man warriors. The refrigerator exploded, spewing its contents, food, milk and whatever else, the motor sparking, blasted to scrap.

Manning heard them crying out their pain, bodies no doubt tossed about like rag dolls out in the living room, arms and legs all but sheared off by what he had to figure were either 12.7 mm or 20 mm rounds. Given their prior experience with the al-Amin terrorists, Manning knew he needed to somehow make his way out into the living room, fearing even a badly mangled survivor might be crawling around, ready to touch off a big bang.

The big Canadian wasn't a believer in second chances, unless a man learned from past mistakes.

Manning crawled toward a doorway to his left. Pelted by glass and wood needles, he homed in on the racket.

He was around the corner when his worst fear was in the process of being realized. A wall of deafening silence fell over the living room, the black-garbed CIA shooters vaulting through the churning smoke like Olympic hurdlers, someone in the far corner shouting that he surrendered, don't shoot.

The box was in the terrorist's hand, the red light on, the figure soaked from the waist down in blood. He was rolling over, toward the CIA shooters, that eerie smile of the fanatic ready to go out in a final blaze lighting up his face when Manning jumped to his feet. Hawkins was right beside him, in tandem, the ex-Army Ranger obviously having the same grim thoughts. They were locked on, and hit the terrorist with twin streams of autofire. Manning went for the hand first, obliterating the appendage in a burst of crimson and bone, then raked him, head to toe until the clip burned out.

"On your face! Get down!"

Lachlin was over in the corner, shoving the lone terrorist who had—as miracles sometimes went—survived what had to have been a thousand rounds ripping into the place. The room was choked with smoke, showering plaster and dust, Manning's senses flayed by the stench of death. The walls, where they weren't obliterated, were streaked with red.

Manning held his ground while the CIA shooters broke past him. They split up, charged down the hall or bounded up the steps. He left them to the chore of rooting out any snakes in hiding. He'd just about had enough of worrying about booby traps and suicide bombers.

Vincent Rousiloux was on his mind.

Manning and Hawkins walked up to Lachlin, who was fastening plastic cuffs on the prisoner's hands.

"Maybe a break, gentlemen," the CIA agent said. "That is if my friend here decides he'd rather sing than squeal in pain."

Manning winced. Torture. That never cut it with Manning, but he didn't intend to be around Lachlin long enough to voice any objections.

"Rousiloux," Manning said.

Lachlin jerked a thumb at the gunship, hovering in the courtyard, rotor wash sweeping away most of the smoke by now. "There's your ticket to ride. My pilot knows the way to where my guys say Rousiloux just showed up."

"I take it you've got better things to do here?" Hawkins said.

"Meaning?"

"Meaning whatever you learn from this one," Manning said, "we're wondering if you're the sharing kind."

"Hey, my friends, this thing is bigger than you know, far bigger than Rousiloux, a goddamn pimp. I've got al-Amin cells spread all over the map from here to Italy, through the Middle East and maybe all the way to Indonesia. I've got—"

"We know what you've got," Manning interrupted. "Let me ask you something. I was wondering how the French intelligence fits into all this."

"They don't. They're a nonfactor."

"And my original question?" Hawkins asked.

"If I learn something from this sack of garbage, you'll be the first to know. Thing is, I'm set to bail France anyway. This thing is just getting heated up."

"Meaning your war machine is rolling onward down the Mediterranean?" Manning said.

"You got it. If you want to tag along..."

"We'll let you know. I want you to tell your pilot

that he is to obey my orders without question,'' Manning said.

''Rousiloux is your party. Knock yourselves out.''

Manning led Hawkins away from Lachlin, bounded onto the mangled sill and forged into the smoke and rotor wash.

''YOU ALWAYS COME to Mama Michelle, my little Vinnie, whenever you're in trouble or need something. Like money. Or Mama's loving.''

Vincent Rousiloux grimaced. His head was still throbbing like a jackhammer, and he needed a drink desperately. The mere sight of Madame Duvraux, all three hundred pounds and five foot ten inches of her wasn't helping to ease the queasy churn in his stomach. The woman had a triple-decker chin, and her flaming red hair was done up in some sort of hairdo that he figured went out during World War I. She had doused herself in some kind of musky perfume that smelled like dog urine, and if he stood too close to her another second, he was sure he would vomit all over the bar. Then there was her voice. Where his voice sounded like a soprano, she had a booming bass, raspy now after three to four packs of smokes per day the past twenty years. Then there was the way she looked at him, rendering him confused as to whether that was a leer or a smirk on lips painted as red as blood.

She might have been a business partner, both of

them sending clients to each other, but he still considered her a subordinate, since it was his money that had originally set her up. Even at that early hour Rousiloux had noted the salty crowd, a mixed throng, merchant marines, a few local hoods he recognized from the city, a politician he thought he should know. Her security team, five at last count, were all armed with holstered pistols, wandering the premises, sometimes stealing a half hour, he knew, to sample the goods.

Any other time he might have admired the posh surroundings and dived in, let the good times roll. Everything was done in silk and satin. Huge oil paintings, mostly nudes. Billiard room. Jacuzzis, saunas. There was a pool on the roof where a lot of frolicking went on, champagne and coke laid on silver traps, Rousiloux having just marched two of his men up there with walkie-talkies. He hoped they kept their mind on business. First reports on the radio, and it sounded as if terrorists had set off an explosion that had knocked out half of la Canebière. Law enforcement personnel, he'd heard from an associate, were crawling all over the city, rounding up anybody known to have underworld connections, ostensibly for questioning. No word on dead or wounded, but as jacked up on anxiety as Rousiloux was, he felt sure Puchain still had people on the prowl. It was no big secret that Madame Duvraux's cathouse on the hill along the coast was his second home. And the way his luck had run the past few years, it would be asking too much of fickle fate that Puchain had been blasted to hell.

"My little Vinnie, have you lost your tongue?"

He went behind the bar, grabbed a bottle of whiskey and poured a stiff one, a splash of ginger, two cubes. "Will you stop calling me that?"

That infuriating smile—or was it a sneer—again.

"Have a drink, my little Vinnie. We sit, then catch up. Like old times."

What old times? Oh, God, he remembered now, killed the drink, built another at light speed. A hundred or so pounds and ten years ago she had been doable enough so that he at least wouldn't get squashed like an insect beneath her. Then it started to come back to him, and he began to see the smile for what it was. He shuddered, recalling some of the games they used to play, stuff that would have made the Marquis de Sade gasp.

"I will need to stay here a while."

"The trouble in the city?"

"Yes," he told her. "Until I learn what happened, if Puchain and his people... I sent some of my men, and two strangers, an American and a Canadian, mercenaries, I think, to go and kill Puchain."

"Ah, Vinnie, Vinnie. Naughty little boy. Always with this hunger to kill the monster, Puchain. I suppose it's good to dream. I know you want to be big instead of little Vinnie. And what if Puchain is out of the way? Then what?''

He spotted a new light shining her eyes. ''I sense you have something in mind?''

''Yes. I have been thinking, perhaps me—we—are long overdue to expand. There are other areas we must consider, if we ever plan to retire and live the high life. Never have to worry about money again. Entertainment is becoming very big in France. Internet, we get our own Web site. We can shoot films using our girls....''

He was thinking maybe she was right, porn was growing in France, a huge industry, and he had long considered finding a way to carve himself a piece of that action. He was about to pursue the conversation, feeling better now, fortified by a few ounces of booze, when his radio squawked.

''Vincent! Pick up! I think we have a problem!''

CHAPTER ELEVEN

Manning felt better, both physically and psychologically, but it was stretching it, he knew, to admit he was one hundred percent. Up until a little while ago, the big Canadian was fighting off the nausea, dizziness, the pulsing headache that had persisted since hauling himself out of ground zero, but the sludge in his body, the chiming in his skull seemed to diminish, due to either time passing or each fresh burst of adrenaline.

And now it was just the two of them, alone again, and that felt clean, away from any devious plans or games that the CIA man might be playing. Not to say Lachlin wouldn't play it straight with them—beyond neglecting to inform them the terrorist safehouse was meant to be a shooting gallery for a Huey gunship, as if the guy had been saving the punchline to some big dirty joke. Whether or not Manning would see the two of them carry on their mission, locked on with Strike Force Scorpion…

Moot. And definitely on the backburner.

If Lachlin was jerking their chain, leading them around by the nose, or simply wanted to discover the truth as to who they really worked for, Manning figured the man would reveal whatever dark machinations he thought he could hide in time.

Right then Manning knew they had a pimp and standing army of brigands to fry.

It was a short chopper ride, maybe twenty minutes, to the estate on the hill. To Lachlin's credit he had left a brief intel packet on the target site, and one on Madame Duvraux. The woman was a business partner of Rousiloux, the little rat man having, according to the synopsis, brought her into the skin trade a decade earlier, her own small force of gun-toting thugs on-site part of their combined payroll. She catered to anyone with ready cash, and Manning wasn't sure who or how many shooters they would find here, maybe a gendarme or two, some local businessman, political brass straying from the loving arms of their wives. Which meant not everyone was fair game.

They were going in blind, but they were rolling in, shoot to kill if it was armed, had that particular cut-throat look both of them had come to see as the face of evil belonging on the whoremonger's goons.

Judgment calls, each step of the way, every bullet fired in anger.

It struck Manning as ironic that for all of Lachlin's blustering how insignificant Rousiloux was, it looked as though the CIA had the pimp on tap for either a roundup or a full-blown strike to topple his operation. Who could say? The CIA, he thought, was infamous for only letting the other guy in on a need-to-know, while demanding everything the other guy knew.

Spook SOP.

It was a postcard perfect view of the lay of the land below the Huey as the gunship streaked in on the target, vectored from the southeast, nearly hugging the rocky, tree-studded coast. Wedged in the doorway beside Hawkins, the big Canadian took in the picturesque scenery beyond the belted Gatling gun. Up and down the rugged cliff he saw clusters of shops, quaint inns, sure there was any number of cafés, restaurants along the harbor for the party crowd. A fishing village lay to the south, every kind of pleasure craft imaginable docked or floating out to the Mediterranean. Just another day in paradise down there, and if word about the devastating explosion in the city had reached this far, they appeared clueless. Giant parasol pines swept up the hillside, but Madame Duvraux apparently had a special place in her heart for the tropical. Palm trees and other prehistoric vegetation, most likely transplanted, ringed her estate, scrubbed white stone, with fancy wood trimming, red tile roof. A large motor pool, roughly twenty vehicles, mostly luxury cars, fanned around a circular brick-paved drive. The cars would be the task of the flyboys, he determined, to take out. No escape. From the few intel pics Lachlin had provided them, Manning had already formed a battle strategy and run it past Hawkins.

The pool on the roof was, even at that early-morning hour, hopping with players, several women slinking around, little more than string bikinis or flimsy nightgowns covering what they were selling, as they led johns across the deck to what looked like some bay-windowed party or upstairs dining room. A quick look through his binos, and Manning framed two hardmen. Both were sitting, armed with subguns, beneath a red umbrella, sipping from some sort of fancy drink with fruit floating near the rim, ogling the flesh show behind dark sunglasses. A second later, they came alive, jumping to their feet, staring at the onrushing gunship. One of them was on a handheld radio, and Manning believed he recognized them from Rousiloux's cathouse in the city.

Lachlin had left him a tac radio by which to raise the pilot. Manning looked toward the open hatch, patched through. "Flyboy?"

"Sir?"

"Drop down near the deck. We jump and go. Your job is to take out that motor pool. I mean I don't want anything left of those vehicles but scrap. You copy?"

"Man said it was your show. I copy."

"Let's do it."

Both of them were going in with Uzi subguns this time out, extended 40-round clips in place, spares fixed to webbing. Any tossing of hand grenades would be a last resort, if a pocket of shooters decided to hole up in a room.

As the gunship lowered near the edge of the pool, the hardmen were up and moving, Manning and Hawkins jumping from five feet up.

The Stony Man commandos marched, side by side, Uzis coming up as the hardmen cut the gap. They balked for a heartbeat, Manning almost able to read their thoughts behind the shades as recognition and the menacing intent set in. They nearly made it, MAC-10s sweeping up, on-line, when the Stony Man warriors blew them off their feet.

VINCENT ROUSILOUX felt his heart sink to his stomach when he heard the American and Canadian mercenaries had just hopped off some sort of military gunship. The first report was they were armed, and looked, according to Pierre, as if they had something very bad on their minds. The fact that only the two of them had come there, alone, none of his soldiers with them, shot some warning flares through his mind. What the hell had happened then at Puchain's? When he heard the shooting next, the screams of whores over the radio as he imagined a stampede had just begun in furious earnest poolside, he barked for Pierre to respond. His bowels now churned like a blender, fear of what was happening grinding away.

Madame Duvraux waddled down the bar, slapping the whiskey bottle out of his hand. "Vincent! What have you done? What trouble have you brought to my home?"

"Quiet!" he grated. "Pierre!"

"Hey, Vince, how you doing? Pierre and his buddy were the first to go, but they won't be the last."

It was the Canadian, he believed, trying to picture the two mercenaries from their one and only meeting. Rousiloux's mind raced with questions but he couldn't find his voice.

"Vince? You there?"

"What do you want?"

"You, Vince. René's history, but before we shot him I think he made a last request. Something about not letting you claim the whoremonger's crown."

"Who are you?"

"Your death knell, Vince. See you in a few."

The doors burst open, Rousiloux swaying, his stomach swollen with bubbling nausea. Who were they? Why did they want to kill him? Maybe they wanted money. Maybe...

Maybe, hell. They wanted his ass. But why?

"Vince!"

Madame Duvraux was in his face, spittle flying, and it was all he could to keep from slapping her into silence, but he didn't think he could reach up that high. One of his soldiers stood in the doorway, calling his name. He was so petrified, he couldn't even recall who the man was, only that he was armed and ready to lead him, somehow, out of this sudden raging madness.

"We need to go, Vince!"

"Yes...yes," he stammered, finding his legs, Madame Duvraux railing at his back as he waddled an unsteady course out the door. "The car!"

"Vincent, come back here!"

He could hear the commotion on the roof, feet pounding, whores and their johns howling. More gunfire, coming from behind, which meant the mercenaries had made the dining room. They were something other than what they claimed, he was sure. But what? FBI? CIA? It was possible, but he didn't think so. No American law enforcement or intelligence agents just came in shooting what they considered the bad guys, damn the questions. And why would they deem him a bad guy anyway? He was just a simple businessman. Ambitious, yes, but all he ever wanted was a little bigger slice of the pie. What was wrong with that?

He let himself be ushered by the arm through the waiting room, now empty as the last of the patrons brushed by, peeling off to go hide in any number of rooms. He considered following that example, but there was something in the Canadian's voice that told him the two madmen wouldn't leave there until he was found, and shot dead.

He entered the foyer, moving toward the massive double doors, now open, his Mercedes limo framed in the early-morning sunlight when one of his soldiers triggered at something, shooting skyward. Then his body seemed to explode, a giant red dam-burst, right before his eyes. It looked as if his right arm had been sheared off at the shoulder, then the head erupted, followed by the complete obliteration of something that was once human. It was all Rousiloux could do to keep the bile down. There was some kind of storm descending, wind rushing down the foyer, causing him to slit his eyelids. The terror was so overwhelming it took more than a few racing heartbeats before he recognized the helicopter gunship for what it was.

And what it was now doing.

Rousiloux screamed, frozen in some hysterical borderland between horror and outrage. The mammoth machine gun was raking the motor pool with a hurricane of bullets that seemed to carve up metal as if it were nothing more than wet paper. The force of the onslaught was so great, Rousiloux watched as his Mercedes was pulverized to smoking metal ruins, lifted off its wheels, hood, roof, the works blown off in shards that vanished to scrap in seconds. Then the killing bird swung, left to right, hosing down the other vehicles, that awful thunder of destruction swelling his eardrums with a painful lancing. Rousiloux was forced to close his eyes, nearly stumbling as he backpedaled from all that glass and metal flying around in some cyclone of destruction, wind and trash rushing through the doorway.

"I need a weapon!" Rousiloux shouted at his man, shaking him out of his shock as he stood there, gaping at the sight of all those luxury vehicles, their escape, reduced to a graveyard of wreckage.

"Yes. The bag, follow me. What do we do?" the man, André something, he now recalled, wanted to know.

"Do? We find another way out of here!"

He was retracing his steps through the vacant waiting room when Madame Duvraux heaved her bulk in his path. "Just like that, Vincent, you leave me here like this! You bring disaster to my home and now you are just going to run away?"

"These men are coming here to kill me! You want to stay, fine. Maybe they will kill you, too."

She seemed to think about that, the fury ebbing in her eyes.

"Stay here, or do we go out the back together?"

"Follow me, Vincent. But when this is over, you and me are going to have a very serious talk."

He should be that lucky he thought, found André beside him, pulling out a mini-Uzi from one of the bags his soldiers had brought. It was a small weapon, but it seemed to dwarf his pinky pudgy hand, his finger barely able to curl around the trigger. This was no time, he knew, to lament over his freakish diminutive curse of nature.

A plan flared to mind, as he eased close to Madame Duvraux, who led the way down a bisecting hall, away from the sounds of gunfire, the madmen on the way down, no doubt. Worst-case, he would use this red whale as human armor, say if he was intercepted in flight by the madmen. If he could stall them, talk some sense into them...

Surely, they wouldn't shoot a woman, not even a hideous beast like this, now, would they?

MANNING AND HAWKINS made the bay windows just as three armed silhouettes rushed into the dining room. The Stony Man warriors fired their subguns together, blasting in the window, washing the hardmen with shards that were nothing more than flying scalpels. They were sweeping bursts of subgun fire, thrown off the mark now as they received bloody facials. The two commandos hit them with long bursts, flinging bodies back in a triple jig step, the dance team crashing down on white-linen tabletops.

Gone, and knocking on hell's door.

Two more of the house goons came bounding up the steps to their left as they surged through the doorway. They locked a heartbeat's gaze with the two Stony Man invaders, pistols jerking up, but Manning and Hawkins nailed them, left to right and back, kicking them down the stairs, all flailing arms and legs, out of sight.

Now the hard part, Manning knew, as they reached the partition that ran beside the top stairwell opening. Below, the big Canadian heard the flurry of activity, voices raised in panic, doors thudding somewhere. Crouched, cracking home a fresh clip, Hawkins likewise reloaded his Uzi, he peered around the corner. It was about a twelve-foot descent to make the first floor.

"Let's keep rocking," Manning told Hawkins, taking the lead.

Uzis leading the descent, they were halfway down when two gunmen whipped around the corner. Both warriors had their adrenaline and combat instincts torqued to maximum lethal. Manning heard and sensed them before they popped into view. He was already holding back on the Uzi's trigger, Hawkins's Israeli subgun stuttering on beside him. The hardmen were chopped up, crimson divots erupting across their chests, their bullpup assault rifles chattering several and way too long nervous heartbeats for Manning, as rounds gouged wood and showered chips and plaster dust over their heads.

Manning raced to the bottom of the steps and took a hallway to his right, hearing shouting, angry voices around the next corner. It sounded as if the speakers were running in the opposite direction.

One way to find out who and what the rabbits were.

A nod to Hawkins to cover his back, and Manning, one long stride taking him over the heaped bodies, wheeled around the corner. One thug was pivoting their way, a pistol cracking out rounds that snapped past his ear. Manning stitched him from crotch to chest, a line of 9 mm lead nearly decapitating him. Two other goons had to have decided they weren't getting enough money from either Vince or the lady of the manor and bolted down the hall. They were armed and dangerous, as far as Manning was concerned. No point in finding them turn up minutes later, looking to get back into the mix, so the big Canadian drilled a long burst up their spines. They were sailing away when Manning heard Hawkins yell, "Hey, Vince baby! Where you going?"

CHAPTER TWELVE

"We're your death knell, Vince."

It was wrong, it was an outrage and it was too much for Vincent Rousiloux to bear. He fought back a sudden urge to break down, hit his knees, weep before the mercenaries, beg for understanding and compassion, aware they were shooting from some point down the hall as he stuck close to Madame Duvraux's waddling gait.

When he heard his name called out, he nearly collapsed. He was wheeling, freezing in midshuffle, legs nearly going out from under him like pasta, when he spotted the American mercenary. It was a face of cold determination staring at him from the end of the hallway, a vision of doom, and he knew he was finished.

André went next to whatever waited in the great beyond, Rousiloux crying out as the American and the Canadian cut loose with subguns together. In the corner of his eye, certain he was dead on his feet, he glimpsed André cut to ribbons, flung back, pinned to the wall, big spurting holes in his chest before he folded like an accordion.

"Vincent! Get me out of this!"

Some dark anger boiled up deep inside him. The outrage of what was happening here snapped something in his mind. He balled up a wad of what he considered her African bedsheet, the whale woman squawking, and stuck the muzzle of his subgun in her spine, at some point just above quivering buttocks that very few chairs, he imagined, could possibly hold up under.

"What are you doing? You little shit!"

"Shut up! Just play this out! They're not going to shoot you!"

THE SIGHT OF the Halloween couple caused Manning to balk for a moment. It was one of the most hideous, paradoxical matchups the big Canadian could ever imagine. She was three hundred pounds if she was...

To hell with it.

"Watch our six, T.J."

Nodding, Hawkins trailed Manning down the long hallway, Uzi up and ready, monitoring closed doors, covering the way behind their death march.

Manning knew what was coming next, the whoremonger hiding behind the behemoth, nearly invisible other than half his face peeking around her hip. It was a momentary lapse of cold logic, the hardened warrior inside him giving way to a fleeting snatch of mercy.

Manning could damn near see the guy's problem, this abysmal failure of a human being. A little man, a freak of nature, he had still nearly climbed the ladder of criminal success. Rousiloux was a vicious, greedy predator, the only world he could live in, tolerate, revolving around and paying homage to him. Maybe his mother beat him up too much when he was a kid, maybe used his tongue for a mop if he missed the toilet, who the hell knew. These days, from France to L.A., Manning had heard every shrink, lawyer and talking head concoct and conjure up every excuse and rationalization for why this thug committed that crime, or why that particular atrocity needed to be understood, victims all but gone and forgotten in the mayhem and carnage left behind.

No one was accountable anymore. Too much sugar made them murder and rape. They were poor, uneducated, disenfranchised, so they sold dope, blaming the system, looking to kill cops who were out there doing their damnedest to keep it all from swirling right down the sewer. Some days, Manning thought, it was tough to get out of bed and even look at it, wondering if the whole world hadn't gone insane. The problem was, if he succumbed to a line of reasoning that it was all beyond hope, evil triumphed and the mayhem went on, unchecked, unaccounted for. Well, he wasn't in the morality business.

"We can talk!"

"Nothing to talk about, Vince. It's over. You're finished. Bon voyage, Vince. End of story."

"Let me go, Vincent, you bastard!"

"I told you to shut your mouth! We're walking out of here!"

"Afraid not, Vince." Manning kept closing, rounding the corner. The pimp and the madam were backing through an open doorway that led to an indoor pool done in some Greco-Roman style.

"T.J."

"Yeah. We're clear out here."

"Take the other side of the pool. Get a clear shot, take him out."

"Gotcha."

"You want money? Name your price!"

"No sale."

That squeaky, high-pitched voice reached new soprano decibels as Manning's ears were hit by panic and terror. The big Canadian held out the Uzi, padding onto the deck.

Hawkins cut off to Manning's right, angling away, then moving up the far side of the pool.

"Why?"

"Because you're not a very nice guy, Vince," Manning said, looking for any opening to squeeze off a few rounds, a foot, a knee. The trouble was, the whale woman made a perfect shield for the pimp.

"That doesn't make any sense. I'm not in a very

nice business. You're going to murder me because I'm not Mr. Nice Guy?''

''Not murder, simple garbage removal. Solving a problem before it starts. You were looking to move on up, Vince. The world's just not ready for you. A year from now, who's to say you wouldn't pick up aiding and abetting terrorists like the late and unlamented Puchain?''

''I wouldn't do that. I could not care less about a bunch of Muslim crazies.''

''You say that now.''

''Let me go, Vince, damn you!''

Whether cracking up under the stress of terror or plain outrage, the woman wheeled on Rousiloux, wrenching free of his one-handed hold on her African smock. A crack across his face, and the pimp sailed into a wet bar. He was still holding on to the mini-Uzi, shuddering away from the bar, torn between targets, screaming something about how this wasn't fair, when Manning and Hawkins ripped free with their subguns.

''No!''

The howl of outrage went to hell with Rousiloux. The combined barrage slammed him into the wet bar, his mini-Uzi stuttering toward the ceiling. A skylight took the burst, shards raining, Madame Duvraux flaying the air with a scream, waddling away from the glass shower, a water buffalo with red hair. Rousiloux, stitched to crimson rags, bounced away from the wet bar, jigged into a weird spiral, riddled on with a follow-up burst, then plunged into the pool.

Madame Duvraux was shaking, staring at them. "Why did you do this? Who are you?"

Manning said nothing, raised the pilot, informed them they were coming out. Sitrep from the gunship was that a small stampede of people was flooding out the front. Time to bail.

"The man's here," the pilot said. "He's coming in, so check your fire. Over and out."

"Lachlin," Hawkins grumbled.

"Yeah, let's go see what might be up his ass now."

Quickly feeding fresh magazines to their Uzis, Manning and Hawkins retraced their steps. They couldn't find any more shooters, but they kept up their guard. They were stepping into what Manning assumed was some sort of holding area where the girls warmed up the clients, when Lachlin entered the foyer, a black box in his hand, an object like a wand held out.

"What's this?"

Manning heard the faint clicking as Lachlin ran the wand over them. He didn't like what he was thinking.

"Not too bad. A long shower should do it."

"Do what?" Hawkins asked.

"My little songbird informed me two things. One, Wahjihab has blown France. Two, the bomb that nearly buried you was dirty."

Manning felt his heart skip a beat. "You mean to tell me the two of us took a depleted-uranium bath?"

"We won't know how high the level of contamination until I can talk to my French contacts. Relax, you two will be fine. Worst-case scenario, twenty years from now you maybe come down with cancer."

Did the guy just grin? Manning wondered, fighting back the impulse to pound a few straight rights into his jaw.

Russia

DAVID MCCARTER CHUCKLED. "How come I'm not surprised?"

He shook his head, grinning, but there was nothing remotely funny about how the ex-SAS commando and leader of Phoenix Force was feeling when he heard the news from Chino.

McCarter, Calvin James and Rafael Encizo were standing down in their quarters at Fort Pavel. They were in Russian Georgia, had been waiting for the DNA test results for what felt like an eternity. The joint venture between the Russian military, the FSK, a CIA black-ops team and Phoenix Force had, in the Briton's mind, been little more than an excuse to tear and blast up a large Chechen village and waste, not only al-Amin scum and Chechen rebels, but to execute just about every living thing in sight, down to the family dog. It still galled him that they'd been attached to this surgical strike, though neither himself nor his men had actively participated in the indiscriminate slaughter of civilians. They had no problem waxing bad guys, and they had assisted in helping tally a massive body count in Chechnya. Nothing of intelligence value, however, that he could see had turned up at the Chechen stronghold. No computers, no paperwork, no weapons of mass destruction, no training or operational manuals, zilch. He had just informed the Farm as much.

He had some idea where they were headed next, but he needed confirmation of something first, and he was getting the sorry news right now.

The grizzled, black-clad Chino tossed the manila folder on the metal table. "It's all there in triplicate. Feel free to fax it to whoever you work for. Hell, if you want, I can courier the arm we bagged up in that compound, have it checked yourselves. It wasn't our boy, Wahjihab, who got blown to hamburger back there."

"Like the man said. We're not surprised," Calvin James offered from a seat at the table. "We're thinking, Chino, maybe you knew all along it wasn't the fabled Sword of Islam. We're thinking maybe you know a lot we don't."

"Your thinking is wrong, pal, if you're thinking I'm holding back, winking in the mirror as I jerk you three around. The CIA is after the same thing as you guys. We want Wahjihab. We want the source of the

Angels of Islam. We want the Kykov Family. We want a bunch of missing Russkie microbiologists who sold their souls to the devil. We want the North Korean connection severed.''

''You want it all, in other words,'' Encizo said.

''What you don't know, friends,'' Chino growled, ''is a lot.''

''We could have gathered as much ourselves,'' James, the black ex-SEAL, said.

McCarter held up a hand. ''All right. So what's next, Chino?''

''Kykov. You asked a while back where Harker is and what he's up to,'' he said, referring to the CIA special op the three Phoenix Force warriors had fought with against al-Amin terrorists in Croatia. ''I've got orders to go after Kykov. Dead or alive, the Russian Don is finished. He's an embarrassment to the Russians, but he's got enough comrades in Moscow who are either too beholden to his cash or are too afraid of retribution to go after him. Harker is gathering some last-minute field intelligence on Kykov and a bunch of North Koreans who are in this country and who have been buying and selling al-Amin the technology to build the Angels of Islam. Talk to whoever you got to talk to, but in a few hours, with or without you, we saddle up and go burn down the entire Kykov organization. Whatever you need to know about the hit, facts, faces, places, is all in that folder. You're welcome.''

McCarter didn't know what to make of Chino, not that it really mattered. He would have preferred that all five commandos of Phoenix Force were together, on their own, away from the clutches of the CIA. But the so-called new war on terrorism had just about every intelligence and law-enforcement agency on the warpath these days. Which meant sometimes tripping over other feet, McCarter thought.

"Think we can get some chow first?" James asked.

"And I don't think he means the slop with the roaches in it you might feed to Chechen rebels the good general keeps in his dungeon," Encizo added.

"I can work that out," Chino said, spinning on his heel and leaving the windowless, corrugated iron hut.

"What do you think, David?" James asked. "We trust heading back into the trenches with these guys again?"

"I think I need to phone home. I'll run it all by our people, let them call it."

"I hate working with the CIA," Encizo groused. "Every time we do, I always feel like I need to take a long hot shower after."

McCarter gave a silent amen to that and headed for the sat link.

CHAPTER THIRTEEN

"Do it. Let us know when it's done."

Three separate sitreps had come in over the satcom in the Computer Room, one after the other during the past hour. After just giving David McCarter the green light to declare open season on the Kykov organization, Hal Brognola weighed the good news and the bad news after the Briton aye-ayed and signed off. One wandering look over the cybernetics team and he found them at their workstations, tapping away at keyboards, lost in duty, but looking torn between relief and worry of their own.

That was understandable, Brognola thought, pacing. The future was as uncertain and foreboding as ever.

And weaponized Ebola was never far from the big Fed's thoughts.

The man from Justice glanced at Price, who was working on a cup of coffee, alone, legs crossed, in her swivel rolling chair, stare glued on the situation map. She seemed anxious to say something that was clearly on her mind, brow furrowed, some look he couldn't peg, but his own mind was churning with the updates, all those dire variables between the problems and the solutions. She was never one to hold back her thoughts or opinions, so Brognola gave her the necessary private time to gather whatever her case.

Good news. Manning and Hawkins were still among the living. Bad news. The al-Amin butcher brigade of Marseilles had touched off a dirty, or radioactive bomb, and there was a good chance both Manning and Hawkins had been coated with some uranium or plutonium poison, given the fact they had crawled out of the rubble of Puchain's mass grave, which had been right next door to ground zero. Aaron Kurtzman and Akira Tokaido were huddled at Kurtzman's workstation, the two of them lapsing into a quiet brainstorming session. Huntington Wethers was now sitting with Carmen Delahunt in the other corner of this intel-gathering lair. The black ex-professor of cybernetics from Berkeley and the stunning redhead, formerly of the FBI, were perusing printouts.

The atmosphere was heavy and grim.

Finally, Brognola glanced at Yakov Katzenelenbogen. The former leader of Phoenix Force and ex-Israeli intelligence operative was speaking in guarded tones on a secured line to what Brognola assumed were some of his former contacts in Mossad.

Katz severed the connection to his contact and approached Brognola. "My source at Mossad believes al-Amin has a large cell operating somewhere in Yemen. No surprise, granted, but the word I get is that there's a Saudi connection, or rather some al-Amin operatives, it appears—two of whom were arrested as of yesterday in Ramallah—have been granted a safe route where Wahjihab's people move weapons and cash up through Saudi Arabia, through Jordan and into the West Bank. They are smuggling in operatives who are dumping off sophisticated time-delayed and radio-remote high explosives and funds for the families of a whole new battalion of suicide bombers they have been recruiting. These bastards seem to be multiplying like cockroaches. It would appear al-Amin is graduating entire schools of mass murderers daily in several countries, from Iran to Syria to Yemen. It sounds as if they have set up an entire network for cash distribution, a life insurance policy, if you will, believed to be courtesy of Wahjihab and maybe his sons, for the survivors of these cockroaches who blow up innocent women and children."

Brognola nodded, grunting around his stogie, and noted the simmering anger in Katz's voice. "I understand your concern for the Israelis, Katz. Unfortunately, and I'm not glossing over the seriousness of the mess over there, but it's one hell on several fronts that can only be addressed by keeping our people running and gunning. No punches pulled. No retreat. No quarter given. This is war, total and complete, until this is wrapped, one way or another. We know this al-Amin organization spreads from the Philippines to the States. We have CIA special ops all over the map, SEALs, Green Berets doing whatever they can to topple al-Amin and al-Qaeda in other parts of the world. We've got Wahjihab sightings, ringers or what have you, from Chechnya to Marseilles, and I don't know what to believe on that score or if we'll ever hunt the real Sword of Islam down.

"What we do know is these murderers have tens of millions of dollars at their disposal, to recruit and arm maybe hundreds of thousands of militants, buy what has turned out to be the most insidious form of mass destruction we've ever dealt with. I've got people at the Justice and Treasury Department in the process of freezing assets all over the globe. We're learning more by the hour, Katz, locations of cells, their connection to Mexican drug cartels and Russian organized crime, but unless we turn up the heat at this point past a hellfire scorch on what has become, by my orders—and it's been cleared by the Man—a rolling execution campaign, we could be staring down the gun barrel of the apocalypse. The existence of the entire free world is at stake."

"I wasn't implying we shift our focus, nor asking for some special consideration for Israel. I concur with you. We hit them where we know they are now. No prisoners. I merely wanted you to know this Wahjihab has a few irons in the Israeli fire. He also has those two sons, Mahdji and Abdullah, you might want to take a very close look at. And I was only going to suggest you do exactly what you just stated."

Brognola nodded. They were all on edge, he knew, nerves raw, the tired and worried lot of them waiting for some new horror to crop up.

"Yeah, you've already hinted these two sons, these Omani bank executives, believed in charge of a chunk of al-Amin change in what Carmen has called off-shore banking units, deserve to go under our microscope. Anything concrete I might be able to have Phoenix run with?"

"I'm working on it."

"When you have something definite, let me know, Katz." The big Fed looked at Price.

"Barbara? I get the impression you want to say something."

The mission controller swung halfway in her chair. "It's the Mexican front, Hal. We have essentially cut the DEA and the Mexican narcotics task force out of the loop."

"At this point, I'm not real concerned about hurt feelings."

"I understand that. What we don't know is who or how many *federales* or Mexican military officials are on the cartel's payroll. In short, Striker and Able are on their own."

"They always were, and the cartel's always owned people down there who pay lip service to law and order. I'll contact the DEA's special agent in charge down there as soon as I get the chance. Remind him of the seriousness of the crisis, just in case it looks like I might have to throw him a crying towel. The Cordero-Ojeda cartel is in bed with al-Amin. We know North Korean operatives are running all over Mexico, the same thugs from the axis of evil who are doing business with the Russian Mob and selling weaponized Ebola to al-Amin. Hell, I need a scorecard just to keep track of who wants to wax who down there at the moment."

"That's not my point. The Mexican authorities could very well turn against Striker and Able. They could corner them, round them up, detain them, dump them in a prison hole somewhere. Torture or worse, if they're lackeys of the cartel. Especially now since it looks like Striker and Able shot up a bunch of *federales.*"

"All of whom were dirty, and all of whom were holding hands with al-Amin terrorists," Katz put in. "A DEA-Mexican narcotics task force did a walk-through in that bloody mess in Ciudad Zapulcha, confirmed those *federales* were on the cartel's payroll. Striker and Able have been cleared. Unofficially, that is."

"We know that," Price said. "But other Mexican authorities may not care. I can't see the rest of the *federales* or the power structure in Mexico City shrugging it off as the cost of doing business with crazy Yankees just so they can keep lining their pockets with our dollars.''

''You're talking political fallout,'' Brognola suggested.

''I'm talking maybe the DEA gets booted out of Mexico altogether,'' Price said. ''If that happens...''

Brognola blew a cloud of smoke. ''Point noted. The flow of drugs goes on unabated if the DEA is sent packing across the border. It's too late, though, to halt what has already begun down there. Right now I'm thinking McCarter has the big game in his sights, at least one of the bigger dragons that needs slaying. That's what's on the table in our immediate future. Word is—according to this Chino's sources, and I've confirmed it with my own Justice Department agents in Moscow—Petre Kykov is en route to meet with the North Korean envoy in this city of Rujik, the town by the Volga that Russian Mob money built.

''Kykov is going down. We burn down his organization, kick the teeth out of the North Korean connection on Russian soil, we might begin to see some daylight on this one. The way I heard it from the FBI and the CIA over there, Kykov is an embarrassment to the Russians, but there are a few comrades of means roaming around Moscow who won't touch him, act like he's the real president of Russia or some damn thing, and the way it's shaping up he might be the real power over there. The Russian military won't touch him, but it's my understanding after talking to the Man and laying out the situation, and after he ran this by their president, the Russians will turn a blind eye to us cleaning up a mess in their own backyard. Now, all of us here know it won't be the first time this has happened. We get the privilege of wiping the egg off the faces of the Russians.''

''When our people hit Kykov, I'd like to think we could maybe snap up a few prisoners who might help steer us toward any clandestine labs,'' Price said, ''which might be producing these Angels of Islam.''

''What can I say to that?'' Brognola asked. ''If they do, fine. If they don't, we'll find another way, and I'll sure as hell gladly take another body count. As long as it's them and not us.''

''Barbara may have a good point about our Mexican flashpoint.''

Now it was Kurtzman's turn, Brognola saw, to voice his concerns. ''The Ojeda brothers, Rodrigo and Julio, are actually the CEOs, so to speak, of the Cordero-Ojeda cartel. What I'm saying is if they own the *federales,* the military, the politicians, they could very well marshal up an entire army, spare no expense to hunt our guys down. Especially when they learn that Striker and Able dropped the net over Cordero. They bagged a big one. When the Ojedas find out, I'm thinking they'll declare war on Striker and Able. They can't afford to have Cordero opening up the whole encyclopedia on their operation. The Ojedas, according to the DEA file, are the real muscle behind the Cordero cartel.''

Brognola paused. ''Our people are aware of that. And to address your concerns,'' he said as Delahunt, Tokaido and Wethers halted their chores to turn his way, ''we all know the risks involved. We've got the best in the business doing what they do, which is seek out, engage and destroy. I gave the green light personally to Striker to make a judgment call on who may or may not be dirty, if there's any so-called official flak flying their way. We—and they—will take their situation on a minute-to-minute, body-count-to-body-count basis. I know how this might sound to some PC bunch, but I'm not scheduled for a *Crossfire* appearance tonight. Mexican brass and politicos have long since been talking out of both sides of their mouths as long as they keep on getting aid from Washington in terms of cold cash dollars. They coddle drug dealers in the same breath they proclaim how they're helping the DEA in the war on drugs, and now they've granted haven to international terrorists who think they have found another and easier way to slither across our border and murder our citizens. In other words, enough is enough. Okay, what's the story on Hawkins and Manning? How bad does it look for them falling ill from any contact with radioactive waste? Anybody?''

''According to Gary, from the initial readings this CIA op took,'' Kurtzman said, ''the level of contamination on their person looks low. So far, other than getting dinged and banged up by the blast, they claim they're feeling no ill effects.''

''If they were, say, buried in debris,'' Tokaido added, ''and they got out of there fast enough, there's a chance there was no real harm done.''

''How will we know for absolute certain?'' Brognola asked.

Wethers spoke up. ''Two to three weeks, maybe less. If nausea, dizziness, weakness, fatigue sets in, you'll know if they took a hot dose.''

''Well, if we didn't need them so bad, I'd pull them off the mission now,'' Brognola said, ''and fly them straight back here. Fact is, depending on how it goes in the coming hours, I may rejoin them with David and the others.''

''I offered to bring them back. Thorough decon, full medical exam.''

''I know you did,'' Brognola said to Price. ''But you heard them turn down that offer. They want to go the distance on this one. Okay. What are the civilian casualties?''

''Undetermined,'' Wethers said. ''Five square blocks around ground zero have been evacuated. Extensive damage to buildings for a quarter mile, windows blown out, structural damage, first reports maybe as many as four hundred dead. Interpol, French intelligence and military, our CIA, all on the scene.''

"Classic quarantine of the area in question," Kurtzman said. "According to CIA intercepts, it would appear the French are on the verge of declaring martial law."

"The lack of details we've heard from CNN makes it sound like the French aren't quite prepared to announce publicly," Delahunt said, "that Marseilles might have been hit by a dirty bomb."

Brognola was trying to digest the enormity of three separate flashpoints, then gave it up. What was done…

Well, it was time to relight the fires all over the map. "Okay, Bear, try to get us sat recon of Yemen, see if there's anything doesn't look right to you. Covert military installations, get a fix on where any of our Special Forces are, like that.

"Barbara, I've got some business I need to go and take care of in Washington. Our people out there in the trenches have their orders and they know what must be done. Keep me posted."

"You know, Hal," Katz suddenly said, "it makes you wonder."

"What's that?"

"What happened in Marseilles. What's been happening in Israel."

"Yeah, I get the drift. You don't need to tell me. How long before an army of suicide bombers finally finds their way into our cities, starts blowing up crowds of commuters, restaurants, theaters, pizza parlors. When does America come under siege like... I'll be in touch."

He wasn't often so abrupt with his own people, but Hal Brognola wasn't joking or exaggerating about the prospect that maybe America, even the entire planet, was shoved to the threshold of Armageddon. They, too, knew as much. The cyberteam was an integral component of the Stony Man operation, Brognola knew. But intelligence gathering, logistical battle mapping, maneuvering all the right pieces into the next flashpoint could only do so much. They were in a nasty business, doing battle with some very bad folks, and the only real solution, the bottom line, he knew, was for their warriors in the field to eighty-six the enemy.

Total annihilation.

End of discussion.

The big Fed marched out of the Computer Room to go see what his shadow man had to offer.

SERGEI KILCOTCHKIN thought there had to be a better way to reach a successful conclusion to their business with the foreign barbarians, but if there was some magic way to resolve the current crisis, it eluded him. The truth was that none of what was happening should have ever come to pass, but this had been Petre Kykov's show all along. Hindsight, though, was for losers and wanna-bes, he believed, and he had seen plenty losing when he'd been a major in the

KGB and mired in the ten-year debacle of Afghanistan. The moment called for decisive action, not all this waiting around for either good or bad news, worrying about the future, the wringing of hands. But what to do? And how to proceed?

Deep inside he knew it was time to declare war. But on whom? The North Koreans? The al-Amin rabble was already being hunted for their duplicity, but that was another matter altogether. So many thorns to remove. And then there was…

Well, rumors that Kykov wasn't happy with his performance lately. The whispers were getting louder out of Moscow more often during these dark and nervous days. Kykov was making noise how he felt his underboss was more interested in maintaining a playboy lifestyle—drinking vodka around the clock, getting hummers from his bevy of international beauties, spending lavishly on clothes and cars and trips—than shoring up and seeing through to a successful end the organization's business. Indeed. As if these endless days of trial and tribulation were his fault. It was true, just the same, that he loved the life he led. But he had earned it, after all, and how he spent his free time was his affair. After years of loyal service, all the shedding of blood for the man, either rivals or policemen or politicians who wished to bring them down, it galled him that Kykov would dare to speak of him as if he were little more than a lackey who needed to be taught a harsh lesson.

How many times, he wondered, had he attempted to warn Petre Kykov that doing business with Arab terrorists would only bring trouble to their doorstep? Kykov saw only more money, but Kilcotchkin had more than once attempted to sway the boss from selling weapons of mass destruction to fanatics, even if it was done through the Asian intermediaries. And the North Koreans, he knew, clearly had their own agenda.

Since returning from Bosnia to Russia, what had been floating rumors up to then about another potential dire straits had been confirmed by his FSK sources. The countryside was crawling with American intelligence and law-enforcement operatives. Welcome, he thought, to the new democratic Mother Russia, where one-time enemies were now allowed free rein to flex muscle, call the shots on his own turf, wooed even by their own intelligence agency. The problem was, he knew the truth on that front. E-mails and sat-phone transmissions had been intercepted by his contacts in the FSK, and both Kilcotchkin's and Kykov's names kept cropping up as the primary salesmen of what the al-Amin terrorists craved for so long to get their hands on so they could sweep America from coast to coast with a horror unlike the world had ever seen.

War was coming—he could feel it in his churning gut. It always began with the rumors, the implied threats, so-called allies or even comrades he had trusted shifting allegiances in order to save themselves from getting tossed into the fire. The blame game would start next, and there was always a scapegoat that needed to get skinned, usually someone high up the pecking order, but a rung or two down the ladder.

That would be him.

It was falling apart, and he had to wonder why. For years, their organization had the magic touch, owned most of Moscow, the best of nightclubs, restaurants, a booming construction business, which had branched out into Europe, most notably Belgrade since that city had to rebuild after the Americans nearly bombed it off the map. Fronts, of course, for all the contraband they moved, legitimate businesses they could use as siphons and firewalls for all the money narcotics, prostitution, pornography and extortion rang up.

He pulled on his black turtleneck as he headed toward the phone on his desk in his study. Had the call come in ten minutes earlier he would have asked who it was, considered the source and told them he'd return their call. Kykov had already phoned, right before he was due to fall into the sack with his Ukrainian playmates, and from his private jet, no less. Kykov was coming down to the small city, this resort near the Volga that Kykov money had erected, to have a personal session with the North Korean contingent under the roof of Kilcotchkin's manor. Kykov claimed there were certain matters his underboss wasn't aware of. That alone raised a mental red flag, considering the talk and the grumbling he'd been catching wind of lately. There was much, or so he was learning from his own sources in the organization, about the North Korean–al-Amin connection he hadn't been privy to.

He had just sent the two Ukrainian beauties on their way, the evening's sport sex reaching its normal blissful conclusion. Being sated still wasn't doing the trick to calm his nerves. He strode for the wet bar, poured a vodka neat. One gulp, and he refilled the glass.

This caller could wait another moment. It was urgent, just the same, the NKs down in the sitting room, casting him those inscrutable looks, most of their time spent on their sat phones, chattering away to those in Pyongyang who were antsy to receive word of how their own special-forces ops had fared in the Chechen strike. Beneath their calm and controlled demeanors, he knew they were angry, as was Kilcotchkin, that the al-Amin rabble had conned them with counterfeit currency. The terrorist riffraff had strolled off with the whole store, in fact. There was sophisticated state-of-the-art technology for their drones that they'd absconded with. They had sashayed off with shipments of VX, sarin, weaponized Ebola. They had scooped up in Kazakhstan five of Russia's most brilliant microbiologists.

So many thorns, so many problems. And when, he wondered, would the knife come tearing into his back?

He picked up the phone. "Yes."

"You are going to be hit."

Kilcotchkin felt his heart lurch. "What? When? Who?"

He listened, heart drumming in his ears, but didn't quite hear the first few words of this harrowing revelation. He was counting up his own soldiers under his roof, a standing army of twenty-two. There were plenty of assault rifles, machine guns, even RPGs. He was looking up, through the skylight, thinking he needed to place a rocket team on the roof.

"Are you there, comrade?"

"Yes, yes. Go on. Tell me precisely what you know, General Mytkin."

CHAPTER FOURTEEN

"Rujik is Russian Mob central. I kid you not. Our Big Daddy Badasski is sticking the middle finger in the eyes of the free legit world, proclaiming for all to hear how he's just a nightclub owner-construction magnate, this is his little fiefdom that his dirty billions built for him and his comrades in crime and any movers and shakers out of Moscow he chooses to woo or blackmail into his kingdom. It's all there in your package. Rujik is Kykov's personal claim to fame. It's bursting apart with the who's who of the Russian *mafiya.* It's got it all. Swank nightclubs, casinos, prostitution meccas, sex factories. They've got a frigging golf course put anything Tiger ever walked on to shame. They've got indoor and outdoor shooting ranges where their goons can refine their shooting talents until they can land themselves in the Dirty Harry category of 'Make my day.' You got the money, welcome to the jungle. I'm talking the cream, the elite of Russian military, politics, the underworld call this place the next-best thing to their own Riviera on the

Volga. Way I hear it from the Feds and the FSK, a little skim off the top of gangster proceeds there does a lot of greasing the skids back at the Kremlin.

"Wake up and smell the whiskey, gentlemen. This whole country is bought and sold by the Russian Mob, big part of the reason why the country is circling the toilet bowl. The thing is, whenever the Russian power structure is called on it, they act like they're helpless to do anything to stop it or too embarrassed or too damn scared to grab up or just outright shoot these assholes when they're more corrupt than any dictatorial regime to ever rise up in Latin America."

A lot of what Chino said, the ex-SAS commando thought, was true, since he had firsthand experience with the Russian Mob on their own turf in the past.

They were sitting in the cabin of what David McCarter assumed was a CIA Gulfstream. Chino had laid out the assault plan when they'd gone wheels up in Georgia, although after getting off the radio minutes ago with the AWOL Harker—who had ostensibly been on surveillance detail all along—the black op just changed the game plan, and when they were in the fourth quarter, the goal line being the clandestine CIA airbase near Rujik. There, Chino informed them, the twenty-four-man strike force would board, fly on and swoop down in prototype helicopter gunships on the massive dacha estate where Kykov's top lieutenant, Sergei Kilcotchkin, was holed up and entertaining a group of North Korean operatives.

Only that was now the curtain call.

McCarter didn't like it. None of it. It was wise to never take the intel of the other guy at face value, although Chino's brief to them made it sound as if he were the voice of the Almighty, every word chiseled in stone. Why was it, McCarter wondered, that he was suddenly experiencing déjà vu? Why was he feeling the ghost of the late Colonel Joe of Croatia disaster on board and talking into Chino's ear?

The intel photos, both sat and what the Briton assumed were ground and aerial pics, were spread out on the table. The crown jewel of the Kykov Family, perched on a steppe near the 3690-kilometer Volga, Europe's longest river, was due southeast of Moscow. To hear Chino tell it, Rujik was the playboy paradise of the Russian *mafiya,* where the criminal underworld could take a vacation from all their killing, extorting and drug trafficking, frolic with Ukrainian and Belarus beauties, chug booze and idle the daylight hours away putting eighteen holes on the green, forgetting their differences and rivalries, one big happy family. McCarter already had that much confirmed by Stony Man Farm, and the Phoenix Force commandos were cut loose by Brognola to, in the big Fed's words, "take no prisoners, burn down the Kykov house." If it was true what Chino claimed, Rujik chockablock with nothing but the worst of the Russian *mafiya* worst, upward of a few hundred to a thousand Russian gangsters or more could turn the small city into an armed fortress, or create a massive rolling wave of shooters coming to cut them to bloody sausage.

McCarter read the grim, dubious set on the features of the faces of his men, Jack Grimaldi included.

"What's the problem here? How come the four of you look like you just bit into a turd sandwich?"

Encizo got the beef session jump-started, tapping the piece of paper with its Cyrillic writing on the table. "For one, this little love note. You plan to stroll right up to Kykov in his club and give it to him."

"The Golden Bear. You heard me on the horn with your pal Harker. Kykov and a squad of goonskis just made the scene, holed up in the club, some big powwow going down. So I rearranged the setup. And I read that note to you in case your Russian isn't up to snuff. I explained what I had in mind already. What's the bitching all about, girls?"

"It's crazy," James said, "this sudden altering of the game plan with a two-minute warning. It's cowboy, and it's going to get us all killed. First, the plan didn't sound too bad, the original one, that is. We blow out the skylight, rappel into his study, two teams move in on Kilcotchkin's estate, front and back. Three of these new Area 51 gunships of yours..."

"They're called Dragons. Fresh off the assembly line, and I never said they came out of Groom Lake, pal."

"Whatever," James said. "Hitting the top lieutenant's house was no problem, since—or so you said—the North Koreans are guests, and they're the ones been dumping off what we hear are called Angels of Islam to the terrorists."

"Again. So?"

McCarter spoke up. "We didn't come this far, fresh off the Chechen slaughter wagon, to commit suicide. Your plan sounds bold, all big swinging balls, but—"

"But nothing. We walk right in there. You back my play. I already mapped out the firepoints my people will be taking when we hit the club. I've got the layout from a reliable source. I know where the big blini sits, I know the numbers of shooters he'll have around him. Kykov has two choices. Surrender to me, Chino posing as your not so friendly American CIA agent in Russia, or he's squashed caviar, right in his club. Since I don't see him willing to be extradited to America and spending the rest of his life in a cell, he's going to give the nod to his thugs. They'll make a stand. We gun them down. End of story. Our gunships will be in the area, ready to extract us for phase two. Besides, I need a body for what I've got planned when we hit Kilcotchkin's digs outside the city."

"This is getting better all the time," James grumbled.

"Listen, mate," McCarter growled to Chino.

"With or without you along for this ride, we don't pledge undying allegiance to you or the CIA."

"Meaning?"

"Meaning the people we work for gave us the thumbs-up to take out the Kykov organization. You're along as a courtesy."

Chino bobbed his head, his eyes going mean. "Courtesy, huh? Is that right. You're using my intelligence, my contacts, my gunships and my men, and you're doing me a big favor. May I kindly kiss your limey ass now or later? You see where I might be headed with this, ladies?"

"You'll leave us behind if we don't go along with your dance steps at your madman's ball," James said.

"Bingo. Are you going to do this my way, or would you like to walk back to Georgia?"

It happened like this, McCarter. He saw it in Croatia when Colonel Joe got himself and a bunch of special ops blown out of the sky when they hit a major stronghold of al-Amin terrorists. Power had become a hunger that was eating Chino up from the inside out. Well, the campaign had been crazy to the point of a suicidal fury almost from the time they dropped into the Balkans. CIA popping up all over the place, threatening to go on the muscle, hell-bent on making any and all final calls. McCarter had his orders, though, and that was to trample Kykov's organization. At this point, he knew he had no choice but to run with Chino's plan. In some ways, he could appreciate the straightforward bulldog tactic, but he didn't like the idea of throwing his own men into a lion's den where they were essentially Christians with rusty spears.

"There's a good chance Kykov and Kilcotchkin know we're coming anyway."

"How's that?" Encizo asked.

"You think I really trust that vodka-guzzling General Pavel Mytkin? The whole time we were kicking ass and taking names in that Chechen village, he stayed up in the air, fresh glass of vodka in hand, two miles or more out, giving the orders. I know a little more about the good general than I've let on."

Chuckling, James looked at his teammates, his arms up in the air.

"He talks a big game about ridding his country of terrorists, but the CIA has a file on him how he's kept his hand out to the Kykov Family over the years. Safe passage for heroin. Recruiting military and intelligence contacts. Keys to the kingdom, figuratively speaking, handed over to Kykov for various chem-bio-nuke installations where the Don has helped himself to the candy store."

James cursed. "Anybody want to tell me why I'm a little nervous?"

"Hey, come on, guys, show a pair, huh? We're about to hit the jackpot. We can wipe out the mother lode of organized crime, maybe restore this country to some sanity, or at least give the peasants half a chance for a better life.''

The guy was nuts, McCarter decided. He nodded, said, ''So much for bettering East-West relations. It's your party, mate. But I have one concession I want you to make.''

''I'm listening.''

McCarter nodded at Grimaldi. ''One bird for the four of us. You do your Santa-down-the-chimney act, but we take the rear of Kilcotchkin's dacha for round two, assuming, naturally, we all make it that far.''

Chino grunted. ''What the hell, okay. I mean, I had to cram my people into three other planes for this ride in anyway, since you four didn't strike me as overly enthusiastic about being part of the team.''

''I don't think we have a problem with teamwork,'' Encizo said. ''It all depends on the team.''

''How long before we touch down?'' McCarter asked.

Chino checked his chronometer. ''Twenty minutes, give or take.''

McCarter looked at Encizo and James, then said, ''Let's break out the goodies, mates.''

''And, Chino, maybe you'd like to cover this big plan of yours one last time? Just so we're all on the same page.''

PETRE KYKOV FELT utterly and miserably alone. He had been robbed of money, millions, in fact, loyalties appeared to be fading around him and enemies, seen and unseen, were lurking everywhere, seeking to take away everything he had spent more than a decade earning in blood and sweat.

He knew a little something about loss and losing, and, after his tenth or maybe it was thirteenth glass of vodka, he was experiencing a tightness of the chest, a sick, sinking feeling of longing and regret over a life that had seen much pain and suffering. It was true that he was a man with an empire to lord over, protect and see flourish, but he was a king without a real family, no one he would leave behind as an inheritor to his vast fortune. Everyone he had ever cared about, or believed he might have at one time loved, was dead and gone. His only offspring, two sons, had been soldiers, killed by Chechen rebels during one of the Russian army's many incursions into that terrorist breakaway state. Their mother, and his wife, he had one awful day learned, had been having an affair with a rival. Sometimes he wondered which—the death of his sons or Natasha's infidelity was more painful to recall.

It had happened during the early years when he was trying to establish himself as an up-and-coming businessman after the fall of the old Soviet Union, when he had been little more than another heroin trafficker on the block, a former and unemployed KGB colonel. The signs had been there—her incessant demands for more of his time, the fits of rage when she felt neglected and her constant drunkenness—but he had chosen to ignore them, turning a blind eye to her wants and needs, the hunger to be more than a drug pusher consuming his every waking moment. When he suspected the worst, he had one of his soldiers spy on her.

He shuddered at the memory, the vision of walking into his rival's apartment, finding them together...

He had shot them both where they lay entwined.

Money had changed hands to cover the crime, and that had been the beginning of buying policemen in Moscow, the ripple effect of payoffs going all the way to the top politicians, those young but rising FSK agents who had their own families to feed on what amounted to little more than the bread crumbs of a civil servant's salary before he offered them a way to be more than just struggling, underpaid government stooges. After the killings he had concocted a plausible story to pass off on his sons, claiming their mother had been gunned down by criminals in the streets. It was Moscow, after all, where violent crime was the order of the day.

He wondered now if the crimes of his past had somehow caught up to him in the present. There was duplicity and treachery wherever he turned, or so it seemed, incompetence and neglect, at best. The playboy, a former KGB associate, had allowed business to slide, overlooking the finer details, he believed, allowing the Arabs to bamboozle them with bogus money, more concerned about his next sexual foray, his next thousand-dollar suit or in which tropical paradise he'd idle his time away. Sure, Kilcotchkin had killed for him countless times, but those were the old days when all of them were hard and hungry. His underboss had grown soft the past year or so, weakened by his desire for pleasure and comfort, living it up, squandering vast sums on his every whim. And as their North Korean counterparts clamored for reprisal against the Arab terrorists while demanding still more hardware and technology that would further their own weapons-of-mass-destruction program, he knew he was faced with a choice that might either topple his empire or steer it back on course, a glorious reclamation of the old days. Or so he envisioned.

The final decision was his, of course, and he wondered if he could actually give the order to execute his underboss. Dereliction of duty was intolerable, and perhaps he should make an example to the next man who took Kilcotchkin's place.

They were having a grand old time in his club, out there on the dance floor, under the strobing lights of the spinning chandeliers, American rock and roll thundering in his ears, pockets of gamblers jammed around the baccarat and craps tables, the spinning roulette wheels in the far gaming corner where they were leaping around and shouting for their lucky number to roll up. They were business associates, rivals even, drinking his booze, throwing away their money, perhaps looking for favors, or stewing in jealousy behind the mask of revelry, sharpening their blades, here to search out some weakness in his operation they could exploit. Beyond the smattering of near naked beauties shaking for the crowd on their raised stages, there were well-heeled women everywhere, glittering in diamonds and jewelry and wearing dresses that most Russian families couldn't afford in five years' worth of pay.

Why did he come here? he wondered. They were playing grab ass, putting aside whatever their schemes for the sake of chasing the night's pleasure—or perhaps here, wolves in the silk suits of playboys on the prowl, looking to engineer bold new ambitions to rise to the top. Perhaps he, too, had grown soft, sitting on the throne too long, building a city to himself, a god among mere mortals, showing off his wealth, inflaming envy that could become his fatal downfall. Had he come here, procrastinating, stalling before he made his final decision?

He slid higher up in his booth, looked at Dmitri Yukov and tapped his glass. The young former Spetsnaz captain poured him another vodka. This one was hard, lean and hungry, he decided as he stared into Yukov's black eyes. He wouldn't drink, he didn't chase whores, no vice that he knew of that could drape a noose around his neck as it did so many men. What he did was kill on command, or break the bones of businessmen, the drug dealers and whoremongers and smugglers who wouldn't pay their tribute for being allowed to do business in Moscow.

Decisions.

Kykov addressed the matter he knew Yukov was most concerned about. "Comrade, when we arrive there, I will take him into the study, after I speak with the North Koreans. Should I say to you 'I wish a moment alone with Comrade Kilcotchkin,' you will give us two minutes exactly. You will not knock. Simply enter, walk right up to him and shoot him in the head."

Yukov's expression didn't change, but Kykov noted the gaze was narrow enough that he sensed the ex-Spetsnaz commando was hoping just such a moment would come to pass. "He will have his own soldiers there. Men who may be loyal to him and resent such a move on our part."

That could prove a problem, Kykov knew. Mentally he added up the numbers on his own crew of shooters. Eleven, including Yukov, the others jammed into booths down the wall, machine pistols beneath their coats, assault rifles in their vehicles out front, in case it all got ugly and mass execution was demanded on the spot. For what could be a most dangerous encounter, an execution and a changing of the top guard, even Kykov had armed himself, a Makarov pistol, in a shoulder holster beneath his jacket. Yes, Kykov decided, he knew about loss and losing, but he would die first before he saw the first stone of his empire crumble.

"If they prove themselves too loyal to him, if I sense they are unwilling to accept the matter, they will share the same fate. It will pain me, understand, Comrade Yukov, if I have to go through with this. I am not without heart, I am not without gratitude for those who have served me. Sometimes change, unfortunate as it may be, is necessary in the interests of survival."

"It was his deal."

"Not exactly. It was my deal—the specifics were his to handle."

"He blew it."

"It is something I need to find out for myself. The fact that he allowed the Arabs to trick us with counterfeit money, or so he claimed later... You see my point?"

"Yes. Since no one but Comrade Sergei and those closest to him ever laid eyes on this so-called funny money, it leaves one to wonder. It begs a certain question."

Kykov was about to pursue the conversation further when he saw some commotion beyond the gaming area, near the foyer entrance. He came alive, his head clearing of vodka as adrenaline fired through him at the sight of maybe fifteen black-clad and heavily armed figures elbowing their way past his security, their hands thrusting something—wallets?—in the stunned faces. They acted official, but there was something in the way they took charge of the moment that began to concern him the deeper they moved into the club, his eyes seeming to cloud over by a dark shroud of fear. He listened as the voice of the head of security crackled over Yukov's tac radio.

"What is it?" Kykov growled, feeling the tension level rise, a coursing of electricity that seemed to crackle through the entire club, his face hot as anxiety tore through him.

"They say they are with the American CIA," Yukov answered, rising, sliding out of the booth, taking up his post beside the table.

Kykov was suddenly more outraged than he was afraid. He knew he'd been under surveillance by American authorities working in collusion with certain factions of the FSK. That Americans would dare to assume they could march right into his hallowed sanctuary, humiliate him in front of rivals who lived in fear of him twisted his stomach in hot fury. Still, if they knew about his dealings with the Arabs...

He watched, his mind racing, as the armed contingent marched and weaved a path through pockets of gamblers and dancers, bodies spinning, this way and that, as if to cover their flanks and rear, grim faces looking hungry to shoot the first patron—many of whom, Kykov knew, were armed—if they so much as twitched for the bulges beneath their suit jackets.

They split up, Kykov saw, sliding into his dining

antechamber. He counted twelve altogether, four men backing up to one side, lining up along the wall like an execution squad. Those four held large assault rifles with attached grenade launchers, and Kykov, old warrior that he was, instinctively knew they were neither CIA, nor had they come to arrest him.

He barked in Russian at Yukov, "Do whatever it is I tell you without hesitating. Tell the others."

"I understand Russian, Comrade."

He was a lean, dark man, wielding an MP-5 subgun, the sort of weapon Kykov knew was used primarily by American Special Forces, not the FBI. The subgun was held low, but Kykov knew a killer when he saw one, and this man had come to kill.

"Then you'll understand," he said, speaking in English, "that the CIA is not welcome here. Have a nice night."

"The party's over, big shot," Kykov heard this impertinent bastard tell him, watching as he walked up to the booth where he flipped a piece of paper on the table. "You're history, Comrade, and I'm not talking about shipping you off to the gulag."

The outrage twisted into some dark rage Kykov felt boiling up from deep inside, like some monster churning from the depths of the ocean, shooting upward to explode through the surface. He felt countless eyes watching him, everyone waiting to see how this drama would unfold. He reached out, picked up the slip of paper, slowly, carefully. He was reading the first few lines, written in perfect Russian, when the beast inside spewed a stream of curses, burst through the surface.

Petre Kykov knew what had to be done.

And he bellowed the order. "Shoot them!"

CHAPTER FIFTEEN

"We know about the Ebola. We know about the five engineers of mass death you sold, fat man. We know you are a drug-dealing, murdering, extorting sack of shit who took it up the ass from a bunch of camel riders called al-Amin. We know you are in league with the North Koreans, selling them technology that they in turn sold to terrorists. Your life is now numbered in seconds. You have two choices, fat man. Surrender and be extradited to America to be put into a maximum security prison and get passed around as everyone's love slave or die right here and now."

It wasn't exactly what David McCarter would stamp as class prose; but it did the trick.

And it was bringing out the killer in Kykov.

McCarter gave James the nod to watch the main dining and gaming area, as the freeze out there turned hot and gangsters in their five-thousand-dollar suits and twenty-grand Rolex watches sidled away from the women, grunting at other gunslingers, their hands sliding up toward bulges beneath jackets. For whatever reason, Chino had stuck the three Phoenix Force commandos with one of his own hard-eyed buzz cut shooters, the black op McCarter knew as Silo on his far right flank. The plan was to make Kykov jump out of his skin with murderous rage, the gangster maybe breaking out the hardware, gunned down where he sat before he or his goons could get off the first shot.

As soon as they'd hit the door, it was clear to everyone under the roof the lot of them had come in, armed to the gills, as grim as death and looking as if they were poised to take on the whole of the Mongol hordes that had so long ago pillaged and burned and savaged this part of Russia. They were weighted down in full combat regalia, grenades fixed to harnesses, big Beretta 92-Fs in hip holsters, nasty commando daggers sheathed across their thighs. The M-16/M-203 assault combos were the most obvious pronouncements of hostile intent for the Phoenix Force trio, Chino's shooters opting for the HK subguns. On the way in, McCarter had tried to take a head count, but it was impossible. Nerves were crackling all over the joint, McCarter catching a few goons talking into com links—Kykov's boys, no doubt—angling down in front of the upraised bars, east and west.

The Golden Bear, according to Chino, branched off to several large back rooms where the sex frolicking took place, with some of the bawdier shows for private entertainment. Which meant once the feces hit the fan it was hard to tell how many gangsters would come running to jump into the mix. How the black op came by all this marvelous intel McCarter couldn't say. He couldn't imagine Harker, the CIA special op who had pretty much been their taxi driver from Croatia infamy, strolling in, rubbing elbows with all the Russian kings of crime, firing off the questions, rolling dice, grabbing ass. It was possible, though, that Harker had done just that, as the CIA was known for working some pretty seedy and unorthodox angles to get information.

Despite the insanity of the play here, McCarter granted Chino two things. One, this could be the mother lode of Russia's bad guys, and a full-scale slaughter here could go a long way in kicking a major dent in the crime juggernaut. Two, Chino had some balls. The guy walked right up to the table, a mean grin cocked on his lips, planting himself in the spotlight, ready to kick it into maximum lethal overdrive.

Petre Kykov was a beefy mobster, flaccid jowls quivering with rage, the storm, McCarter saw, building behind the eyes as the revelation and the insults sunk in, his mind churning for a way out. The change shadowed the mobster's face, a slow fall of a veil, something McCarter tagged as suicidal fury. His gunmen were lifting themselves out of their booths, digging for hardware when Kykov shouted the order.

McCarter didn't understand what the Russian said, but the meaning was obvious.

About a dozen goons went for broke, all snarls and feral wrath as they began to make their last stand.

They were there to execute, plain and simple, McCarter knew, but where it all went from that point on...

First order of business was to wipe the scourge of Petre Kykov off the underworld face of the earth, so McCarter, James and Encizo joined Chino and his firing squad, a burst of noise and a flying wrecking ball of lead that jump-started the massacre.

McCarter swept the enemy gunners left to right with M-16 autofire. The scissoring lead storms clamped them in, hardmen dying on their feet, blood and shredded cloth hitting the air as the combined fire of Phoenix Force and the CIA black ops kept drilling into the enemy. As such moments in battle often went, it seemed to McCarter to go on forever, aware they had their backs exposed to a herd of potential killers, the Briton ready to pivot and find out who was going to do what out there in the main room. As Chino had outlined, half of his shooters had been ordered to swing their aim after capping off a few rounds, hose down any imminent threat out in the main room.

The doomed gangsters spun, machine pistols stuttering, drilling wild rounds into one another. They bounced off the booths, slammed walls, bringing down an oil painting or two now running slick with blood.

Kykov was the last to go, and not because he had avoided getting scythed during the initial barrage. He was holding on, a crimson-drenched puppet man, winging off wild rounds from a pistol. McCarter was aiming for the chest, coring big holes spurting red, but some of Chino's shooters cranked out head shots, bursting apart the mobster's skull.

The Phoenix Force leader's ears were ringing from the barrage, bodies flopping off tables, but he made out the bedlam in the main room. Feeding a fresh clip to his assault rifle, he turned, found a sea of rage staring back. Women were screaming, darting pell-mell, a few of the less brave already tracking their retreat for the front doors.

"Move it out," Chino said. "I've got a mental file on the A list of Russia's mobsters," McCarter heard the black op inform him. "I start shooting, you guys are on your own. We're out of here."

McCarter grunted. As if they had to be told that, he thought.

A moment later, a few goons began breaking out the hardware, a mixed bag of machine pistols, subguns swinging up from behind the bar.

Chino, surging past McCarter and into the main room, cut loose with his subgun, selecting what he considered prime targets.

CALVIN JAMES HAD sensed the racial animus directed toward him from some of the mobsters on the way in, but that was the least of any concerns at the moment. Blacks, he knew, were pretty much a rare sight in Mother Russia, and he could only imagine the hostility and hatred stewing behind the faces he viewed as he headed out into the main room, M-16 up and ready to nail any armed blockade.

Three goons, shouting something unintelligible, although James could fairly get the gist with the brief baboon comments, were swinging stubby machine pistols his way, focused solely on him. But McCarter and Encizo were right beside him, hosing down other threats, bodies crashing into roulette wheels, the air choked with smoke and the stink of blood. The ex-SEAL's trio of trouble was blown off its feet by his autofire, heaped on the craps table.

Snake eyes.

James was wheeling, shot another goon who popped up behind and flung him to the floor, a smear of blood trailing his outstretched form.

"Goddammit!"

A glance to his left revealed that one of Chino's shooters was down, another black op stepping in, hefting the body over his shoulders in an awkward fireman's carry. The sight of one of his own biting the worm torqued the crazy Chino's killing wrath up another notch or two. The east-side bar became a focal point for Chino and his shooters to vent their rage. Four tuxedoed hardmen were standing tall, firing AKMs when the sustained bursts from Chino and company blew them apart, tossing them like rag dolls in a cyclone into the racks of liquor, all flailing limbs bringing down the best booze dirty money could buy. Another Chino casualty, though, kicked into a pillar, crumpling to his haunches.

James checked on his teammates, then kept heading for the front doors. The exit was at the far end of the foyer, the giant Golden Bear, standing twelve feet tall on hind legs and mouth open to display huge razored teeth, still seemed like a mile away. He noticed the shooting diminish, the crowd in full stampede for the doors now.

"Hold on, mates," McCarter called out. "We're almost there."

Chino got on his tac radio, called in the Dragons for liftoff.

Then James heard Grimaldi raising McCarter, the ex-SAS commando having been given a special unit by Chino to tie him into their ace pilot's radio. James tuned his ear into the grim report. "G-Man to Mr. M."

"M. here."

"You've got a welcoming committee setting up, circling the luxury wagons. They'll be on your nine and three as you come out. A gauntlet. I'm counting fifteen hostiles, and they're getting reinforcements as the fun bunch beat it out of there."

"Can you make a clean sweep of that problem, G-Man?"

McCarter had no doubt in Grimaldi's ability to clear the street. The specs on the Dragon had been reviewed earlier, and the Briton knew Grimaldi had quite liked the doomsday package. A cross between an Apache and a Huey, the wing pylons on the Dragon had sixteen Hellfire missiles. Throw in one M-230 chain gun and a cousin GAU-8-A Avenger, a Gatling gun likewise in 30 mm, both in the belly turret…

They weren't there yet.

Chino, McCarter saw, was spraying pockets of runners, armed or otherwise, sliced and diced bodies sailing over banisters, baccarat tables, hammered into the bar. As far as McCarter was concerned, their mission here was done. Whether Russia would be left a little kinder and gentler place without Kykov was a question left answered only by time. The next problem he saw—beyond getting down the foyer and exfiltrating—was this Sergei Kilcotchkin getting word a strike team was on the way.

Later.

They were hitting the foyer when five goons came swinging around the edge of a spiral staircase that led to some second-floor playground. Why play games? McCarter decided, and let a 40 mm frag round fly from his M-203. The explosion tore the gangster barrier apart, flinging bodies and gore in all directions, the blast close enough to the front doors that they were shredded.

McCarter relayed the word to Chino, who stopped cursing and killing long enough to listen to the problem awaiting them outside.

"Tell your boy to blow them off the street!"

"I thought I just said as much!"

Chino looked set to pursue something, his eyes wild, McCarter wondering about his sanity.

"Torpedo!" he shouted at one of his shooters, as he kicked at a form twitching out on the landing near the foyer. "Grab this sack of garbage!"

It made McCarter wonder what that was all about, but a moment later, he turned toward the smoking exit, heard death from above come thundering from the night sky.

YURI DMITKIN KNEW an opportunity for career advancement when he saw it. It was damn near dropped in his lap, but on a silver platter overflowing with the blood of fallen comrades. As head of security at the Golden Bear, he was long since overdue to step up into the ranks of the Kykov Family, he figured, as a bona fide soldier who had bloodied his hands in combat, soon to be admired and respected among the hallowed ranks of Kykov shooters. With a wife, three kids and a mistress to keep happy, he had been searching for a way to make a career move into the inner circle, tired of being a mere servant or bodyguard to the Russian Mob elite. Keeping them happy and secure in the knowledge they were safe and welcome at the Golden Bear had worn his ego thin over the past year or so. He wanted more out of life, and he knew this was his moment to shine.

The problem was that Petre Kykov was dead, slaughtered minutes ago, where he sat, supposedly by the American CIA. There was still the late Don's second in command, Kilcotchkin, though, and if he pulled off this ambush of the American murderers he was certain he would be rewarded with a top post in the Family.

It never hurt to dream, he knew, but without action dreams didn't come true.

He had rallied close to twenty of what was left of the security detail, outlining the plan for them on the way out the door, barking orders, taking charge, the savior of the hour, getting the vehicles out front moved and ringed just so. They were all armed with AK-47s or AKMs, hunkered low, spread out behind the cover of a dozen or so luxury vehicles, most of them stretch limos. Two firepoints, and the gunmen, he figured, would have to come out the same way they brazened their way inside the club.

The blast blew off the front doors, and Dmitkin, raising his assault rifle over the hood of a Mercedes limo, passed the word over the tac radio to his men to be ready, but only fire on his signal.

Wait, he knew, until they blundered through the smoke, caught in the cross fire.

Where were they? he wondered, his heart throbbing in his ears.

He cursed, growing impatient when he heard the whapping drone, one of his men shouting, pointing toward the Hotel Kykov.

Dmitkin froze at the sight of the winged leviathan boiling up over the hotel roof, swooping down, the cries of the panicked patrons all but lost as the monster helicopter gunship cut loose a flaming rocket while simultaneously opening up with twin fingers of fiery wrath.

McCARTER HEARD them screaming in terror and agony beyond the wafting barrier of smoke. He led Encizo and James down the foyer, past the giant bear statue, heard the pounding of chain gun and Gatling fire hurled into the storm after the initial explosion, figured a Hellfire had gotten the ball rolling. One look back down the foyer, and he found that the survivors in the main room didn't look eager for another try to reclaim the night, gangsters or whoever shuffling away, lost to sight. Those goons were more career-minded, looking to step up and fill in the power vacuum now rather than risk tossing away futures promising them more power and money.

Not his problem.

If Chino wasn't happy with his body count…

Screw it.

McCarter, crouched, hit the jagged teeth at the demolished opening. He found them dying quick, hard and ugly. Grimaldi was in the process of sweeping a rolling wave of doom over the ambush site. Vehicles were pounded to little more than smoking trash, bodies savaged by heavy steel-jacketed projectiles, erupting human minefields vanishing in dark clouds before his eyes. Grimaldi held the Dragon in a hover, maneuvering the death bird left to right, pouring it on, riddling man and machine with long hammerings.

McCarter, James and Encizo helped nail it down, triggering concentrated bursts as shadows tried to rabbit down the street.

Grimaldi patched through. "M.!"

"M., here, G-Man."

"You're clear."

"Tell your boy to drop it down. We're bailing."

McCarter found Chino at his rear, the black op squeezing past, calling in his other Dragons. He stood there, admiring the carnage, McCarter getting a little more edgy about the man as he grinned and bobbed his head.

"Not too shabby. Not quite the kill count I came here looking for, but I'll take it."

"You mind if I ask, Chino," McCarter said, nodding at the black op lugging the lifeless sack of the Russian gangster on his shoulders, "what that's all about?"

"Special delivery," Chino replied.

McCarter stared into those laughing eyes, knew the

man was long gone. The other two Dragons were vectoring in, one from the east, the other black-winged demon lowering onto the street to the west.

Chino's grin widened. "I'm going to wrap that gift package up with C-4 for Kilcotchkin. Drop it right through the skylight."

"Guy's flipped," James muttered, sliding up beside McCarter as Chino walked on. "Out there in lala-land."

Chino looked back over his shoulder at James. "You got something to say there, save it for the celebration later. Let's get out of here."

The stink of smoke, leaking gas and running blood and guts in his nose, McCarter nodded at his commandos to move out, led them for their Dragon now parked on the street.

"Flipped," James muttered.

CHAPTER SIXTEEN

Sergei Kilcotchkin wasn't certain if he was more angry than he was afraid. There was a definite sense of mounting desperation, however he chose to sift through the writhing mass of emotion that had his stomach knotted and his brain pulsing with blood pressure he was sure was off the monitor.

Life as he knew it was coming to an end. Unless he rallied the troops. Unless they understood they were to fight to the death.

This was no time for speeches, he determined, no time for blaming any number of the oversights, misjudgments and miscalculations of the past few months since the deal with the Arabs fell through and he was left explaining to Kykov how in the hell he—the organization—got snowed out of something in the neighborhood of ten million dollars. It was time to find out who under his roof was worth his outrageous weekly salary and who was on the way out.

Fight or die. Life or death. It didn't get much more simple than that.

He was barking out the orders in his study, all hands assembled, assault rifles handed out from the secret armory stash hidden behind the oil painting of Ivan the Terrible. Vasily, Boris and Vladimir were the rocket team, Kilcotchkin snarling now for them to move it out and secure positions on the roof, the tac radios passed around. Shoot first, shoot anything.

When they had their various assignments and posts determined by him and he was alone, Kilcotchkin moved double-time for the wet bar, grabbed the bottle of vodka and drank deeply. This was no time to lose control of himself, drown his anxieties in booze. He was a kick-ass, take-charge type, despite whatever Kykov might think of his promiscuous lifestyle, no doubt the boss believing he no longer had what it took to tackle a battle that now threatened to topple the entire organization. His soldiers were depending on him to steer them to victory against the coming raid, which meant at some point he would have to dive into the melee and lead the way. Despite the fact he knew he owned a track record that saw no backing off from a fight to the death, he feared he was about to lose everything. Money. Power. His life.

And what was this CIA strike all about? he wondered, reviewing his agonizing twenty-minute conversation with his bought-and-paid-for General Mytkin. Slice it any way he wanted, instinct had warned him before the first shred of bad news was reported by Mytkin that the CIA knew about the Ebola, his association with the terrorists, in short, everything. Mytkin had confirmed as much. He had been branded a terrorist sponsor in the eyes of the CIA, and they were coming for him. The goddamn Americans, he thought, were all over the world these days, plunking down black-ops bases wherever they pleased, hunting down terrorists and all manner of international criminals. They saw themselves as the world's policemen, answerable and accountable to no one. Each piece of news that came out of Mytkin's mouth kept swelling the gangster with paranoia, and the bad news didn't stop with word the CIA wanted him terminated with extreme prejudice. The NK contingent, shipped out by General Yong downstairs, had been wiped out, and Mytkin, safe and snug in Georgia, had simply told him he could do whatever he wished with that piece of grim news. They had gone to Chechnya, arrangements made by himself through Mytkin intermediaries, to execute the treacherous al-Amin terrorists, criminals who had…

Forget the counterfeit money scheme, which, he knew, had also left him holding the bag, but no one, not the NKs, not Kykov, seemed to care he had lost his ass on that deal, too. And now he wondered about the sudden silence on Kykov's end.

He had attempted to raise Kykov after hanging up with Mytkin. Instead of speaking with the boss, he had ended up being informed by one of his soldiers that Kykov was at the Golden Bear, in conference, not to be disturbed, they would see him shortly. When Kilcotchkin flew into a rage, demanding the insolent bastard's name, the soldier calmly told him he was Boris Sveltin. And in a tone, Kilcotchkin thought, that fairly told him he could kindly kiss his ass. Kykov wasn't ready or willing to speak to him, so he could wait, stew, sweat.

Which meant trouble. Or, rather, more trouble.

Despite telling himself he needed to get control of his emotions, Kilcotchkin practically flew through the air on wings of fury. He was ready. Bring them on.

He would have to tell the North Koreans something, he knew, as he nearly ran for the doors. But what? That their vaunted special ops had been, not gunned down during a firefight with al-Amin terrorists, but shot up by his own people? He'd figure something out, wing it, lie, if nothing else. How could they possibly corroborate whatever his version of events as relayed to him? They had died, brave soldiers, in battle against the terrorist criminals. Simple enough.

He was through the door, his ears buzzing with all that burning desperation when the walls began to shake, and the faint rattle of autofire and the shouts of his men pricked his ears. He was nearly at the top of the staircase, then taking two steps down when the roof itself seemed to ripple with some tremendous thundering from directly above the house.

"What is happening?"

He looked down into the hallway and spotted General Yong and lackeys, a few of them with pistols in hand, but frozen figurines in their expensive suits, clearly worried now as the racket outside intensified.

Kilcotchkin moved like a zombie, three steps down, or like a man, he thought, taking the final few steps to the firing squad.

He stifled the sudden urge to begin eliminating any and all problems by sweeping the NKs with a long burst of autofire. He was reconsidering doing just that when the world blew up around him, a fireball the size of a domed cathedral roaring through the doors of his study. The force lifted him off his feet, trash in a hurricane. He was tossed through rubble and smoke, then he was tumbling, head cracking off marble before the lights winked out.

DEAN HARKER FELT the smile tug at his lips when their Dragon gunship, guided in by his GPS signal, touched down, claimed a clearing in the birch, fir and pine forest. He was on his feet, cramped from being outstretched on the knoll, having scanned the underboss's massive dacha to the south through infrared binos for the past hour. Thank God, he thought, MP-5 subgun in hand, he was back in business with these three. Unflinching, unhesitating under fire, they didn't mind wading right into the killing zones, but they weren't suicidal maniacs like the late Colonel Joe of the Croatia disaster who had nearly gotten them all blown out of the sky. They were stone-cold professionals, assessed and analyzed every angle of a surgical strike, poking holes in the enemy's weak spots before...

Bottom line, he thought, they were the best of the best, whoever they really were, whoever their employers.

They bounded out of the belly of the gunship, Mr. M., Mr. C.J. and Mr. R. After getting the next round of action, as proposed by Chino, he could only imagine what these three kick-ass commandos thought of the black op in charge of this mission. Most likely they viewed him as another glory-hounding, crazed gunslinger. One look into the big Briton's eyes, as the commando, lugging his M-16/M-203 combo and leading the other two shooters, and Harker read the serious doubt about the kamikaze drill about to go down.

"That crazy Chino," Harker shouted into the rotor wash, figuring he was back in the saddle with these guys, "is going to drop his package first and bring the roof down. That's the game plan."

"We know all about it," Mr. M. said. "You want to tell me why I'm seeing the resurrection of Colonel Joe in that madman?"

Harker shrugged. "What can I tell you? The war on terror has brought out more than a few lunatics who only care about a body count."

"Do tell. Thing is, our man framed three hostiles on the roof."

Harker froze as the sounds of autofire strafed the air, working their way in growing decibels with each passing second through the edge of the forest.

He listened as Mr. M. gave their flyboy his orders, the weapons fire rattling on, then the Dragon was lifting off, gone to aid and assist.

"Let's go join the party!"

And Harker gladly followed the commandos down the trail.

Back in the saddle.

DAVID MCCARTER KNEW no one needed any brain surgeon on this surgical strike to see it was destined to go to hell.

A Croatia rerun, but a death dance on the Volga, was being acted out on the rooftop.

The ex-SAS commando was leading the pack, James and Harker on his left, Encizo to the right, weapons ready to a man, all of them cutting the gap at a hard jaunt across a grassy stretch of no-man's-land when it happened.

McCarter saw the armed shadows, charging up the back side, outlined in the house lights, there, gone to blackness, there again.

The rooftop was getting strafed by chain gun and Gatling fire, a double hosing of heavy metal thunder that caught one dark silhouette and blew him over the side as the Dragon held a dangerous hover position, one hundred feet up, by McCarter's reckoning, above the skylight. To make sure the body package went through unimpeded and into what Chino stated was the study, the black op was in the fuselage, firing down with his subgun, blasting away at the pyramid shape jutting up in the distance. Another op then wedged into the hatch beside his commander, hauling up the gruesome spectacle.

"Hold back, mates! Hit the deck!" McCarter ordered, uncertain how much C-4 poundage the corpse was wrapped in.

"One o'clock!" Encizo yelled.

"To our nine!" James added.

They hit the ground on their bellies. Six, maybe seven hardmen were vectoring all over the back side, shadowing away from an ivy-trellised gazebo, firing up at the gunship.

McCarter glimpsed the package get the boot out the door, sailing down, bombs away, gone from sight, then the big blast was touched off by Chino's remote touch. He hadn't gotten a good look at the structure, or counted windows, but the blinding detonation, the roar of thunder and the number of windows punched out, along with huge sections of the wall obliterated, left little doubt that Chino had added considerable weight to his special-errand corpse.

And the Dragon gunship was getting a dose of its

own hell, no sooner had the big one ripped through the dacha.

McCarter joined his commandos and Harker in laying down a blanket of weapons fire, riddling whatever shadows they could, hardmen howling and dropping, but the damage was already in the process of being done.

Two, maybe three RPG warheads were up and away, then slammed into the cargo hold of the Dragon, a massive fireball blossoming, hurling bodies out into the night.

"Goddamn!" Harker roared.

A burning figure leaped from the hull, tumbling to the roof, shrill cries tearing across the distance and seeming to go on forever as McCarter watched, cursing Chino for taking another batch of professionals with him to the grave.

The Dragon went into a half spiral, then plummeted in some weird slo-mo dive, looking sucked down into the fireball still shooting up from the hole left in the roof. Another titanic explosion knocked out more of the back wall.

"Come on!" McCarter yelled, leaping to his feet, sighting down on another hardman, holding back on the trigger of his M-16 and kicking another goon off his feet.

Anyone left standing inside the dacha would be shaken by the shock wave, choking on smoke, McCarter knew, reeling about.

Now was the best time to nail it down.

"I guess you're in charge now, Harker," McCarter said to the CIA man.

"Not unless you want the honors."

"Call in Chino's other gunship," McCarter told him on the run. "Tell them we're going in, so they can hold off on any more renovating."

"Gotcha!"

A tremendous delayed blast belched out another section of the back wall. That was another problem, McCarter knew, M-16 fanning the dark, searching for live ones. Hellfires, cracked and leaking fuel, getting touched off by hungry flames.

There was no choice but to bull inside, he figured, hearing Harker on the tac radio, the CIA man falling behind long enough to keep the Dragon from breathing any more fire while they combed the wreckage.

McCarter led his commandos into the smoke and the stink of burning fuel and flesh.

Into the fire.

THE INTENSE HEAT revived Kilcotchkin. For a second, hearing then feeling the flames reaching out from some point above and behind, he was more concerned about being roasted alive than any threat in human form that sounded from some distant point down the hall. It was one hell of a time, he briefly considered, to be worried about his good looks, since the whole damn sky was falling and he was sure his men were dying, aware he was next on the chopping block. He had to strain his ears, but he made out the long rattling of autofire, beyond the churning smoke, men crying out in pain.

He dragged himself up and out of the rubble. He spit the slimy goo out of his mouth, felt the slick warm mask on his face, ran a hand over his features and came away with nothing but a mass of dripping blood.

Where the hell was his assault rifle? He peered into the smoke, aware then the NKs were nowhere to be found, assumed the cries he'd just heard belonged to them, or his own soldiers getting mowed down by the CIA hitters. How many were coming? Did it even matter anymore?

He kicked through stone and rubble, his toe stubbing the barrel of his AK. He was grabbing it up when he saw three, then four armed figures barrel through the smoke.

Kilcotchkin knew it was a lost cause, that it was over, no time even to curse these CIA bastards or his own rotten luck.

He was bringing up the AK-47, finger taking up slack on the trigger when four fingers of doom erupted.

"THAT WAS Kilcotchkin, right?"

"Indeed it was," Harker answered McCarter.

"Cheer up, guys, you helped bring down one of the top crime families in Russia. Chino...well, it sucks, I know. He took a lot of good men with him. Bull-headed SOB was going to do it his way, no matter what anybody said or did."

The ex-SAS commando was leading them down the pillared steps, toward the motor pool of luxury vehicles. The Dragons had just received their orders, which was to unload some Hellfires on whatever was still standing of Kilcotchkin's burning tomb. Rubble, smoke and fire permitting, they had checked a few rooms for survivors, but given the destruction done by both Chino's special delivery and the downed Dragon, McCarter had to believe whoever they had encountered and gunned down on the way in was all there was for the taking.

Quickly they moved down the drive, McCarter not sure how he felt about what he considered another half victory. Sure, they were heaping up body counts wherever they hit the enemy, but nothing of real intelligence value was turning up, since every time they struck it seemed nothing but a raging inferno was left behind.

Maybe, he thought, that was good enough.

This was war, after all.

"I wouldn't have minded having a few words with those North Koreans," Harker grumbled. "They could have been an intelligence gold mine. Too bad they went for it."

"Yeah," McCarter said. "Could have, should have, would have, didn't. This whole mission..."

The Briton let his words trail off, glancing at Encizo and James as the first few Hellfires slammed into the funeral pyre behind them. He sucked it up, shrugging off whatever disappointment he felt, the night lighting up with a marching line of firestorms. Where it went next...

The Farm, he hoped, had a few ideas who was up on the hit parade. He was fresh out of answers, leads, but the quicker they put Russia behind the better. Chechnya. Rujik.

The ghost of Chino.

The whole damn bloody mess.

He'd had enough of letting the other guy call the shots. From there on, McCarter was doing things his way, and his way only. No more CIA hotshots. No more tag team with questionable allies.

Phoenix Force, more than ever now, was on its own.

CHAPTER SEVENTEEN

It wasn't Hal Brognola's first rendezvous with the shadow man. Whoever he really was, whichever alphabet-soup agency the man vowed allegiance to, he had proved himself an intel-gathering wizard in the past. His gems of information had often guided Stony Man operations to daring success when the warriors in the field appeared to be staring down the final, ticking doomsday numbers and all looked lost. Touchdowns aside, there was always something about the magic man with all the answers that made Brognola a little uncomfortable, and the big Fed was always left wondering if there was some marker the shadow man would think he could call in someday. If he knew so much, often even about ongoing Stony Man operations, it seemed, he could garner intelligence from every conceivable avenue of local, federal and international agencies at what amounted in Brognola's mind to little more than peering into a crystal ball, reading the future, well…

It could be that the shadow man knew, or at best

thought he knew about the existence of Stony Man Farm. It had happened before, the big Fed knew. Infiltration of the Farm, conspiracies involving the CIA, KGB and such, Stony Man having come under attack in the past, its very existence nearly obliterated, full-frontal assaults, no less, that kept his own memories short, grim and alive about everything that could go wrong and often did. That might have happened in the distant past, when Stony Man was either nearly exposed for what it was or destroyed by enemy attack, but Brognola was always grimly aware that very little in the intelligence world remained secret for long. Thus, he was always on the lookout for present and future threats to the Farm's security, whether home-grown and wrapped in the Stars and Stripes or otherwise.

The big Fed was out of his sedan, found the vehicle parked in the bowels of the underground garage in D.C. exactly where he was told he'd find it, reading the numbered slots on the concrete as he walked. It was black, a luxury vehicle of indeterminate make, government plates, no factory markings or brand name to indicate its assembly line origin. Dark-tinted windows, the vehicle backed in against the wall, so the occupants could see him coming, monitor their surroundings.

The driver in dark suit and sunglasses opened and unfolded out the door. Brognola figured he had to be the size of Godzilla's firstborn, clearly packing as he held open the side door. Brognola hunched and slid into the well, claimed a seat, his back to the black-glassed, and what he assumed was a soundproof partition.

Privacy? Brognola wondered. Or designed for something more insidious? Such as an execution? He wanted to laugh that notion off as wildly absurd, gunned down by some intelligence operative from the No Name Agency, but since the beginning of the Ebola campaign he felt his own paranoia and fear of the future mounting to a boiling point, unwilling to trust anyone outside his own immediate Stony Man circle. He was grateful right then that he had packed and holstered his Glock 17 for this sit-down.

Shadow man shut the door, and Brognola watched as the guy poured a whiskey from the wet bar.

"Join me, Mr. Brognola?"

"I'll pass. It's a little early for me."

The shadow man's smile indicated to Brognola it was never too early for a good stiff belt. He was neatly groomed, dark brown hair tinged with gray on the sides, *GQ* all the way on the surface, but a demeanor that radiated an aura of dark truths and bad knowledge earned from blood experience. He had one of those ageless faces, Brognola decided, the eyes shielded by sunglasses, could have been anywhere from forty to sixty, not a wrinkle. Trim beneath the creaseless tailored suit jacket, wingtips, a bulge on the left side, hardware next to a muscled bicep that flexed as he took a long sip of whiskey. He lifted a fat, white 8×11 envelope, handed it to Brognola.

"I understand there's a nasty little covert war going on over in Russia," the shadow man began. "I understand the Russian *Mafiya,* or a sizable chunk of it, namely the Kykov organization, pretty much no longer exists thanks to some wildmen who also laid waste to a Chechen breeding ground for terrorists. I understand there's an ongoing covert war in Mexico, in the process of ripping out the guts of a major drug cartel that's sleeping with al-Amin terrorists who are the spawn of al-Qaeda and Taliban rabble. I understand some *federales* are on the warpath down there in Mexico, but there seems to be a pipeline, like the voice of God," he said, chuckling, gesticulating at the roof, "from the White House to Mexico City that's going to hold back the Alamo part two for this elite crew of black ops. Amazing how things can happen in this strange, strange world of ours, huh?"

There it was, Brognola thought. The man was laying it out, the feelers, telling him he knew something, reeling him in. Brognola wasn't biting. "To what do I owe this honor?" Brognola said, dumping the intel packet on the seat beside him.

"I know you can make things happen, certain activities that can win the day, shall I say, but that would have those ball-less pukes on the Hill demanding not only your job but would want to see you strapped to a gurney for treason, maybe even lit up for public entertainment, pay-per-view, just so they can remind us little people who's in charge. But what do they know? All they see is reelection, guest appearances on various sundry talking-head shows, sucking up to whatever the PC mantra of the day, speeches at colleges where they 'rape' in outrageous fees for feeding the young and impressionable their spin of deceit and self-aggrandizement."

"Now that we know you're apolitical, maybe we can get on with this?"

"We're living, my good friend from the Justice Department, in the most perilous time in human history."

"Spare me the doomsday speech."

"Extreme measures are the only thing that will keep the barbarians from breaking down the gates of freedom. No speeches here, just the facts. What I know has not, and cannot reach the White House, or I would have to personally kill those of loose lips. If the public at large, even the power structure knew how close we are to Armageddon in the form of the mother of all black plagues, there would be mass panic, anarchy in the streets, the end of America as we know it, in short. Martial law, and so on, Washington emptied out of all its stalwart leadership, running to the hills of West 'by God Virginia' or stashed away with their briefcases in NORAD, waiting it out for the savages to devour each other in the city streets. A tactical nuke or two set off on our own citizens perhaps, just to get it all back together on 'their' chess board."

"I'm already aware of the present crisis."

He smiled, sipped his drink. "Really? If that was true, the crisis, as you understate it, would have already been dealt with to a successful conclusion. In that little gift package I just gave up, is everything you need to know to clean up the Ebola nightmare. Yemen. That's where it's happening. Truth is, certain factions of our government have known about this clandestine facility in Yemen for over six months. It's all there, hell, it's practically a road map to where they're building the Angels of Islam. Appreciate you not asking how I know all this, small talk and like that, so I'll get right to it, as long as you're keeping the faith. The technology came in from Indonesia, the North Koreans using Indonesian freighters to smuggle both the technology and the killing agents into Aden, those devils north of the thirty-eighth parallel having acquired what they sold from the Russian *mafiya* of late Kykov notoriety. In time, fear not, the North Koreans will be dealt with, but the way I'm hearing it a decent chunk has already been carved out of their operation. But, like I said, fear not, Kim Jong is on the way out."

"Wait a second. You're telling me the buck stops in Yemen? We have special ops over in Yemen...."

"Right, right. Come on, now, I know you're not that naive. It's all sleight of hand, you show me yours but I show you what I want. Saddam had the game down to a fine art. The Yemenis, as I'm sure you know, are as bad as the Saudis, our, uh, so-called allies over there. They talk big about cooperation in our effort to exterminate Islamic extremists while espousing the virtues of holy war against us infidels behind our backs. English for our cameras, Arabic out of the other side of their mouths when they think we're not listening."

Brognola had to give the shadow man that much. "Telling me this facility has been marked by sky spies for what it is, and what? No one sees fit to do a full on-site inspection?"

"No one wants to."

"How's that?"

"Those factions within our own government I mentioned. There's been an ongoing plan, to give you some background, at least on the drawing board, to attempt to foment the unrest in the Middle East, get it all past the critical-mass stage, step back and see who's left standing after the big one. The thinking is the world will someday run out of oil."

"If you're heading where I think you are, I'm aware there's been conspiracies involving a military strike and seizure of the Saudi oil fields."

"You make it sound like it couldn't happen."

"What's this have to do with any Ebola factory in Yemen?"

"Everything. It's exactly what 'they' have been

waiting for. Say this plague is unleashed, in a controlled-experiment scenario, by our own side, on selected 'targets' of the U.S. population. Hey, don't look so constipated, chief, it's happened before. The CIA—"

"I'm aware of that, CIA experiments on our own, so on and so forth. But what you don't—or they don't, whoever the hell 'they' are—understand is that if this agent is released it will be unstoppable. It will spread and infect the entire population of the United States within weeks.

"Not unless the controlled experiment involves quarantine of the target area. The thinking goes on along this line. The blame would be dumped solely on the Arabs, or so the White House would march out their mouthpiece for the media and state with overblown passion, rattling the saber, demanding blood justice. It would then give us an excuse to launch a full-scale invasion of the Middle East."

"And take the oil."

"It's the only reason we even bother to acknowledge their existence. This country imports sixty percent of its oil, gobbles up ten percent of the world's production and those numbers are growing by the millions of barrels by the week. Think about it. The world's population will be something like fifteen billion plus in twenty years. More mouths to feed, more cars to gas up, our own cities swollen to capacity so that no one will even be able to walk down the street.

New York alone, what with mass immigration, is going to make Calcutta look like a vacation hot spot in about ten years. Crime will be the only thing by which the masses will be able to support themselves, since those of us in the know are aware it's only going to take another Enron or two before the whole economy bottoms out. And when a whole nation is out of work, starving, historically either man-made or natural calamities get it all back in balance. An entire planet dying, natural resources a luxury only the rich and powerful will able to afford. Our nation's citizenry armed to the teeth, a few guys at the Pentagon with their fingers on the button. Think I'm crazy? Making this up? The drug war alone, so-called, should clue you in that it's all a sham, a game where a few who have the most will continue to take more, and will do anything to hold on to what they have. Like Mount Everest, climbing it—greed in this case—because it's there."

"And you? What's your angle here with all this big help, being as you see me as a guy who can get things done?"

The shadow man paused, studied Brognola for long moments behind his shades. "It's real simple. Consider me one of the last heroes of this great republic. A patriot. No more. No less. I'm here, giving you what I know—facts—at the considerable risk of my own life. I don't know. Call me a Christian, but one who's done turning the other cheek."

Brognola felt himself spiral inward, his guts churning, wondering if the man was playing it straight. Whatever was in the package was worth checking out, the Farm running down the facts, whatever they were, that the shadow man had provided him. And if he dismissed the shadow man as some conspiracy kook?

He wouldn't. Instinct warned him not to let this opportunity slip away.

"We can win this one, Mr. Brognola. I'm sort of counting on you to pull it off. Thing is, once you've discovered I'm not blowing *X-Files* smoke in your face, this facility...well, if there's Ebola there, and there is, the bioengineered kind that can wipe out this planet in about two months, I'm thinking the area in question will have to be, uh, thoroughly 'sanitized.' Do I need to spell out ADM?"

Brognola felt the ice walk down his spine, and no, the shadow man didn't. *If* what he said was true...

The shadow man lapsed into a long silence, Brognola sensing the powwow was over, as he poured another whiskey.

"Good luck, Mr. Brognola."

And that was that.

The big Fed scooped up the package, dismissed, was rising when the shadow man, staring into his whiskey, said, "You ever wake up some days and wonder where the world thinks it's headed?"

"Lately...too often."

"Keep the barbarians from the gates, Mr. Justice. Stay frosty, guy."

Was that a grin on the shadow man's lips? It was something he and Bolan often said to each other. Again, Brognola felt his paranoia blipping all over the radar screen. He got out of the vehicle, then took a few steps back. He stood there, as the engine fired up, the boat pulling out, the shadow man gone moments later as the vehicle hit the exit ramp.

Hal Brognola stared at the white package and wondered, if this was the end of the beginning, or the beginning of the end to the Ebola nightmare.

Only time, and the blood of the enemy, he knew, would sort it out.

ATOMIC DEMOLITION Munition. Thoroughly sanitize the area in question.

"Stay frosty, guy."

Ebola.

Hal Brognola was indulging a rare afternoon Scotch on the rocks. With what was on his plate, having already run it by the President, who told him he would call back in two hours at Brognola's Justice Department office, the big Fed figured he'd catch his breath, sift through his options, mull over his encounter with the shadow man before what could be the biggest play of his career was set in motion. It wasn't his call, but in the end he would be the one to sound the order to the troops on the ground.

He was sitting alone at the bar. Before entering this joint, which catered to the late-lunch Perrier crowd around the Federal Triangle, he had passed a nudie bar, grinned to himself, frozen in time, it seemed, tempted to go inside and find out what were all the cheap thrills that got Lyons and his guys so wound up—and where this whole mission actually got launched down in Miami, thanks, to some greater or lesser degree, to Able Team's shenanigans and prurient approach to R and R. The married man in him dumped a case of conscience in the end, and he shuffled on.

He glanced at his briefcase, undecided whether what the shadow man had given him was Pandora's Box or the Holy Grail.

Both, perhaps, and neither.

He had spent twenty or so minutes in his sedan, perusing the package. Sat pictures clearly showed a military build-up of some sort in the Wadi Hadhramaut of north-central Yemen. Russian APCs, three T-72s, low-lying aboveground installations ringed by chain-link fences, sat dishes, antiaircraft battery, including a dozen SCUDs. Then there were tunnel-boring machines, huge trucks to haul away the rubble and the framed hardmen with the traditional skullcaps of Yemenis adding fuel to Brognola's fires of paranoia and agitation, the whole nine yards that whatever was going on there wasn't kosher. A brief written synopsis listed several intelligence contacts in Aden, their handles, addresses and numbers, HUMINT on the ground who, or so claimed the shadow man, had the roster and the layout on the Angels of Islam factory. Apparently it was a primitive operation, but the essential technology was in place, courtesy of Pyongyang, with the bulk of the sinister alchemy brewed in a small underground city, dug deep into the mountainside.

Where al-Amin terrorists monitored the progress of the five errant Russian microbiologists. A neat package? Brognola wondered. Gift wrapped and dropped in his lap, open at his own peril? A setup, some devious ploy by the shadow man to flush Stony Man operatives out into the open?

Brognola didn't think so, or, rather, hoped not.

Far too much was at stake.

If Stony Man got the green light from the Oval Office...

ADM. Sanitize.

Of course, there was another option, once Phoenix Force cleaned the AIQ of hostiles, and that was to simply roll in a HAZMAT team to sanitize the situation, retrieve and isolate any doomsday agents. Political fallout? Not his problem.

He had already touched base with Price. He had ordered her to get the next phase in motion, whatever it took, pull off the logistical magic to get Phoenix Force assembled, on the ground in Yemen and moving. Manning and Hawkins were in Italy, cooling their heels in a CIA safehouse, supposedly on the trail of Wahjihab, but Price was working on getting them to the American air base at Aviano. With the dirty little war against the Russian *mafiya* apparently over, McCarter, James and Encizo were catching flak from the FSK at the CIA base near the beleaguered Rujik. Another red-tape mess, right then getting scissored by State Department, CIA and Pentagon officials who were intervening at the request of the President.

It was going take time, Brognola knew, twenty-four to thirty-six hours—a goddamn eternity—before Phoenix got a hard look at this factory of Armageddon.

And then?

Brognola drank deeply, willed himself to relax for what could well be the last time in a long time.

Why not?

He was no conspiracy buff, but most threats to national security involved a secret circle of collaborators and traitors and assorted savages, and he doubted the shadow man was blowing that *X-Files* smoke in his face. He had come through before, but everything in life had a way of changing, people especially, the void of the shadowy intelligence world always spitting out the worst of the worst, traitors who chased their own agendas.

Brognola knew he had no choice but to run with it.

"Tough day?"

Brognola looked up. The bartender was a cute little brunette, her eyes searching what he knew was a haggard face, his eyes, no doubt, sunken, reflecting a soul weary and worried to its core. He wondered about her life for a moment, her hopes, dreams. It felt good, clean to sit there and have a total stranger—even if it was the job acting on her—make a polite inquiry....

Did she have children? A husband? If she only knew, he thought, like everyone else there, eating and talking away an hour or so before they headed back to whatever made their own lives click, churn and move ahead, unaware, or maybe simply wanting to ignore the evil in the world.

Brognola smiled. "That remains to be seen."

She nodded at his empty glass. "Another?"

Brognola considered it, checked his watch. "One more."

"It's on the house."

"Thanks."

There was rarely a free lunch in life, he thought, even when generosity seemed to float down out of the sky on blinding light. Still, she was sincere, kind enough, and Brognola found himself wondering about his own strange mood.

She came back with his drink, Brognola peeling off a fifty for the one drink. "Ring me up."

He took another minute, working on his drink, the bartender laying his change down, thanking him, but moving off, sensing he simply wanted to be alone.

The weight of the world, he knew, was on his shoulders.

He drank up, stood, thanked her, gathered up his briefcase and left the change on the bar.

Give a little, get a little, he thought.

CHAPTER EIGHTEEN

"You know, a man lives long enough, he sees everything, wonders what the hell's left. No more surprises, no thrills, no new horizons, no nothing, like he's a balloon or something—life sticks a pin in him, he slowly deflates. He's lucky he gets out of bed in the morning with a piss hard-on. But this deal here with you guys?" DEA Special Agent Chuck Baldwin smiled, chuckled. "You four might as well hang a shingle out front wherever you go—Black Ops R Us. Maybe something along the lines like 'assassins for hire in the name of national security, we do the dirty jobs nobody else wants.' Have to tell you, I really appreciate you guys bringing the Gaza Strip south of the border—everything but the suicide bombers—me being a mere little civil servant of the United States government and all. You know, I have to hand it to you after your little Wild West show. You four are either special crazy or you got special kinds of balls of steel. Hell, who knows, maybe they're both the same thing. All I know, I'm about to grow major wood here over this Kabul, or the West Bank comes to Mexico."

Bolan and Able Team were in what the Executioner assumed passed as a command-and-control center in a stone hovel on the southeastern foothills of the Sierra Madre Oriental. Little more than a wall map of Mexico, a file cabinet, two computers, a radio console in the corner. Two black Huey gunships parked outside, one of which had transported the Stony Man warriors from the carnage of Ciudad Zapulcha and dropped them off here at what Bolan guessed was a roving intel operation, the DEA able to pack it up and move on in the time it took to smoke a cigarette. The warriors had put some distance to the scene of slaughter hours earlier, Bolan calling in the DEA-Mexican drug task force cavalry for a pickup. The task force had combed through the massacre, questioning eyewitnesses, one Major Raul Benito none too happy—or so Special Agent Chuck Baldwin had informed the four of them when evacuating them far south of the killzone—about assassins taking the law into their own hands on Mexican soil.

The Executioner had his hands on the war table, intel pictures of target sites, photos of the next round of bad guys up on the list, various grid maps spread out before him, names of DEA contacts, numbers and addresses, hot sites of enemy lairs circled in and around Mexico City and the Yucatán Peninsula. Bolan gave Baldwin—a tall, lean, dark-haired figure in brown desert camous, a Beretta 92-F in shoulder holster and tac radio attached to his belt—a sideways look.

"Yup, I must have missed the updated playbook on Justice Department operations. Take no prisoners. Scorched earth."

Baldwin gave his head a slow shake, but in the strange smile he showed them, Bolan read the closest thing to admiration they'd get. The short speech had been delivered without rancor, judgment or criticism, and Bolan read the man as old-school military. Which meant he didn't have to explain this was war, and they were down there, carte blanche from powers high up the chain of command back in Washington, to waste any and all enemies of the United States, drug traffickers, terrorists and anyone they had purchased safe haven from, whether politicians, *federales* or the Mexican military.

No tap dancing. No diplomatic coddling anywhere across the board.

No bullshit games.

The SAC went to the file cabinet, produced a bottle of whiskey, five shot glasses, brought the whole package back to the table. "Tell you what. If those *federales* you blew up and shot up weren't all cartel lackeys and known executioners and torturers for Cordero and the Ojedas, you four would be in a world of feces. I know, I know, before you say it, you didn't start shooting at anybody who didn't shoot at you first.''

Lyons, Blancanales and Schwarz were grouped around the table, alternately watching the SAC play bartender and scouring the DEA's intel spread.

''Won't exactly raise a toast to you men,'' Baldwin said, passing out the drinks, ''but there's a few pluses and somehow I've managed to calm the churning waters before they get too chummed, meaning I ran a shitload of diplomatic interference for you guys with the *federales* and the good major before you got tossed to the sharks. Best I keep you guys moving around, away from the major. Cordero, though, is a nice catch for us, especially now, considering his state of mind. When you handed him over to me, he practically hit his knees like the DEA was all of a sudden his only ticket to salvation.''

''Mutual cooperation,'' Bolan said, sipping the whiskey. ''He's all yours from here on.''

''Right. Least you could do, huh. We'll sit on him, keep picking his brain. He's so damn scared after seeing his hacienda blown halfway back to Texas he's already giving up what are elaborate tunnels along the border, details about these terrorists you guys are hunting. Apparently the tunnels were how they planned to smuggle in these al-Amin terrorists and whatever their ordnance. Of course,'' Baldwin said, cocking a grin, ''I had to make certain promises. Such as no extradition back to the States, handing him over to Mexican authorities instead, where he can do his time working on his tan and his golf game, but, hey, my memory's not what it used to be. As for El Condor, he stays with me. I can use him to infiltrate a bunch of mules I've got marked on my own hit list up north. Bottom line, I have my orders, gentlemen, and that's to give you four blanket cooperation, and some voice of God in Wonderland pretty much hinted if I like my job I will see no evil where you're concerned.''

''There will always be another cartel for the DEA when this one is burned down,'' Lyons said, gulping down his drink, looking at Baldwin, who gestured at the bottle to help himself.

''And on goes the drug war, I hear you,'' Baldwin said. ''But there won't always be cells of Arab terrorists running around in Mexico. If you four have something to say about it.''

''We're losing daylight,'' Bolan said, anxious to get their war machine cranked up again and rolling on the Ojeda brothers. ''What else can you tell us about the Ojeda–al-Amin connection?''

Baldwin started rifling through the photos, flipping them around the table. ''This is older brother Rodrigo's place, where you say you want to hit next, being it's the closest in a leapfrogging campaign of kick ass and take names and no prisoners. First, our phone and e-mail intercepts, our informants in Mexico City confirm that Julio has packed up his toothbrush and vanished into the jungles of the Maya lowlands in the Yucatán. They're splitting themselves up now that they know war has been declared on them. There's a compound somewhere near the village of Chiaxa, but deep in the jungle, rife with gun-toting rebels, Indians, smugglers, killers, rapists and thieves who prey on wandering Yankee tourists."

"Ciudad Zapulcha in the Yucatán," Blancanales commented.

"Worse. There's more cutthroats, like times ten what you saw up north, according to our information, and they've got a lot to lose if they bite the dust. Somewhere in this stretch of jungle is where the Ojedas store mass shipments of cocaine that comes up from Panama, through Guatemala. It's also a prison compound, we've heard, where a number of our own informants are believed to have been made to 'disappear.' Likewise anybody they brand a threat, politicians, cops who can't be bought.

"Kidnapping's become a booming business down here, especially with the Ojedas, who employ a mini-organization for just this kind of work, only those abducted rarely make it back to the bosom of their loved ones. Now, Rodrigo, he's the real badass of the two. These days, he sits around dipping heavy into his own snow supply. When he's not smoked up, sniffed up or boozed up, he's always got a dozen or so women lounging around the premises, guy strutting around wagging his ding dong and doing the dirty in full view for our sky spies. He never, even when he's humping away, strays too far from his Uzi submachine gun. He's a psychopathic killer, enjoys doing his own dirty work, and he's been known to torture to death several of our informants. His favorite gig is to drop some poor sap into a well where, at the bottom, is a nest of every poisonous snake from cottonmouths, imported from Louisiana, to fer-de-lance and whatever else in South America."

"Snakes," Schwarz muttered. "I hate snakes."

"His, uh, home, if you want to call it that," Blancanales said, "doesn't look like any standard hacienda. It looks more like a spaceship. A straight silver cylinder, roof fanned out like a...saucer."

"Yeah. He calls his compound El Chupacabra."

"The Chupa what?" Lyons asked.

"It's Mexican folklore," Baldwin answered, smoking, refilling his shotglass. "Little gray men coming down from the sky, abducting Mexican peasants and taking them away to the mothership. Rodrigo spends whatever sober time he can manage, sitting around, watching *X-Files*, old *Outer Limits* reruns, word is he's also—get this—a big *Miami Vice* fan, and *Scarface* is his favorite movie. Got the whole collection on all three of his favorite shows, videotapes."

"Chupacabra," Lyons grumbled. "Guy's a flake."

"But a dangerous one. Hell, this is Mexico, and between the Chupacabra and all the claims of UFO and Virgin Mary sightings half the peasant population ought to be in straitjackets, it's lala-land down here. Like most of these big-time dealers, the Ojedas come from dirt-poor villages where they retell myths and legends—hell, it's almost like a badge of honor to be a believer. Anyway, east of the Chupacabra is where he repackages the blow, cutting it, or cooks it up into bricks of rock, then ships it out." Baldwin tapped the black-circled area on a sat picture outlining a large stone structure. "That's the warehouse. All told, reprocessing factory, the main compound, you're looking at thirty of his best shooters. Guess it would be too much to ask if you four need a little helping hand on this one?"

"Not this time," Bolan said.

"What I figured. You're not going in to arrest the man. What the hell. I've got my own work to do, playing tunnel rat and all. One more thing. We've learned, and confirmed it with the CIA, that one Irqhan Rabiz fled your little party earlier. He's on the run, but regrouping with a cell that Rodrigo ordered to move to his jungle compound. One corrupt dirtbag *federale* by the name of General Miguel Santos, holed up at his own compound, just outside Mexico City, is making the travel arrangements. He's also the one responsible for a bunch of those North Korean hitters being in-country. It's all there, gentlemen, take what you need."

"We'll need one of those Hueys and a pilot at our

disposal,'' Bolan said. ''Also any refueling sites you can manage.''

Baldwin killed, then poured another drink. ''You guys. What the hell. Maybe you'll put a major dent in all this crime and corruption down here, who knows. You're going to do it your way, so good luck and good headhunting. *Federales*, terrorists, whoever else. Like I always say anyway, since I been in this business. Everybody's guilty of something, everybody's weak in some way, everybody's got a monkey on their back. Even me,'' Baldwin said, winking at the four commandos. ''You guys want one more before you head out?''

Bolan glanced at his commandos, Schwarz and Blancanales declining, but Lyons held his glass out.

''Look like a man I could have a decent night on the town with,'' Baldwin said.

''Only if it's Miami. And before you two make a date, you might want to get this guy to define 'decent,''' Schwarz said, drawing a scowl from Lyons.

RODRIGO OJEDA KNEW all about the life expectancy of a major trafficker. He knew all about the Pablo Escobars, the Gachas, Ochoas, to name a few who were no longer among the living. Eight to ten years was about how long he figured he could stay in the drug business before he was either arrested, smoked out by a rival or hunted and gunned down by the authorities.

Which was why he figured he owed it to himself to live a little, even in these times of trouble. It flew in the face of good business sense to savage so heavily his own supply, getting hooked, he knew, on his own stuff like some migrant field hand or rich gringo. But if anybody, even his own blood, had a problem with his indulgence, he or she was wise enough to keep the talk well out of earshot. After all, didn't his hero, Scarface, enjoy a good high once in a while?

He figured he was somewhere past the ozone on freebase already, but dropped another rock into the glass bowl, fired away with his mini-propane torch, inhaling deep, feeling his brain light and swell up with the desired ecstasy.

"Sweet, lovely," he sang to himself.

Times of trouble? he thought. No problem. Everything in life came to an end. Good times, bad times, life itself. Enjoy success and all his world had to offer, earned by his own blood and sweat, while he could, while it lasted.

Even still, if the end came for him, if the kingdom was destined to be destroyed, then he would find a way to somehow save himself.

Options. Fight back? It depended on who and how many came for his head. Kidnap one of the enemy? That made more sense. The Americans didn't like the idea of one of their own being abducted, tortured, threatened with death. They cherished life, spoiled children never willing to sacrifice their own blood if they could squirm or buy their way out of a crisis. The more he thought about it, taking another hit, the more he liked the idea of snatching one of the *americanos,* their gringo counterparts fretting about, capitulating to his demands to back off, or else they'd find their man in so many body parts littered all over the countryside for the buzzards. It would be a message to them. If he could take one of their own so easily, he could always abduct another, a thief in the night, the very human embodiment of the Chupacabra.

He was sitting at his personal table in the auditorium, alone, watching his favorite *Outer Limits* episode on the big screen. Man, but he loved it, he thought, Robert Duvall, an assassin for the Americans, transformed into an alien to infiltrate an extraterrestrial camp where a UFO had crashed, telling the general he was going to a warm yellow planet now with his newfound alien friend.

A kiss-my-ass gesture, he thought.

Just as he needed to do if the DEA came storming his palace.

Life hadn't always been this good, he thought, soaring away on enough coke smoke to shroud half the screen and blot out Bobby and his new buddy. He'd been a petty thief, leg-breaker and assassin years ago, for the Ochoas, but it had been a rocket ride, shooting straight to the top when they'd gone down under federal guns. Somebody had to step up to the plate. Why not him? Of course, his brother, the accounting wizard, the diplomatic brains behind the cartel, had been useful, his educated tongue swaying all manner of political, police and military brass to keep their organization afloat, weed out those so inclined to uphold the law with a trip to the Yucatán.

He was thinking, as he felt himself shoot right out of his body, floating away on a cloud of euphoria, that maybe his brother no longer had the smarts or the nerve to stay in business with him. Sometimes a changing of the guard was necessary for survival, removal of weak links assuring the chain remained strong and together. His brother, he recalled from their earlier phone conversation, had come unglued when he'd heard the news about Cordero, some four-man mercenary army that had mowed down his *federales*, half his mules in Ciudad Zapulcha. The DEA and its Mexican cronies in the so-called war on drugs had come in after the battle, the four killers gone in the wind like ghosts, so that left him wondering exactly who and what these four men were. CIA? Rogue assassins? Well, his North Korean and Arab guests had also been gunned down in the killing spree, a bitter feud having erupted between those two parties over counterfeit money being handed over to the Asians in exchange for some terrorist ordnance dream come true he didn't even really want to know about. There were too many human factors—problems—

running around, chasing their own agendas, at his expense, and perhaps his very continued survival.

Then there was Cordero.

Word had reached him, earlier in the day, about their associate getting snapped up by the DEA. Cordero, he feared, would break, give up the tunnels. The man was more interested in his lavish lifestyle lately than taking care of business, might even point the finger his way, claiming the brothers were the geniuses behind the smuggling routes.

Rodrigo had the entire compound on full alert, but depending on who or how many came storming in...

He needed prisoners more than he needed bodies. He needed information about why, all of a sudden, he was on the radar screen of the Americans.

It was the business with the Arab terrorists, he had to believe, that had brought this ghastly trouble to his kingdom. His own purchased general in the Feds had backed him up on that line of reasoning. Still another whining human problem in Santos, the general more concerned about...

Selfish bastards, he thought, everywhere he turned.

Thus he knew he needed to conclude this half-assed venture with the Arabs and the North Koreans before the sun rose tomorrow. Already he had put in the pertinent calls, Rabiz and General Duk Jung being rounded up for a short flight to the jungle to settle their differences.

It was pretty simple, the way he saw it. Whoever

came up with the most money first would live. Or maybe he'd personally take a trip to the Maya lowlands, foment their agitation, anger and feelings of betrayal, arm both sides, step back and watch them shoot each other to so many bloody pieces to feed to the beasts of the jungle.

He was loading up another fat nugget when Octavio Quito burst in, a stream of panic-stricken words encroaching on his buzz.

"Two men, boss. Armed. Big assault rifles with grenade launchers. They just breached the southern edge. We have them on the cameras."

"Slow down, Octavio! I am anxious enough without you jabbering away at me like some nervous woman! Gringos?"

"Yes, it appears so."

They were being hit, he knew. But, he wondered, only two men had turned up on their monitors? Yes. That was it. Where there was two...

The four mercenaries.

It was his turn.

His mind racing, his heart hammering in his ears, Rodrigo put together a quick plan.

"This is what you are to do, Octavio. Take six men with you. Place three on the balcony facing where they will be coming. Do not kill them unless it is absolutely necessary. Use the sleeper canisters, drop six, seven on them. I want them out with the first cloud of dispersing tranquilizer!"

His second in command looked confused. "I do not understand. Why—?"

"Do not question me! Take those two men alive and bring them to me and have the helicopter ready at once!"

"We are leaving, we are—"

Rodrigo picked up his Uzi, stepped up and into Octavio's face. "Running? Were you going to say running?"

"No, boss."

He softened his tone. "If you are worried we may lose the shipment in the warehouse, there is more stored in the jungle."

"But, it is seven tons."

"And there's plenty more where that came from. If we lose it, we lose it. If my own home is blown down like Cordero's was, I will have another built. Go, but first bring me a knife, a pen and several pieces of paper."

Rodrigo Ojeda turned away as Quito flew out of there to carry out the orders. He would not go down, like Cordero, without a fight. If he could pull off an abduction, though, he knew the battle for his survival had only just begun. But if it was the four mercenaries, and he managed to grab two…

He would be able to dictate the terms of their own demise at his place and time of choice.

And if he was destined to go the way of his predecessors?

He dumped another rock into the bowl. Torching up, he recalled a line from one of his favorite *Miami Vice* episodes.

"Nobody lives forever."

CHAPTER NINETEEN

T. J. Hawkins couldn't remember when he'd felt so good. The ex-Army Ranger gave Lachlin a smile that was all teeth and said, "We're out of here. Have a nice life. Wish I could say it's been swell."

"Hold the fuck up there, you two!"

Manning had just shut the briefcase with sat link hookup, Hawkins getting the word they were due to fly to Yemen on a classified military flight just arranged by the Farm. Next stop—the American air base at Aviano. They were back in business with their teammates, McCarter, Encizo and James already in the air from Russia, en route for the next leg of the mission. What little Hawkins had overheard from Manning, he knew something big and badass was brewing in Yemen. The gist of it was there was a final showdown, the big score to settle up with al-Amin, something about an Ebola factory. He could get the particulars in the air. Right then he just wanted to grab his war bag, have Lachlin get them the hell out of there and on their way.

The Stony Man warriors had been sitting in a villa in Calabria for hours on end after the flight in a Gulfstream from France. It was, Hawkins assumed, a CIA safehouse, perched on a rocky cliff overlooking the Ionian Sea on Italy's east coast, but the view was hardly enough to keep him there when their teammates needed them. They were showered, shaved and Lachlin had some decent food on hand in the refrigerator. Good news was that the level of contamination from the dirty bomb was near nonexistent, according to Lachlin's digital readout on his Geiger.

"That's it, huh," Lachlin growled. "Free at last?"

"You are to chopper the two of us to Aviano air—"

Lachlin cut off Manning. "I heard. I don't know what kind of clout Barb Price wields these days, but I'll get your asses to Aviano."

"Hey," Manning said, standing, moving around the sofa, injecting a little steel into his eyes and voice. "We've got a job to do, we're gone, that's that. I don't have time to nurse any hurt feelings, Lachlin."

The CIA agent chuckled. "You two have real short memories. If it wasn't for me, I daresay the French authorities would have you sitting in jail."

"Skip all that noise," Manning growled. "We damn near got our heads blown off because you neglected to tell us back at that al-Amin safehouse your gunship was going to turn that place into Swiss cheese all along."

"You made it out all right."

"It's over, Lachlin," Hawkins said.

"Not for me. Wahjihab is here in Italy."

"Wahjihab's gone," Manning said.

Lachlin's gaze narrowed. "And you come by this information how?"

"My gut."

"Your gut." You guys. How do you like this for gratitude. I mean, I've got maybe twenty or more al-Amin scumbuckets strewed around Italy, I could use the extra guns."

"Maybe some other time," Manning said, hauling up his war bag. "Now. Is that chopper out front going to take us to Aviano?"

"Yeah, yeah. Get your asses in gear. I was getting sick of looking at you two anyway. Waste Puchain and Rousiloux," he grumbled, moving through the archway for the foyer, "I guess you got what you wanted. I'm just a glorified taxi driver."

Manning fell in beside a grinning Hawkins, shot him the thumbs-up. "Free at last. I kinda like that."

"DIG IN, dig deep and get it up."

Words the Executioner had passed off during the brief to Able Team to live and fight by on the short chopper ride to El Chupacabra's outer perimeter.

The gunship was circling to the east, hugging the low chain of hills, ready to drop the hammer as laid out and timed by Bolan. Schwarz and Blancanales had been dropped off first, moving in on the spaceship compound of El Chupacabra right then, weaving a course through a manmade forest as Bolan and Lyons scaled the rock-littered incline, their own handheld IR turning up two bogeys, a hundred feet above, to their one o'clock.

The Executioner hated to split up the team again, but they needed a synchronized one-two knockout, the double whammy set to go off in less than three minutes as Bolan checked his chronometer.

Once the clock struck, it was all blitz and burn.

Their gunship, tagged Thunderbird, would hit the warehouse with an opening barrage of 2.75 mm missiles from the fixed rocket pod, the door gunner going for armed hangers-on with the Gatling gun. Supposedly there were peasant workers doing the cutting and refining of pure Colombian poison inside the warehouse proper. Bolan had no intention of gunning them down, but they were going in hard, bent on nailing anything armed and angry. He could only hope the workforce had the good sense to duck or run.

NVD goggles on, Bolan saw two green-gray ghosts rise up along the ridge. He slung the M-16, drew the Beretta 93-R, its sound suppressor snug in place. A hand motion for Lyons to hold on, and the Executioner lined them up in the sights. It was a one-two chug, head shots, subguns falling from lifeless hands as the two figures sagged to the ground.

The poison factory was just over the rise.

First the factory, then Bolan and Lyons would link up with their teammates. Two could play at the Ojeda dirty game of abduction, and the Executioner was going in next—unless Pol and Gadgets beat him to it—to bag another big fish.

They topped out, crouching, both warriors' M-16/M-203 combos ready. The motor pool would have to go, either Thunderbird or their own M-203s about to reduce about ten vans and trucks to scrap, whoever got there first. NVD goggles off, Bolan and Lyons took in the armed figures, ten in all, scurrying around in the glow of hanging halogen lights.

They were made, Bolan knew, as they pointed up the hill.

"Do it," Bolan told Lyons as he heard the whapping bleat of Thunderbird, then saw the black warbird soar down and unload the first few rounds of fiery destruction.

The Executioner and Lyons triggered 40 mm warheads into the panicked mass of hardmen.

SCHWARZ KNEW something was wrong the second he breached the last ring of what he assumed were transplanted palm trees. The spaceship compound, up close, was massive, a dully shining steel cylinder with squared-off windows that told him the structure had at least three floors, a balcony ringing the second level. Schwarz could sense, then heard movement in the distance, a soft rustling of brush.

"We've got live ones, Gadgets," Blancanales said, stowing his IR monitor.

Schwarz checked his watch. Right on time. The show to the east had already begun, he knew, as he heard the distant crunching thunder of explosions.

"Six on the balcony, ten o'clock, two more—"

That was as far as Blancanales got. Schwarz was bringing his M-16 into target acquisition when several objects, spewing clouds, came snapping through the foliage above, two more small canisters erupting to his left.

Several large billows of smoke immediately enveloped the two Stony Man warriors, Schwarz angry they'd been caught with their pants down, aware of what was happening.

"Run!" Schwarz yelled at Blancanales, triggering his M-16 at the shadows bounding through the thick vegetation.

Too late.

He glimpsed Blancanales wilting as he attempted to burst through the wall of smoke. Schwarz heard himself cap off a few more rounds, felt a brief stab of grim satisfaction as someone howled in pain, then a fog settled over his eyes. Then he was gone, tumbling down, nauseous, into a black hole.

ALANO PANTANCHEZ KNEW that one day either his prayers would be answered or his nightmares realized. Working for the number-one narco-trafficker in all of

Mexico held only two bottom-line realities. The prayer—he could abscond with two or three bricks of pure cocaine during a raid by either the DEA or the Feds, skulking off while his security detail did all the fighting and hopefully dying. It would be difficult, but not impossible, assuming he made a clean break, to resell the drugs in Mexico City. There were plenty of small-time dealers he knew in the big city, fledgling traffickers looking to step up into the ranks of the big leagues, some of whom might question how he fell into such sudden good fortune. He had a family of six to consider feeding, though, and he would take his chances since the dog scraps Rodrigo Ojeda fed him to watch these peasants and make sure they didn't get sticky fingers wasn't putting much more than a few tortillas on the table.

The nightmare—arrest, and imprisonment in what he had heard were some of the worst prisons in the world. He had no wish to rot away and die behind bars, but another shadowy vestige of the nightmare saw Rodrigo Ojeda, wise to his pilfering, and a pack of killers with machetes coming to pay him and his family a visit in the middle of the night. But, he knew, desperate times called for desperate measures. He was sick and tired of being poor, seething inside while other, less worthy men made it in the world, growing rich off the slavery and the suffering of others.

The first series of explosions nearly blew down the front wall. Chunks of stone and wood were flying all over the warehouse interior, the workforce sounding off long, pitched cries of panic, muffled bleats behind their filter masks all but lost next to some terrible pounding of a big gun that he saw blowing apart several of his security men just beyond the roiling smoke. This was no DEA operation, he knew. This was a full-bore slaughter. The who and the why didn't matter.

It was time to cut and run, and grab up some goodies on the way out.

The stampede was under way, Pantanchez raging at the peasants to move out the back door, his plan coming alive as he saw them abandoning the cutting tables, flying past the vats where the cocaine's purity was diluted, ground up with a vitamin supplement. One worker, Miguel he believed his name was, apparently had some ideas about making his life a little better. He was plucking up a green plastic-wrapped brick from the pallet, when Pantanchez lifted his Uzi and drew a bead on his white smock. Miguel's eyes went wide, brick in hand, a sound like "Nooo!" coming out from behind the mask, but Pantanchez was already chopping up the white smock into red ruins with a long burst of Uzi fire.

Two voices, rife with fear, came flaying from both sides at once. Santiago and Purez were all over his flanks, Pantanchez cursing them for their cowardice. "You have weapons! Get out there and deal with this!"

They looked uncertain, the workforce rushing for the back exits, the eyes of his own security men wandering all over the pallets heaped with white gold. He knew what they were thinking, aware he would have to make some token gesture of leadership.

"Move it out! I will make sure none of these peasants steal from the boss. I will be right with you! Go! You saw what this one just tried to do," he bellowed above the racket of gunfire and screams of men dying in pain, kicking at the scarlet mass at his feet.

They shuffled off toward the smoke and the sounds of battle.

Pantanchez watched them go, looked around, found all eyes were either focused on a way out or fixed on the hell that had descended on the warehouse from outside. Quickly he grabbed two bricks, wishing his camou jacket were a little bigger, and shoved them in the waistband of his pants near the small of his back.

He took several steps toward his gathered force, barking at them to shoot.

BOLAN AND LYONS WADED into the slaughter zone, popping off one 40 mm round after another, blasting apart man and machine in a frenzy of sudden, thundering doomsday. Vehicles were blown asunder on fireballs that swept through the hardforce, figures sailing away on the crests of flames and blossoming smoke. Rotor wash was pounding over the enemy gunners who were backpedaling for the ruins of the front wall, subguns and assault rifles flaming skyward, but the Gatling door gunner, smoking out hundreds of rounds in the time it took to blink a few times, was scything through the ranks.

Marching ahead, the two Stony Man warriors chose targets, driving long raking bursts in a viselike pinch that sealed their doom as six or seven more hardmen held their ground.

They spun, flying away from fiery wreckage, drug watchdogs crying out in final spasms of pain.

Senses choked with smoke, Bolan and Lyons made the obliterated opening, the Executioner, com link now in place, ordering Thunderbird to hold its position outside. Two crabbing moaners were treated to mercy rounds by Bolan and Lyons, then the Executioner led his Stony Man teammate into the warehouse proper.

It was empty, except for a sprawling mother lode of poison, then Bolan spotted a figure in a green camou jacket beating a hard run for the back exit. He bumped into a table, looked over his shoulder, then gathered momentum again. Bolan and Lyons hit the triggers of their M-16s in tandem. Steel-jacketed sizzlers tore up his back. The eruption of cloth and crimson was dappled with white puffs hovering in the air as the thief was launched to the floor, skidding up and slamming headfirst into a vat. Whatever his ambition, Bolan thought, it just went to hell with him.

"Ground Control to Thunderbird, come in!"

"Thunderbird here, Ground Control. You're clear out front."

"We're coming out. Drop down, we're out of here."

The command rogered, and Bolan and Lyons armed incendiary grenades. The Executioner indicated to Lyons to dump his at one o'clock. Lyons tossed the white phosphorous egg and it settled up against a pallet piled six feet high with poison, bursting into a blinding flash to begin its raging consumption. The soldier winged his to the opposite far corner. For good measure, the two warriors pitched another round down the middle, rolling them up under the worktables.

They were moving at a jog, scanning the carnage for live ones but finding only the dead, when the cleansing fireballs went off.

Time, Bolan thought, to help Pol and Gadgets bring the spaceship-designed Chupacabra in for a crash landing.

CHAPTER TWENTY

Reality proved a painful awakening for Hermann Schwarz. He felt the open-handed slaps stinging his face like a thousand wasps going berserk at once, his tormentor lashing flesh so hard his eardrums felt set to burst. He was swelling with anger first, his brain on fire, then fear boiled up from deep beyond the sparks of electric agony as he struggled to get his arms moving, fight back at whatever bastard was taking potshots.

And realized his hands were bound behind his back.

The kicks drilled into his ribs next, deep, driving blows, his eyes almost opening, then snapping shut with each hammering to the side that punched air out of his lungs. A few kicks speared him in the kidneys, leaving him wondering how many days—assuming he lived that long—he'd be passing blood. His ears were ringing like a thousand church bells at high noon on Sunday, someone hollering in his face, demanding to know who he was, whom he worked for, how much did he know.

Know? he thought, brain searing with pain, his mouth opening as he heard himself sucking wind. They were prisoners—that much was obvious—but he'd die before he gave up Bolan and Lyons and their mission parameters, which, he knew, were damn well about to change to full-tilt boogey the likes of which these savages could never imagine in their most frightening nightmare.

Then the stink of tequila pierced his senses, some asshole dousing his face, the bitter liquid flooding into his mouth, choking him. He hacked, gagging on the liquor, twisting away, but the same asshole kicking in his ribs went back to the foot-stomping routine.

Pol? he thought, fear for his friend tearing through him, winding up into terror. Was he alive?

Schwarz forced his eyes open, a snarling dark face behind the misty veil somewhere in his sight. The central core of his skull felt swollen with cotton balls, his limbs weak, limp rubber, then he remembered the incident.

Ojeda's thugs had brought them down, he knew, with some sort of sleeping gas. He grew angrier at the memory alone, ashamed for a moment, thinking he'd let down Bolan and Lyons.

Then cold rage put some more life back into his body when he found Pol was still alive, bearing witness to what they had done to him.

They were in some type of aircraft, he realized, leather chairs, the kind of plush carpeting and walnut or teak tables found on private jets. Or maybe it was a chopper—hard to say, since he could barely hear anything beyond the hissing, growling hyenas in his face.

Blancanales was a bloody mess, Schwarz saw, two long-haired cutthroats holding his teammate up by the arms while another savage slammed punches into his gut. Pol was buckling, whoofing air, but forced to stand and take it. His friend's face was a lumpy patchwork of cuts and bruises, and God only knew, Schwarz thought, how long they'd been working him over. A few more piledrivers into Pol's gut like that, and Schwarz knew his friend would hemorrhage.

"Amigo," the goateed hyena rasped in his face, "I asked you a question. Who the fuck are you?"

Schwarz sucked in a deep breath. If he told them anything, he knew both he and Blancanales were dead. They were probably going to be killed anyway. He took some degree of satisfaction right then that their deaths would be avenged.

And God pity these bastards once Bolan and Lyons hunted them down.

Schwarz winced as his hair was wrenched, his head shaken like a wet rag. The face was becoming clear now, and he recognized Rodrigo Ojeda as his tormentor.

"I'll kill you and throw you off this helicopter this instant if you do not tell me who you are. Well?"

Schwarz steadied his breathing, grinned and said, "Bond...James Bond."

Ojeda slapped his face, shouted, "Stand him up!"

He felt their hands claw into his shoulders, then realized they'd left his feet untied. Their mistake, and Schwarz let the bearded face rolling his way know all about this error in judgment. He slammed the tip of his combat boot into the man's scraggly jaw, heard the sickening crack of bone, teeth flying through the cabin, the bearded jackal tumbling over a seat. He was hoping he'd killed the son of a bitch but didn't get the chance for confirmation as someone chopped a rifle butt against his skull, bringing on a light show of supernova dimensions. He was on his back again, Ojeda's mask of rage fading in and out.

Schwarz thought he was going to vomit, his mouth filling with blood and more tequila rain. The drug scum was shaking his head again.

"Amigo, you have guts, I give you that. We will see soon enough just how tough you and your friend here are. I have a little surprise for you waiting at the end of this ride.

"Leave them be for now!" Ojeda ordered.

Schwarz saw Blancanales tossed to the floor, but the kicker couldn't resist one more shot to his ribs.

And Schwarz passed out.

"THIS FEELS all wrong, Striker."

"Tell me about it."

The gunship was vectoring in on the massive cylinder of El Chupacabra at what Bolan assumed was the back side, given the pool and cabana ringed by a coral rock wall. The Executioner was squeezed in beside Lyons and the door gunner, his gut instinct nagging him like acid in the belly the closer they bore in on Ojeda's personal statement about his eccentricities. There were lights on in various windows, but the place had an eerie, empty feel to it.

And the soldier had given up trying to raise Blancanales or Schwarz.

He didn't want to fear the worst—that their teammates were already dead—but if there had been a pitched battle here there were no indications, bodies and wreckage, flames and smoke, all the telltale signs they had gone to the mat with Ojeda and his thugs.

"Drop us over the pool deck!"

The gunship was lowering when Bolan spied three armed figures stepping through an opening on the far side of the pool, rushing out to greet the invaders.

"Hit them!" the Executioner ordered the Gatling gunner, who cut loose with his spinning wheel of murderous lead.

The trio didn't stand a chance against a weapon that could spit out several thousand rounds per minute. They were eviscerated where they stood, blown back from wherever they'd come.

Bolan and Lyons, M-16s up and ready, 40 mm charges down the chutes of the M-203s, hopped out of the fuselage. The Executioner was pumped, angry and worried, but knew runaway emotion was for amateurs, and got it under cold control. If their friends were...

Stow it.

The Executioner wanted answers, some dark foreboding settling an icy chill over his gut. "If there's one to be taken," he told Lyons, skirting around the edge of the pool deck, "I'd like him alive."

Lyons nodded, as grim as hell, and Bolan caught the worried look in the ex-LAPD cop's eyes.

Cautious, they slowed their jaunt, sidestepping the litter of corpses. Beyond the opening Bolan took in the sprawling opulence of a massive living room. Smack in the middle of the floor was a huge aquarium, a kaleidoscope of exotic fish fluttering around bizarre fan-shaped vegetation.

Two hardmen came running around the corner of a TV screen the size of a small car. Armed with subguns, they went for it, bringing them up, but Bolan and Lyons were already holding back on their triggers. One was chopped off at the knees, howling like a banshee, thrown by his own agony into a mad pirouette, his chattering subgun blowing out the aquarium. A damburst of water and flying fish bowled the screamer to the floor, the flood driving him halfway across the room. Number two was grabbing at legs chewed to scarlet ruins, but he was holding on, firing wild bursts, trying to adjust his aim.

Bolan needed only one, and cored his chest open like rotten squash with a figure-eight burst of 5.56 mm tumblers.

"Watch our backs!"

Lyons grunted his assent as Bolan sloshed his way to the downed hardman, kicked his subgun away.

"Two men—gringos—where are they?"

The hardman choked out the words through gritted teeth. "Ojeda took them prisoner...he left...a message...auditorium...down the hall..."

"Where?" Bolan demanded, but had a pretty good idea.

"Jungle...Yucatán..."

"Only five of you left here?"

"*Sí*...yes...please..."

Bolan thanked him with a mercy round. The two men headed down the hall where the Executioner spotted flickering shadows beyond the open doorway. Crouched, he peered around the corner.

"There is nothing wrong with your television set...."

Bolan looked at the movie screen at the end of the auditorium flashing *The Outer Limits,* took in next the rows of seats, empty, or so they appeared.

"There's something stuck on the screen," Lyons said, and Bolan noted the piece of paper impaled with what appeared a knife in the middle of the screen.

Heart pounding, Bolan walked down the aisle, his finger curled tight around the M-16's trigger, pivoting side to side, checking the seats for ambushers lying in wait. He could feel the emptiness around him, and his gut knotted up with anger the closer he came to the screen.

He ripped the paper off the knife. The message was written in misspelled and broken English, but Bolan got the gist of it. He handed it to Lyons, who swore.

"This bastard takes our guys hostage," Lyons growled, "and now he's telling us leave the country. If we even come after him, says he'll kill them."

"If he thinks that," the Executioner said, "he's dreaming."

ROBERTO MUNOZ WAS worried, but he had work to do. Counting millions of Yankee dollars was both time-consuming and nerve-racking, since it was someone else's money, and he was responsible for every dollar, and under the threat of death.

Reports of disasters and disappearances—a missing Cordero and an errant Julio Rodrigo—from Ciudad Zapulcha to El Chupacabra had come screaming in over his phone by way of General Santos and his own cadre of soldiers the past five hours since his return to Mexico City from Los Angeles. Allegedly, Cordero was in the custody of the DEA, and Rodrigo's younger brother had gone into hiding. Until whatever was happening was sorted and figured out, settled, one way or another, Julio, rumored to be not so brave of heart anyway, would remain in the Chiaxa compound, surrounded by a small army.

With all this mystery and death and destruction, Munoz didn't know what to make of it, stories of sightings of four faceless, nameless assassins burning his ears like all those stories he'd heard about the Virgin Mary floating down out of the sky while growing up in Chiapas. Lately the peasants in Mexico City were seeing flying saucers soaring and hovering around the skyline of Colonia Centro, downtown. The pollution of Mexico City was legendary, and he had always dismissed that sort of fantastic babbling as too many desperate and unemployed mariachis and tortilla vendors with more imagination than money and breathing in too much of the city's poisonous fumes....

Tales of UFOs and the Virgin Mary, he knew, didn't rank up there with four killers on the loose in his country. Not when there was a body count nearing triple digits to back up all the panic and terror flying his way.

He had to concern himself, up to a point, that he might be somewhere on the hit list. His own informants, inside his country's special narcotics task force, had learned these four men weren't DEA agents. Then what? And who were they?

No one had an answer. Munoz detested both the vague and the fantastic.

An extra guard had been stationed out in the hall, just in case.

The Yankee dollars, five million and change, were churning away at lightning speed through the money counting machines. Rodrigo Ojeda, he knew, would be anxious to know how much cash the four of them had brought back from their distributors in Los Angeles. He had considered phoning the man he called *Commandante,* confirm what had to be wild rumors about gringo gunslingers on the rampage, but Ojeda never wanted to hear from him until he had the money counted, bagged and delivered. No exceptions, under any conditions. It was far too much money, what with all manner of legal eyes watching their people in America, for their distributors to simply stroll into a bank and make a deposit. The days of Scarface, Rodrigo's personal hero, were long gone. It came south then, bundled up, stuffed into duffel bags, Ojeda's private jet bringing them and the loot home. Every two weeks, like clockwork, Munoz and his men made the trip to Los Angeles, dropping off the bricks, picking up the cash. The *commandante,* despite his reputed growing addiction to his own merchandise, still knew the math, how much product was dropped off, and how much money should be coming home. If Munoz was one dollar off...

Salazar, he saw, went to the vault, plucked two bricks from the stack, the *mordida,* for Santos who, in turn, he knew, sold it to rival dealers. It was something he needed to discuss with the *commandante,* Santos and his soldiers going into business for themselves.

Competition wasn't good, since it led to an inevitable street war.

He was wrapping the first bundles of cash with rubber bands when the door blew in with a muffled peal of thunder. Stunned, his eyes flashed to Salazar, Jésus and Carranza. All of them were reaching for the Italian Spectre subguns on the table, Munoz wheeling at the toppled steel door when two big black-clad figures in black ski masks burst inside. Their subguns lanced out of the smoke, the long, burping stutter telling Munoz they were silenced and these wraiths had come to kill. There was a second of paralysis, Munoz wondering how they had breached the corridor, how the guards could have so easily allowed two gunmen…

Another heartbeat, rage beginning to balloon in his belly, as he wondered if his own men had set up some sort of rip-off.

That clearly wasn't the case, as he caught a fractured glimpse of bodies flying into the wall, all blood and flailing arms, one of those subguns sweeping his way and…

Munoz felt the burning tear down his arm, his subgun falling from numb fingers. The cry of pain was nearly past his lips, but the black-clad invader moved like a bolt of lightning. Lights blazed in his eyes, and he realized he was falling, the invader throwing out a punch so fast it wasn't even a blur. He was on his back, fighting to focus on the iciest blue eyes he had ever seen.

"You don't have time to pass out, Roberto."

"Who—"

"Speak only when spoken to. Take this."

It took a full second, peering through the haze as the swirling fire in his brain threatened to drag him off into blackness, before he realized the invader was holding out his cell phone.

"You're going to call Rodrigo and give him a message."

It was a voice that Munoz could only imagine came from the bottom of a tomb, cold, backed by death itself. He heard rustling, looked over and felt outrage bring him back all the way. The other invader was stuffing their duffel bags with Ojeda's money.

"Look at me," the voice of doom growled.

Munoz did.

"Don't worry, that money will go to a good cause. Plenty of churches here in town will appreciate your contribution to helping the poor."

Munoz took the phone in a trembling hand. "What if I can't reach him?"

"Your life depends on it," the blue-eyed man told him in perfect Spanish. "Here's the message—repeat after me. Get it right the first time or you're on your way to hell."

"I'm dead anyway."

"You don't know that. You know what they say about where there's life..."

Some hope, then. Munoz listened to the message, nearly screamed in horror at what he was being ordered to tell the *commandante,* a certain death sentence. He dialed the number, mind racing with terror, aware that he was a dead man, either way. Perhaps he could talk his way out of there; he had more money stashed in Julio's office next door. If they let him live, he knew he would have to flee the country, Ojeda holding him, whacked out on coke and jacked up on paranoia these days, personally responsible for this robbery.

He heard Ojeda's voice come rasping over the line. "*Commandante,*" he said in Spanish. "It's me."

"You're back?"

"Yes..."

"You sound funny...."

Munoz was about to explain himself, beg for understanding and mercy, then felt the muzzle of the sound suppressor jammed to his forehead. "Listen. Two men, they tell me to give you a message. They tell me to tell you, 'You have two of our friends. If there is so much as a scratch on them, there will be nowhere on the planet for you to hide.'" Munoz heard the silence on the other end, wondered if Ojeda was still there. Then the drug lord blew up, a stream of vicious curses erupting, but before the barrage blew into full-blown threats, the blue-eyed American snatched the phone, severed the connection, dumped it on the table.

The invader stepped back, the thief sliding into view, duffel bags in tow.

"Now what?" Munoz asked.

"Now you're retired from the drug business. Forever. You'll be lucky if you leave prison an old man."

Then Bolan drove the butt of his weapon into Munoz's temple.

CHAPTER TWENTY-ONE

Even if he was so inclined, Hal Brognola wasn't about to break out the champagne if and when the present nightmare ended.

The jury, as in the Stony Man warriors, he thought, was still out.

The big Fed marched into the Computer Room, found the cyberteam hard at work but looking his way, grim to a face. The word had already come down from the Oval Office, and he wasn't sure if it was good or bad news. Hours ago, he had touched base with Price again, alerted by the mission controller that Phoenix Force was en route for the complete five-man linkup in Aden. Before signing off with Price, he had simply told her, "Make it happen. Pass that on to Phoenix."

Brognola's stomach was a roiling vat of acid. He already knew the score, that they had, in all likelihood, with a little help from the shadow man, pinned down the Ebola factory. It was crunch time, plain and simple.

Kurtzman and Tokaido felt compelled—most likely their own nerves as badly frayed, Brognola reasoned, as his own were—to spell out what they had on purloined sat imagery, running down the numbers and the layout of what the big Fed already knew was a clandestine facility with all the trimmings of a war base. He half listened, moving into their workstations, chomping on his unlit stogie, perusing the sat pictures burglarized from an NRO satellite now parked over the AIQ.

"Hal," Price said, "now that we know the Man won't let our people take it out with an ADM, we need to give Phoenix their other options. David, Calvin and Rafe are in the air, their C-130 set to land at our Special Forces base outside Aden in approximately four hours."

"David, T.J. and Gary," Kurtzman said, "were emphatic about going in alone. No more CIA black ops. The Company's reckless abandon nearly had them cuffed and stuffed by the FSK. If it weren't for the State Department..."

"I know, I know," Brognola said. "This is it, people, the home stretch. One choice, God help us all, and spell it out for David. The President won't risk an international incident with the Yemenis, and given the fact there's a village of innocent bedouin or whatever too close to what would be ground zero, I have to agree. We start irradiating women and children, we're no better than these al-Amin killers."

"Hal," Katz said, "we have bases in the area. We have B-52s, Stealths, F-15 and 16s, we can just as easily—"

"Option one, out the window. I ran that by the President, also," Brognola said. "No thermobaric bombs, bunker busters, all that earthquaking fanfare that will have CNN, Fox and every journalist on the planet parachuting in with a mike stuck in the faces of our people. The Man wants this to be quick, quiet, clean. Easier said than done, I know. A Special Forces biohazard team will go in after Phoenix has taken out the enemy. The Man wants eyeball confirmation of kills and complex. He wants this Angels of Islam technology, assuming it's down there in the cave complex or whatever David and the others will be facing, the Ebola confiscated and taken out of Yemen by the Special Forces."

"Meaning no options on the board," Kurtzman said, "other than our five men penetrating the compound, somehow getting into the cave, going down… Hal, you know what this could mean?"

"Damn right I do. The Man wants no big numbers of our own Special Forces taking this place down, the usual politics in play, no air strikes this time out. Our guys will be completely on their own, basic grunt work, butcher's chores. How they do it…how they get it done. God help them, God help us all. The waiting game, people, is on. If anyone here is the praying sort…"

Brognola let it trail off, as he felt the mood darken, an enveloping wall of mixed dread and hope that nearly knocked him off his feet.

"Anybody hear from Striker lately?"

The big Fed got a round of head shakes and negatives that shook up the bubbling lava in his belly a little more.

THE EXECUTIONER COULD FEEL the stress smoldering like a hot coal off Lyons as they piled out of the deep-cover DEA man's van for round two on a three-stop hit parade.

The former LAPD detective's simmering wrath was far too understandable, Bolan knew, aware the two of them were on the clock, and it was either winding down or it was already over before they had a chance to hold back the eleventh-hour hand of doom. To his credit, Lyons didn't voice or even give the hint of a look that he had found fault on his part in the planning of the strike on El Chupacabra that now saw...

Regrets aside and even still, Bolan was only human, felt responsible, being in charge of the mission and the lives of Able Team, that Schwarz and Blancanales had fallen into enemy hands. Only decisive action, he knew, would turn the tables. Worst case, their friends and teammates were already dead, but Bolan didn't think so, and neither he nor Lyons broached that subject. The Ojedas were running scared, and Bolan was betting the lives of both the good and the bad that Rodrigo would keep them breathing as his ace in the hole.

They could have gone straight to this Chiaxa patch of jungle, but Ojeda had a head start, a good hour or so by chopper, according to DEA satellite tracking, and it would take the DEA and their sky spies and HUMINT in the vicinity a little while longer to pin down the exact location—once the bird landed—and map out the path of least resistance through the jungle to the compound.

What was done was over, and the soldier was never one to second-guess his decisions, or kick himself over what now appeared a basic oversight in not using the Huey gunship to blast the Ojeda Bell JetRanger off the ground before they had made their move on the compound.

In the meantime, Bolan having made a judgment call on the way out of El Chupacabra, they could relay a strong and undisputed message to Ojeda.

Touch our friends, so much as ruffle their hair, and suffer a pain that would make the enemy beg for the fires of hell.

The Mexico City pitstop, the soldier hoped, might just buy Schwarz and Blancanales some critical time. Two hours tops here, then Bolan needed them to be out of the city, in the air, and going for the throat of the Ojedas while the drug lords were, hopefully, sweating it out in the jungle, wondering if they should or shouldn't.

Bolan put the worst-case imaginings of what could happen to Schwarz and Blancanales out of his mind.

The first of what Bolan had marked, mapped and laid out as three hits on the Ojeda organization in Mexico City had been the easiest, but, in his experience, it often worked that way. First hits were usually no fuss, no muss when staging urban-guerrilla surgical strikes, surprise and brutal daring being the key elements. Once the enemy got wise they were being hunted like wild animals, they beefed up the guns and numbers, laying in wait. That's when it got dicey. But Bolan was prepared to brazen it out, take on all comers.

Round one was a wrap, and Ojeda knew by now he had grabbed the bull by the horns, and the goring was just around the corner, if Bolan and Lyons had anything to say about it. The four moneymen, essentially errand boys, according to the DEA file, were merely appetizers. Bolan had dumped off an incendiary grenade on the way out, another statement of things to come for the Ojeda brothers. The money-counting hole had been adjacent to Julio Ojeda's real-estate office complex, the younger brother catering to the rich and famous who could afford beachfront real estate in Acapulco, Cancun, all the ritzy hotspots of fun in the sun primarily for wealthy gringos. The Executioner wasn't in the business of displacing the poor, putting them out in the street because of his own War Everlasting and his own goals, but on the walk up to the smoking sentry outside the building he had seen that the complex sat alone, worthy of nothing else but a cleansing fire.

Julio Ojeda would have to build himself another front, assuming he even lived another twenty-four hours.

BOLAN HAD RADIOED in the SOS, put the situation and his intent to the DEA SAC. Within minutes, Chuck Baldwin had put into play a DEA deep-cover operative, known only to Bolan and Lyons now as Robert, at their full and unquestioning disposal. Robert had been waiting in a dark blue Chevy van at the classified DEA airport north of Mexico City. The choking sprawl of the most populated city on the planet—a grossly conservative twenty-three million bodies spread out over a thousand miles—had ground up precious time. But it had given Bolan time enough to feel out the deep-cover man, read he was legit, relay the hit list, what he needed and what he wanted the man to do. Robert was proving himself the best damn taxi service in a city notorious for cabbies either not knowing where they were going or robbing their customers.

It was working out, so far. That was all Bolan needed to know.

Their sound-suppressed MP-5s in special swivel

rigging beneath baggy black windbreakers, pockets filled with other weapons of war, Bolan and Lyons moved swiftly down the narrow alley, alert for shadows, roving muggers or staggering drunks in the night. Robert was in motion, gone to circle the block, his tac radio tied into Bolan's frequency, ready to alert them if unforeseen police problems turned up.

There were supposedly, according to DEA surveillance, six to eight of them behind the black door of the squat stone building at the end of the alley, a one-story affair.

They called themselves El Mordida, "the Bite." The irony wasn't lost on Bolan. They were the Cordero-Ojeda "round up" artists, as indicated in the DEA file. Kidnapping was their claim to notoriety, and they were so feared that a sizable percentage of the police, politicians, military officers and local businessmen paid them to keep from being abducted and whisked off to the jungle, never to be heard from again.

Within minutes, "the Bite" would be bitten and out of business.

As Bolan moved up on the target, he spied the small skull-and-crossbones painted on the door.

Right place.

Ski masks pulled out of their pockets and in place over their faces, Bolan eyed the single lock, bringing out the subgun. It looked like flimsy wood, nothing special, no extra dead bolts, locks, El Mordida having thrived and prospered so long on reputation alone, the DEA packet tagged them as beyond arrogant. An informant claimed they wiled away the nights, boozing it up and huffing coke, the lot of them usually glued to the giant screen TV in the main living room. As pumped on adrenaline as he was, the wood barrier proved no match for a thundering boot heel from the Executioner.

After the intel given to them about the numbers and interior layout on the Ojeda money bunch, Bolan knew they were both too far along to not trust the DEA's surveillance abilities.

Charging in, Bolan caught the excited chatter, edged with fear, through the beaded curtain to his left. As planned, Lyons had a flash-stun armed and ready to fly. Subgun fire chewed up the archway, beads blowing apart, stone chips slashing the air, as Lyons went low in front of Bolan, the steel egg getting an underhanded pitch into the room.

Bolan and Lyons, backs to the wall, heads turned away from the coming thundering supernova, rode out the crunching blast. The blinding light show raised the human racket to ear-piercing decibels when Bolan and Lyons made their move to put them out of their misery and terror.

The Executioner went in low and fast, peeling off to his right, six of them reeling about the living room, the television set smoking as the blast had blown out the picture. Wild rounds sought out Bolan and Lyons, but they had them dead to rights where they staggered and yelped. The Executioner dropped two with a double precision burst to their shoulders, flinging them to the floor, crashing through the coffee table, white powder billowing in the air.

They were choking, crabbing all over the floor, spidering through glass and wood, Lyons kicking subguns out of their reach. Bolan, combat senses on overdrive, moved down the hall, Lyons watching his back. Three bedrooms, a bathroom, Bolan going into each, checking closets, under the beds. All clear.

The Executioner moved to one of the moaners, bent and raised his voice, asking number one in Spanish, "Can you hear me?"

A jerky nod.

Lyons went into the kitchen and returned with a cell phone.

"I want you to call Rodrigo Ojeda," Bolan said, "and give him a message."

"You're crazy, I can't do—"

Bolan drilled him in the chest with a 3-round burst, then turned to number two and found he was fully back to his senses. "How about you? Can you dial up Rodrigo for me and give him a message?"

"*¡Sí!* I can. I will."

Lyons handed him the phone, and Bolan gave him the message to relay to Ojeda, told him to repeat it, get it right the first time, Spanish or English, it didn't matter. The hardman began to punch in the numbers.

CHAPTER TWENTY-TWO

General Miguel Santos hung up the phone, the ten-minute diatribe, bursting with accusation, blame and threats, still ringing in his ears.

Rodrigo Ojeda, he thought, had essentially told him that if he was finished, on his way out, then Santos could expect his own fate to rival or surpass whatever befell him.

He stared directly, for some reason, at the gold-trimmed base of his opulent study, shaking. Feeling the hot edges of emotion cutting through his bulk, double chin quivering, aware he needed a drink in the most desperate way, he suddenly felt ashamed of himself. A man of his stature, two decades of service to his country, more medals to his name, he thought, than the Ojedas had murdering thugs, and he was treated like one of their common street dealers, or, even worse, a mongrel that deserved nothing but a well-aimed kick.

Despicable, he thought, how he had just been talked to.

With a track record of daring victories over two of his country's fourteen major rebel groups that, in the past, had threatened to topple even the presidency, stunning military success, albeit when he was a mere captain, fifteen years and a hundred pounds ago, and actually led campaigns from the front lines...

That he could have just allowed some narco-trafficker to curse and berate him with such vile language, insulting everyone from his dead mother to his wife to his mistress to his children...

Santos wasn't sure why the image of himself as some fat slug—as Rodrigo Ojeda had finally called him before hanging up—hung in his mind. The picture of himself as a slithering, slimy mass, squeezing through the base of the wall blessedly vanished.

Santos then became afraid, and angry. He had his own world, after all, to protect and save.

Ojeda had blamed him for the current crisis, four gringo madmen on the loose—two of whom were now prisoners of the trafficker—killing dealers, middlemen, cutouts, mules, demolishing the homes of both Cordero and Rodrigo Ojeda that cost enough to feed this nation of ninety-six million for an entire year. He was being accused of dragging his feet where the al-Amin terrorists were concerned, playing games, stalling, perhaps even setting in motion his own agenda to save his skin. It had taken time, getting one of the Ojedas' customized executive jets, he had explained, to find a suitable landing site where the

Arabs were holed up near the foothills of the Sierra Madre Oriental. He had been having great difficulty convincing their leader, Rabiz, to board the aircraft, take all of his men to the jungle compound to meet with what was left of the North Koreans after the massacre in Ciudad Zapulcha. He had already convinced General Duk Jung, after an hour-long faceoff, that it would be in everyone's best interests if his party made the trip to the jungle, solve their differences with the Arabs. That, of course, he knew, according to Ojeda's scheme, meant both sides would come to the table, armed, and hopefully slaughter each other, a lead aspirin for Ojeda's migraine. The drug lord wanted to go back strictly to moving tons of narcotics, no more of this international intrigue that was now threatening to destroy the entire cartel, Cordero already in DEA custody, and who knew how much he had told the Americans. Well, he had manipulated all the human chess pieces as Ojeda had demanded, phone calls and tense conversations the entire day, and yet he was being made to feel as if…

Well, as if his life was on the line.

And, in fact, it was.

Ojeda had informed him that key cogs in the organization's narcotics juggernaut had been destroyed, his prime money men slaughtered like so much cattle, brother Julio's real-estate office burned to the ground, El Mordida, little more than the worst street thugs in his mind, shot dead where they sat in their safehouse, which, as it turned out, hadn't been so safe. All of this Santos had confirmed by the chief of police in the city, who was also on the Ojeda payroll, and, like himself, was in hiding, alone in his second house, his wife and children a safe distance from any line of fire.

It was falling apart, and Santos had to lay a lot of the blame on Rodrigo. Lately, the older brother was getting closer to the edge of self-destruction, his body, mind and soul warped and twisted by all the drugs he consumed.

There it was, he thought. Self-destruction.

They—the narco-traffickers—all went down in due course. They were like shooting stars, but ones that flamed out because of greed and often senseless violence, foolish abductions of even DEA informants and agents that brought the hellhounds of legitimate law enforcement howling for their blood. The multibillion-dollar business would always go on in the event of one or many demises in whatever the current drug regime—it just seemed like some undefined, even supernatural law of nature—but a new cartel would spring up and almost overnight, like pond scum rising to the top or cockroaches skittering out of the cracks when the light wasn't shining their way. Corruption, he knew, was an industry all by itself in his country, the only real democratic face, he had heard come out of the mouth once from Rodrigo, on Mexico. Money was the bottom line the world over, but it was especially true in Mexico, where a few wealthy and powerful controlled and contained the peasant masses who wondered where their next meal would come from.

It occurred to him next that no one—not his own informants, his lesser-ranking officers or business associates he used to peddle his cocaine—was returning his calls. He had left messages on their answering machines, e-mails asking if they could offer some assistance, as in an avenue of escape out of the country or additional security forces. It was a time of need, of peril, no less, his darkest hour of desperation. He needed to call in a few markers, but all the people he had helped become rich, spreading around the *mordida* personally, had suddenly vanished.

He was on his own. So be it.

He chuckled bitterly, his hand falling over the butt of the 9 mm Browning holstered on his hip. Funny, he thought, how a man found out who his friends really were when the bottom was falling out.

It was time to decide a positive course of action, take care of his own future.

He realized he would have to leave behind his mistress, and his shrill, never satisfied wife, but at least his children were grown, living their own lives, out of harm's way. The imported Lincoln Towncar would get him to, say, Mazatlán or Puerto Vallarta on the Pacific Coast. There he could lie low, buy refuge, information, a security force, perhaps wait out the coming storm, return and see who was left standing.

With any luck, both the Ojedas would be killed, a new trafficker stepping up to claim the crown, fresh blood, hungry with ambition, he could offer his services to. He certainly couldn't remain in Mexico City, a veritable walking target with a bull's-eye stenciled on his back, since it appeared two of the four madmen were at that hour on the rampage, and so very close.

Cursing those ungrateful associates and cowardly subordinate officers who had abandoned him, leaving him to marshal up a mere three shooters—thugs he had purchased from a dealer who sold his cocaine through a cutout in the Mordida chain—Santos went to the wall, sliding back a panel, his fingers spinning the dial to the safe with rapid and angry twists.

He opened it, hauled out the small nylon bag and began to stuff it with stacks of U.S. dollars. He considered calling his mistress after all, since he would need companionship, comfort in the anxious days, or weeks, to come, then decided he could simply buy another woman when he arrived safely on the west coast.

Santos heaved his bulk to the wet bar, poured a tequila, one for the nerves and the journey.

The money bag in hand, thinking there was hope yet, reasons to live, and leave whatever disaster behind for the Ojedas to deal with, he felt lighter on his feet, bolstered by his decision to flee.

He was through the doors, barking the names of his three-man security detail when he found two of them beyond the archway. Anger boiling, he found them, chuckling, leaning up against the bar in the living room.

"Where is the other one?"

The one he knew as Jorge threw him an insolent look. "Out front."

"What?"

"You said no smoking in your house."

Santos scowled. It would be good to be free of such scum, if only for a while. "We are leaving. Grab your weapons. Now!"

He stood in the hall, glaring at them as they took one last drink and picked up their submachine guns, weaving a little as they made their way toward him, all but telling him he had fairly wasted good money on this trash while they bullshitted around and scarfed up his tequila. They took their sweet time getting out into the hall, falling in front to lead the way. Santos was growling at the one he wanted to drive, then he noticed the smoker had left the front doors cracked open a few inches.

Snarling curses to himself, he hurried forward to close it, filling his mind with visions of a temporary life on the beach, all bliss and freedom from worry and anxiety, if only to keep hope alive he would be safe and on his way in the next few minutes. He felt the smile nearly form on his lips, then he heard the twin burping retorts beyond the doors.

He froze as the body came crashing through the

doors. Thick jets of blood seemed to suspend in the air in his horrified sight, the body thudding, coming down the foyer in a bizarre slow-motion skid.

There were two of them, and Santos, even though he didn't know their names, their features hidden by black ski masks, knew he was facing his own death sentence.

It was an outrage, an injustice, his mind screamed, his hand, propelled by the reflexes of terror, pulling the pistol. For a heartbeat, he was shielded by the two street thugs as their bodies absorbed volleys of lead, remaining upright but spasming as if they were plugged into fifty thousand volts of electricity. Blood hit him in the face, the gunner who had practically laughed at him falling back, a mauled puppet jerked on an invisible string.

Santos was firing, all reflex, but his aim was thrown off, the black-clad killers actually appearing to march straight ahead, unflinching, eyes blazing with some unearthly wrath that told him he was next, and dead on his feet.

Santos nearly tossed away the pistol, the scream rising in his throat, then he felt the hammering blows to the chest, pulverizing his insides, a millisecond's awareness he was plunging.

Then there was nothing.

"I'M NOT GOING to stand here and squeeze my package and ask for a pat on the back, gentlemen, since I know your friends are in imminent danger, but you two have no idea how close the military was to grabbing you. Good thing both sides, even the good guys, know when and how to play the *mordida* game.''

Bolan looked at Baldwin, nodding his thanks. The DEA SAC had been waiting at the private airfield outside Mexico City proper. The man had gone the distance, risking career and life to get them as far as they had. He wanted in, to finish it by their side. Given the total enemy numbers they'd be facing, Bolan had to agree another gun and a second gunship could well help them savage the odds in a hurry.

Mexico City was behind them. The last hit, severing the cartel's big link in the chain of corruption, had been the most nerve-racking for the two Stony Man warriors, Bolan aware that time was running out as the DEA deep-cover man monitored the police bans closing the net. They had scaled the wall of the Santos estate, gone straight for the smoker, blasting away, inside next. Ojeda's general, who helped keep the cartel's operations oiled and running, had been cut down, though the Executioner's intent had been to take him alive.

It didn't work out that way.

They were in the Huey gunship, heading toward what amounted to a gathering of savages in the jungle.

''Mind if we thank you later?'' Lyons asked.

''Understood. I appreciate you guys letting me in

on this. You guys, well, let's just say you revived a fleeting hope I've had for years that we can actually make a difference in the war on drugs down here. Of course, there's going to be political flak, heat coming my way, but I don't give a damn anymore. I've got my reasons for maybe tossing it all away."

Baldwin smoked, went on, "If possible, I would have brought a small army of my own people, but they're in the process of taking down the tunnels Cordero gave up, and Cordero confirmed what these buildings are. We're going to need to refuel, and he indicated the fuel depot is tucked back in the jungle, actually a tanker truck, east of the airstrip. Okay, as you can see by those pics, your guys are clearly still alive." He tapped one of the photos. "They're in that building."

Bolan listened, taking in the layout of the jungle compound and airfield, a veritable parking lot in a narrow strip slashed out of the jungle itself, choked with a variety of twin-engine aircrafts, choppers and executive-type jets. The DEA, Bolan knew, had taken something of a bad rap over the years, too many pundits out there squawking how the war on drugs was hopeless, not enough money to compete with the traffickers, who had more cash than God to throw away on everything conceivable.

This was one war, Bolan determined, they were going to win. Baldwin had come through, HUMINT, high-tech, the whole outstanding package to get and keep them hunting. Sometimes the Executioner gave consideration to the fact that a cosmic justice was at work in his War Everlasting, a guiding force that put him in the right place, the right time, with the right warriors meant to be steered, perhaps bloodied but standing, out through to the other side, come out on top simply because they fought the good fight.

Baldwin, cigarette perched on his lip, pointed out the command post, pictures detailing a number of Asians, the DEA SAC giving the two warriors a guesstimate of enemy numbers.

"There's a big showdown about to get under way," Baldwin said. "With our phone and e-mail intercepts, the conversations we monitored from Santos, it sounds like Rodrigo has had enough trying to calm the storm between the North Koreans and the terrorists. He's bringing them together. The Arabs, I understand from both an informant and our wiretaps, are due to land there in twenty minutes. That puts us ten minutes behind. I'm thinking Ojeda's cleaning house. He's going to play out the drama, step back and let them kill each other. Being whacked out on coke isn't exactly bringing him peace of mind."

"What's this?" Bolan asked, pointing at what appeared to be some sort of pulley with rope over a hole in the ground.

"That's Ojeda's snake pit."

Lyons cursed, and Bolan could almost hear his thoughts.

"As far as I know," Baldwin said, "they're still breathing."

Bolan factored numbers, time frames between their arrival as opposed to the Arabs getting there, layout, and put together an attack plan. "Can you work that Gatling gun?"

Baldwin smiled. "Work it? Hell, I gave the course to new DEA blood for two years, and God help them if they even blink with intimidation when they step up to that monster."

CHAPTER TWENTY-THREE

Rodrigo Ojeda felt the volcano of rage rumble in his knotted gut, found all eyes fixed on him, as if he were the one and only source of their salvation.

Or a scapegoat to pin the blame on.

Feeling on the verge of erupting out of his skin, knowing—or believing simply out of a mounting and relentless paranoia—the end was coming, coated in running sweat, the air so stifling hot it was hard to breathe, aware the ninety-percent-pure cocaine was at once both helping and hurting, he was tired of waiting for something, anything, good or bad, to happen.

Beyond the open doorway of the command hut, the caws and cries of wild birds, the incessant buzzing of thousands of ravenous mosquitoes sounded as if it was amplified to rock-concert levels. He flinched, even jumped at the slightest sudden noise or flickering shadow. Even the soft glow of hanging halogen lights outside began to hurt his eyes, the hum of the generator rising in volume with each line he huffed up from the brick broken open on the table. It almost sounded like thunder out there, or was that just the wild jackhammering of his heart?

He turned, watched the ten North Koreans watching him, thinking, no doubt, crappy little thoughts, judging him, believing him weak for indulging at such a time of crisis. They were spread around the room, the smug General Duk Jung in his sports shirt sitting at the table, no expression, the man looking dead to him in the naked hanging light and the greenish tint thrown off by the radar screen. Ojeda had put it to them as simply as possible. The Arabs were coming, and they were to work it out however they saw fit. Armed with a mix of subguns, assault rifles and pistols, they weren't fooling him. They were going to massacre the Arabs as soon as they walked through the door, which, he thought, meant he and his men were last on their slaughter scorecard. He damn near picked up the Uzi and started shooting. Forget the Arabs; he wasn't waiting any longer than another five minutes.

Horror was raging on in his wake, crisis points that demanded his immediate attention, return to Mexico City. His business was being dismantled in Mexico City, his people forced to relay threatening messages of doom slated to find him in the jungle. Two gringos, friends of the prisoners, he knew, telling him his life was numbered in hours. He would see about that. He needed to know who his enemies were, how much they knew and how they could so freely and easily move from his places of business, killing his men, stealing his money, burning down everything in their wake. None of the cops he owned were able to come up with a definitive lead or answer.

Nada. Nothing but blood and mystery dogging him wherever he turned, or ran from.

It smacked, somewhere down the line, of betrayal. There was no other way they could do so much damage so quickly unless they had help from inside his organization.

He needed to know the truth.

Rodrigo caught the disdain in the general's eyes, his soldiers shifting from foot to foot, glancing at one another. He impaled the knife into the table. "Something you wish to share with the rest of us, General?"

"In time."

"Whatever the fuck that means."

"Rodrigo."

He wheeled on the shadow in the door, Uzi up, finger tightening around the trigger. It took a full second before he recognized one of his own men. "What?" he barked.

"They radioed. They will be landing in three minutes."

Time enough, he decided, to find out who his nameless, faceless hunters were. Even if he killed them, they were two fewer problems he would have to deal with later.

"Rodrigo, wait. What—?"

"Shut up and stay here with them!"

He glowered at Julio, his brother looking like the frightened child he remembered as a boy, recalling how he always had to fight bullies who were always tormenting him. Very little seemed to have changed even as he became a man and his brother... Well, he still remained what he had always detested in Julio, which was a coward now inside the body of an adult. Out of nowhere he suddenly realized how much he detested his younger brother, fought off the temptation to fling insults in his face, tell him he was sick and tired of having to carry him. That he needed to stand up and be a man for once.

That it was time to fight, and kill.

"They are here, General."

"So I heard."

"Anything you wish me to tell them?"

"Yes. Tell them there is no motherboard."

"A mother what?"

"They will understand. Also tell them we can perhaps make other arrangements."

He would pass on the message, all right, thinking how he could slightly alter the words, add a little more threatening spice to them.

Outside, jumping at the swarm of bats fluttering overhead, he pulled his gunner in by the arm, whispering in Spanish, "Go meet them. Take six men with you. Tell them there is no motherboard, that the North Koreans, we all believe, mean to murder them."

He shoved the man away, picking up the pace, anxiously closing on the hut holding his two prisoners.

Answers.

With what he had in store for them, one of them would squawk. A trip down into the snake pit always loosened the tightest of tongues.

It had yet to fail.

THE STENCH of decaying flesh so close brought on the queasy churn of bile in his stomach, but the stink of rotting bodies and body waste seemed to keep him from passing out. The mere vicinity of death, for some reason, kept him alert, and hopeful.

Schwarz had glimpsed the bodies stacked in one corner of the stone hovel right before he and Blancanales were tossed into the hole. He had also caught a fleeting glimpse of several large furry creatures poking around the bodies—rats, he thought—even believed he'd seen spiders the size of grapefruits scaling the walls. It begged the question of what else could be crawling or slithering around in the dark.

Their captors had left their hands bound behind their backs. Feeling as if he'd been run over by a freight train and dragged for a hundred miles, Schwarz sat in the dirt, away from the wall. In the pitch blackness he couldn't see Pol, but heard his friend coughing, the vile odors working on Blancanales, as well, he suspected. The stench was overpowering, swelling a brain already pulsing from the blows to his skull and face with nausea, the miasma seeming to hang in air so hot it felt to Schwarz as if he were sitting in front of a furnace. His side ached with a throbbing fire, a knifing pain tearing up and down his ribs, certain one of them was cracked, every breath he drew shooting hot needles through his torso.

"Pol?"

"Yeah, Gadgets?"

"We have to hang in there."

"I was just going to say the same thing to you."

The door creaked open, light spilling into the hole, outlining three armed shapes.

"You! James Bond! Get up and come out here!"

Ojeda.

Schwarz was rising, looking around the hovel when he spotted the tarantula vectoring straight for Blancanales. Exploding with fury and hatred for their tormentors, Schwarz lifted his leg, stomped his boot heel on a spider that looked as large as a softball.

"I have no time for this!"

Even as he squashed it, prepared to deliver another crushing blow just to make sure, hands were digging into his shoulders, hauling him toward Ojeda.

"I think I have a solution to get you to tell me what I want to know."

Even as he saw the black hole, a wood pulley with rope near the edge of the jungle, he suspected what was at the bottom.

A moment later, the laughing bastard confirmed his worst terror.

"I hope you like snakes, my friend. No? Not to worry, I am sure they will love you."

IRQHAN RABIZ KNEW it was over.

He was no sooner off the drug lord's jet than he received the message relayed by the North Koreans through one of Ojeda's lackeys.

There would be no motherboard. His mission, then, was a failure. None of them would leave the jungle alive.

He laughed for reasons he couldn't fathom, then seethed in silence, turning, making certain his men, fourteen in all, were following. It was speech time. The Mexican messenger was babbling that the Asians were in the largest building, the one with the satellite dish on top.

"How many?"

"Eleven."

He stopped, lifting his Uzi, holding up his hand. In Arabic he addressed them, chose three volunteers who would be the first through the door. He watched Salim closely, aware the man was wondering if there would be a repeat performance of their first encounter with the North Koreans.

No, he told himself. There had been time enough to feel shame, to pray for strength, ask that he willingly accept God's will.

Even if that meant sacrificing his own life.

The jihad would simply have to go on without him, but he believed heaven was calling his very name, urging him to lead his holy warriors into a final battle in this jungle hellhole.

Asians. The drug criminals.

Infidels, all. And they would all have to be slain.

There would be another source of technology to build a weapon of mass destruction; he was sure of it. He wouldn't be around to see the cleansing hand of God crush the infidels, but knew that someday, from Paradise, he would look down on Earth and witness the judgment day of his enemies, smile into the face of God as they were cast into the fires of Hell.

He took a minute to tell his men as much, saw the fire of jihad relighting their eyes, hands gripping subguns and assault rifles tight. If Salim had pulled any of them aside and related the truth about the battle in Ciudad Zapulcha, his fleeing while leaving their brothers in holy war to fight and die, then he couldn't find the first indication in their eyes they believed him a coward, nothing to tell him they hated and resented him for shirking his holy duty, unwilling to martyr himself.

They were ready, all of them prepared to be martyrs, but only if they saw their treacherous enemies here slain first.

"All of us will then charge inside," Rabiz said, winding down the speech. "We will kill them all. If any of us are still alive, we will then eliminate whoever remains beyond the North Koreans. If there are drugs here, we will take them. They are worth money, and whoever survives and leaves this infidel land of crime can return home and sell them to further the cause of jihad. God is great!"

They raised their weapons, and Rabiz even heard Salim join the chorus.

PAIN AND FEAR GRAPPLED with each other for the release of vomit in his stomach. Keeping it down was a further challenge, as he was hung by his ankles, upside down, jerked up a foot, then lowered another two or three feet toward the twisting mass of reptilian flesh.

Schwarz figured another fourteen or sixteen feet, and it was over. He just hoped it was quick, figured one bite to the face or neck, the toxin setting in, coursing through his body, which was so dehydrated and physically punished by beatings his heart should stop within seconds.

There was no point counting the serpents, but as Ojeda shone a light on the writhing, multicolored nest, Schwarz saw he wasn't the first victim to get fed to the snakes. A few vipers of indeterminate species were coiling around skeletons, a fat rainbow serpent squeezing out between the teeth of a skull, another snake twisting through the empty eye socket.

Schwarz had wheeled on his captors, hardly one to

go quietly to such a hideous death, lashing out with kicks as he was pushed and pummeled by rifle butts toward the black hole. There had been one final blow to the back of his head that had doused the lights, rendering him helpless.

He wasn't sure how long he'd been out. He heard Ojeda above him now, his laughter trapped by the tight confines of the walls, echoing down, ripping into the thunder of his heartbeat in his ears.

More tequila came showering down on his neck and head, the bastard wanting to make sure he was fully awake and aware of what was down there, shining a light around.

The liquor coursed over the gashes on his scalp, stinging, and ran off his chin, mingling with blood and sweat, the gory concoction, he saw, seeming to inflame the serpents as they were drizzled on, reptilian brains aware a meal was on the way.

"Each time you do not answer my questions, my friend Paco here will lower you another few feet. It has been some time since they last ate. Think about it. You can save yourself!"

Schwarz closed his eyes, ignoring the barrage of questions, felt the rope giving way, jerking, as he descended a few more feet. He conceded his death.

He knew that Bolan and Lyons were still alive, that his death would be avenged.

He was thinking about Blancanales, sitting alone in the darkness, among the rats and the dead and the stink and the tarantulas, waiting his turn. He hoped Pol fought like a savage on the way here, forced them to shoot him down before he faced this sort of abomination.

"Last chance, American, then Paco releases the catch, and away you go! Goodbye! Snake food!"

"Go to hell," Schwarz said, braced to plummet.

He felt his heart lurch, all but freeze, limbs rigid, waiting...

Was that autofire?

He twisted his head, making out the faint but distinct sounds of battle beyond the roaring in his skull, men howling, voices shouting in panic. A great gust of wind ripped down through the hole, forcing him to shut his eyes against the dust swirling down, choking him with grit.

He couldn't be sure what was happening, but men up there were shooting away as if there were no tomorrow. And that whapping sound he heard was like the music of angels singing in his ears.

The cavalry, a two-man force of death and vengeance, had arrived.

CHAPTER TWENTY-FOUR

"Go! I've got you covered!"

Carl Lyons feared they were too late, and God have mercy on the first poor bastard who dropped into his sights, because he sure as hell wouldn't.

The war thunder had burst, unleashing a hurricane of death that was blowing all over the compound, an international hodgepodge of gunmen mowing down one another, he saw, bodies sailing everywhere. Lyons didn't have any thermal imaging, heat-seeking screens, all that high-tech jazz at the disposal of their pilot to know who had been hung down into the black hole or what was at the bottom.

If he had lost one of his friends...

The trio of human garbage, Lyons thought, littering the ground near the black hole where he and Bolan had just blown them off their feet with an M-16 greeting and farewell, had better hope they were long gone and on their way to hell. If they were still clinging to the final bitter breath, and if Pol or Gadgets or both were dead, they would beg him for death, Lyons determined. And it would be long, hard and ugly in coming.

A spinning cylinder of mass death from Thunderbird Two was already laying waste, Lyons saw as he jumped from his gunship, a perfect landing on his feet, M-16 flaming and catching a few of his own international hardmen on the fly.

The strategy now was to drive the enemy up and back and into the command hut. Once Pol or Gadgets was freed, Lyons knew, keeping hope burning alive, the flyboys would initiate a sustained barrage of 2.75 mm rockets. The Executioner's original plan was already shot to hell, thanks to whatever problems the savages here, Lyons knew, couldn't resolve, but the more they shot each other up, the merrier. The four buildings comprising the compound were edged up against the jungle, forming a rough half circle. The clearing, either burned out of the jungle or delivered to the enemy by Mother Nature or the long since dead and forgotten Mayas, was arena shaped. The squat structure closest to the trail was where—Lyons hoped—at least one of his friends was still sweating it out.

Lyons veered right off toward the black hole, Bolan at his side. "I've got this!"

The Executioner, com link in place, threw a nod, vectored on, running and gunning from the hip for the prison hut, waxing a few hardcases on the way.

Hope.

Lyons veered around the dead. He was almost afraid to look down into the inky blackness as he grasped the long wooden handle. He couldn't look down. With all the racket of weapons fire, rotor wash and bad guys screaming in pain, he skipped calling down into the hole, would know something one way or another…

Lyons began cranking the handle as hard and fast as he could, embracing hope but dreading what he might bring up.

THE BLOOD RUSHING into his skull was ballooning his brain until he felt his ears set to burst from the pressure. Whatever was in his stomach was gone. Schwarz, dry-heaving now, wondered how far he was from the nest, and if snakes could climb.

The battle seemed to rage on, but from a great distance, as if whatever was happening was now floating away.

He felt his legs stretch, jerk, then his whole body was yanked.

Up!

He was ascending.

Whoever was hauling him up, though, wasn't real gentle about it, his battered limbs feeling the furious twists and turns grinding away through every racked and flaming nerve of his body. His head banged off the wall, but the pain was somehow a thing of beauty right then, and the thunder and the wind and the relentless racket of autofire were growing louder, but bringing on the bliss to Schwarz as he rose up and away from the bowels of a hell he knew he wouldn't soon forget.

Rough hands dug into his legs, hauling him away from the hole. He was on his face, gathering his senses, squinting, adjusting his eyes to the hazy sheen of light, speechless. He thought he recognized the voice—"Roger that, looks like they both lucked out, then"—trying to pin it down, but the din of weapons fire was doing its damnedest to drown the words of some response from his unseen savior that instinctively flared another round of hope in the runaway freight train that was his heart. That was a knife, slicing away the ropes, he knew, wondering if he could even move his hands and legs. A great but nervous relief was washing through him, clearing away the cobwebs. Those same clawing mitts flipped him over.

Schwarz sounded a chuckle, staring up at Lyons, Ironman sporting the most beautiful, wicked smile he'd ever seen.

"Well, well, here we are," Lyons said, bobbing his head a couple times. "You and Pol—yeah, he's still with us—I can't leave you two out of my sight for five minutes and you screw up. That reminds me, Gadgets, something you said before you and Pol got yourselves snatched. Think you can now define 'decent'?"

Schwarz felt the smile frozen on his face, the relief

boring straight to his heart. "There will be a revised definition in Webster's with your name beside it. What can I say? I know I'm a smart-ass, I know I'm not perfect."

"Who is?"

"Besides you, Carl, I don't know. I guess this means I buy you a few rounds when we get back to Miami."

Lyons had to nearly shout over the din, glancing around at the warzone, M-16 ready. "I don't know, but I think I got the Miami monkey off my back. That town's about as shallow and superficial as L.A., and that's L.A. on even a good and deep and substantive day."

"But you love it, right?"

"Just like rock and roll—yeah, I do. And don't say it, that I look so good to you you were thinking about kissing me."

Schwarz cracked a grin. "Actually, I was going to say you're getting a little too old for rock and roll, that maybe you ought to think about growing up a little bit."

"Man, oh man, if you could only read my thoughts right now."

Lyons was jacking him to his feet, ready to unsling and hand him the MP-5 subgun he'd brought, when Schwarz saw the figure rise up from the earth behind the leader of Able Team. Wild eyes shone like two burning coals, the Uzi coming up...

Schwarz felt a terrible rage explode out of nowhere, galvanizing him, a bulldog reacting on pure killing instinct, unchained and going straight for the throat. He shoved Lyons to the left, away from the hole, three steps forward, the kick drilling into Ojeda's gun hand, his Uzi spinning away. Schwarz noted the ragged holes pocked high on Ojeda's chest, aware the drug lord was so jacked up on his own supply of blow that he couldn't feel the pain.

No matter. He was a done deal.

Schwarz threw a straight right into Ojeda's nose, stunning him, the mashed beak and flying blood, he determined, about to be the best of his pain and fear.

Ojeda staggered back and Schwarz, already grabbing a handful of hair and shirtfront, spun and slung the drug lord.

Schwarz watched as Ojeda flew over the edge, the king of cocaine and terrorist backer screaming, throwing his arms out. He nearly grabbed the wooden beam, slapped at the rope, almost had a grip, wailing the whole time, then lost his hold, and he was gone and on his way down. Schwarz didn't have to look into the hole. It was sickening enough to listen to the shrill wail echoing up from the bottom.

"I take it you didn't like that guy, Gadgets?"

"BURY THEM!"

Baldwin rogered the order. The Executioner had just cut the ropes off Pol's hands, turned over the HK subgun. He was momentarily caught up in the group relief, Lyons and Schwarz finishing up their reunion, one of the three tormentors cast into the snake pit a second ago.

Celebrate later, assuming, Bolan knew, they lived out the coming hour. Right then there was still plenty of butcher's work to do. Baldwin had tagged runners on the gunship's IR thermals, ten in all, vanishing into the jungle, on a beeline for the airstrip.

The Executioner had that covered coming in, knew a good many of the savages here would bolt when the heat was on.

The usual bail job when a cannibal's marker was called in.

Bolan and Blancanales stepped out of the doorway, side by side. Together, as Schwarz and Lyons poured out the killing touch, the Executioner and Blancanales cut loose with their weapons. Wounded and mangled rose, staggered, here and there, a few throwing their hands up, begging for mercy, their cries unheard.

Runners and those who chose to hold their turf began dropping like dominoes. Both Thunderbirds, hovering over the jungle tree line, started unloading the 2.75 mm burial.

RABIZ COULDN'T BELIEVE his luck, then told himself it was simply the will of God taking them to victory.

Paradise could wait.

He was focused on sending them all to Hell. He felt alive, reborn, redeemed after even he had questioned his courage coming in. He was tuned in to only his hunger for vengeance, some unholy racket outside under way, Ojeda's men dying and screaming, most likely, but he'd deal with them when this was nailed down.

He had been third in line through the doorway, his Uzi joining the barrage, sweeping the North Koreans, all of whom looked stunned for a brief moment before the floodtide of holy warriors bulled through, weapons blazing. There were casualties, but Rabiz had expected as much, the Asians shooting back, bullets snapping past his ears, two, then three of his warriors tumbling to his side. Runners, three or four, didn't have the stomach to stand and fight, diving out the window at the far corner of the room.

He cursed their cowardice, but he would chase them down.

Someone was hollering his name as he burned out the clip, ramming a fresh magazine home.

Salim, he saw, wheeling, something about gunships…

Rabiz was checking the carnage, when Salim or someone began to scream.

And the room blew up, a great ball of fire eating up the world, it seemed, Rabiz sailing with the flames. He heard himself scream for a heartbeat, aware he was engulfed in fire, then the thunder and the shrieking faded to black.

HE WAS RUNNING, terrified, through the jungle, bladder set to burst and soil his pants, but disgrace was the last thing on his mind. New pants he could buy. A new life he couldn't purchase.

When the crazy Arabs had burst into the hut, shooting up the North Koreans, he had bolted to his feet, a headfirst dive out the window. Others, his own men, had joined him, rushing around the shooting gallery of the command hut, falling in.

He despised himself for fleeing, leaving his brother—most likely dead, and he strangely, perversely took some degree of comfort in that speculation—behind. But hadn't it always been like this?

It seemed to Julio Ojeda he had been running all of his life, uncertain of his own abilities, his manhood, no machismo he could find anywhere in his soul, always shying away from anything confrontational or unpleasant that might reveal all manner of weaknesses, character flaws and such. Whatever good life he had cherished—money, power, sex—was most likely a thing of the past. There was a chance, he thought, provided he made it out of this hell, that he could regroup, salvage what was left of the organization, make a few phone calls to Cali, and spread some money around to see what happened.

He looked down at the pistol in his hand, wondering if he could fire on a man in anger, since he'd never shot anyone in his life, always leaving the dirty work to street soldiers or his brother. And what good would a mere handgun do against machine guns, assault rifles, helicopter gunships that were now blowing up whoever was left standing back?

He turned, slowing, counting heads. Faces of fear blinked back at him like neon signs in the glow of firelight. Ten, he believed, all of them looking armed with subguns.

"Who can fly?"

"I can, you know that!"

Of course, it was Mindingez, his personal pilot, barking at him as if he were an idiot asking such a stupid question.

Julio Ojeda said nothing, running on, a break in the jungle showing the aircraft beyond.

His way out, his only hope, salvation a mere hundred yards or so away.

THEY NEARLY MADE IT to the first aircraft at the edge of the dirt runway, Bolan almost able to feel their hope swelling to joy, savages giddy with relief, thinking they were home free. But the Executioner had the net poised to drop all along.

A gunship bombs-away send-off, he knew, coming in right about...now.

The four Stony Man warriors marched off the trail, fanned out in a skirmish line, weapons ready.

The gunships blew over them, soared on, rockets already streaking downrange, smoking fingers of doom coasting on to seal it. The blast wave took out the survivors' intended ride to freedom first, then rolled up the line of aircraft, all sound, fury, fire and flying bodies and wreckage. A gale force of fire and thunder pounded every piece of flying machine to trash.

The Executioner and Able Team rolled toward the outer limits of the firewall, two flaming scarecrows flailing and shrieking from that hell, propelled by mindless agony and rushing their way at superhuman speed. The Stony Man warriors cut loose, chopping down the burning human comets, three more mauled gunmen rising, lurching from the flames.

Adios.

They spread out, Bolan's nose filling up with the odors of roasting flesh, burning fuel, wreckage floating down from a sky flickering overhead, a black mirror reflecting the sea of fire.

Baldwin patched through, informing the Executioner the gunship's screens were clear.

Nothing in the jungle, either.

A FINAL WALK-THROUGH of the compound, and Bolan and Able Team checked for any survivors.

All dead and accounted for.

Clean sweep.

The gunship had landed, rotor wash hurling away smoke but kicking up a dust storm around the four warriors. Baldwin was right then coming out of the ruins of a structure the soldier knew was the coke storehouse.

"Unbelievable," Baldwin said, stepping up to the warriors. "Not a live one here to be found, but most of what I figure has to be eight to ten tons of bricks were hardly touched. You guys spare me a couple thermites?"

Bolan smiled for the first time in days, plucked two incendiary grenades off his webbing. Blancanales and Schwarz, he knew, were in bad shape, and he needed to get them medical attention within the hour.

Baldwin took the steel eggs, searched the battered faces of Blancanales and Schwarz. "I'm happy for you guys, all four of you."

"You're a class act, Baldwin," Lyons said. "Not sure we could have saved these two knuckleheads in time without you." He paused, smiled and said, "You ever been to Miami? I know a great place."

Grinning, Schwarz cut Lyons off. "Hold on a second. Before you go anywhere with this guy, Baldwin, have someone define 'class.'"

CHAPTER TWENTY-FIVE

Abdullah Wahjihab was pleased with the progress, but the jihad had only just begun. The fact that five of the holy leaders of al-Amin, chosen personally by his father—the Sword of Islam and the holiest of the holy, who had been blessed by the sheikh to carry on the jihad—had arrived safe and unmolested in Muscat, was a sign from God that glory for all Muslims and victory against the Great Satan needed only continued unwavering faith and the will to succeed. That they were now gathered at the white marble table in the white stone-walled conference room under his roof was something of a logistical marvel all by itself.

They were one magnificent step away from achieving, he thought, what their father had been chosen to do in the name of Islam, soon to be the greatest leader the Muslim world had ever known.

All five mullahs, he thought, were marked by their enemies as terrorists, when, in truth, they were merely instruments of jihad, holy men fulfilling God's will. Two of them had flown from Karachi, where they ran *madrassas* in northern Pakistan, what the infidels railed about and lied to the world were schools grooming young boys to be future suicide-bombers. One cleric was from Syria, a recruiter of young men in that country, an army being groomed now that would soon flood into Israel, a rolling and unstoppable wave of martyrs, capable of erasing entire city blocks with the latest in sophisticated explosives. The two Lebanese were just as critical to his father's plans, what with their military contacts in their own country, able, he understood, to rally officers and soldiers who wanted nothing more than to launch an all-out attack on the Israeli border.

They were dressed in expensive suits, were met at either Seeb International Airport or picked up by his personal chauffeurs at his father's private airfield west of the city. All eyes were turned his way. He smiled at each in turn.

Magic, he thought, getting them there, though in reality he had shelled out considerable amounts of money, fake passports and visas delivered to them by courier, the month-long orchestration risking discovery by the CIA to bring them all to his home, same time and place. Even though they were in what the Great Satan called a moderate Arab country, there was nothing to betray them as militant Arabs, those Muslim fanatics the racist infidels stereotyped. No kaffiyehs, no facial hair. They could have been European businessmen or tourists simply visiting Oman for a few days. A different strategy and new tactics had to be employed these days; intelligence and foresight, thinking like and staying one step ahead of the enemy every bit as critical in achieving their goals as was showing the courage of lions in battle.

He looked at his younger brother, Mahdji, seated at his right hand, waiting on him to begin the holy meeting.

It wasn't quite the Grand Islamic Council he envisioned in his dreams at night, aware he couldn't safely round up all ten leaders of various cells spread around the Middle East. Perhaps someday, he thought, when they triumphed, every imam, ayatollah, mullah and holy man in every Arab nation, every leader from Saddam to Arafat, the sultan of his own country, and even the Saudi royal family would make the trip to his palace, paying tribute, giving father and sons honor due them.

The new conquerors, the one voice and the avenging sword for all Islam.

When they left, though, new orders and the vision of the future known to them, they would spread the word that the faithful of the Muslim world were about to rise up as one people, one army.

That total war was about to be declared on the infidels.

"I know all of you are perhaps tired and hungry," the elder Wahjihab began. "I am having a meal prepared for you, and afterward you may retire to quarters I have arranged here. I suggest you rest as much as possible tonight, for in the coming days much will happen, a big event that will shake the world, and perhaps bring America to its knees.'' He paused, savoring the moment, the focus of their undivided attention. ''My father has arrived safely at the site where the greatest gift ever bestowed us by God has been created and is about to be delivered at a destination yet to be revealed even to me. I have spoken personally with my father, and he extends his gratitude that you made the long journey to my home.

''There are to be certain changes made by each of you, what you might want to call marching orders. We must see through the eyes of the devils if we are to defeat them. Which is why my father has asked me to pass on his wishes. We must make an attempt to begin recruiting non-Arabs as operatives to infiltrate America. If you have objections, take heed, I do understand them, even before you voice any protest. Yes, it will be difficult for us, going outside our own blood, recruiting the godless, but sometimes even wild beasts have their use. Money is one of our greatest weapons. We have accumulated dossiers on individuals, most of them with criminal backgrounds, mercenaries and such, most of them from Europe, all of whom, if they are approached and made to understand large sums of cash will be... Well, I am sure you see where I am headed with this.

''Second, we must begin to recruit future martyrs

at younger ages. We need more, many more soldiers for the time of war that is coming. You will remove them from their families, again using money as our weapon. They will fall exclusively under the guidance of all of you here. I may suggest that we indoctrinate them slowly at first, tone down the rhetoric, since even the devils can turn those of us weak in faith against us, infiltrate our religious schools.

"Moderate Arab countries, Jordan and Egypt, are beginning, I believe, to turn against the infidels, and in the future we need to look their way for recruitment. At this time, several operations are in the planning stages, but the big event will happen first. When it does, these other operations, which you will be made privy to all pertinent details, will be launched on the heels of the big event."

He smiled. The big event. He liked that. It sounded like something the sheikh had said.

One of the Pakistanis, Rajh Hammadi, spoke up. "We have heard something about this new and fantastic weapon. Is there any chance that we will be allowed to either hear about it, perhaps even see it for ourselves?"

"I am glad you asked that. Part of the reason for your journey here is to be taken to where the greatest instrument for the glory of jihad has been created."

"When?"

Hassan Murad, the Syrian, looked anxious.

"Tomorrow. We leave in the morning. Arrangements have been made for all of you to behold the coming glory of Islam. Be patient, have faith. The time is nearly upon the infidels, and when the big event occurs, God will smile down from Paradise on each and every one of us who have kept faith and carried out His will. Come. Let us eat, then rest. We will talk later. I have given you enough to think about, and I am sure you will have some questions.''

They rose together. A meal to share now, but a vision to carry out, one, the elder son thought, that could wipe out the entire population of the United States.

HAL BROGNOLA WASN'T sure he'd heard Price correctly. ''What? You're positive?''

The respective members of the cyberteam were all working at a furious pace in their stations, fingers flying over keyboards. Kurtzman had just explained what was about to happen in basic language that Brognola understood. A CIA Predator was holding a steady course right then over what Phoenix Force had tagged as Target Site One. The five commandos were being fed real-time imagery from the Predator. Some sort of special visual adapter, Brognola had been informed by Kurtzman, was being hooked into their sat link modem, which, in turn, would relay back to the Farm what the drone's eyes were seeing.

''The CIA and the NSA,'' Price told Brognola, ''confirmed it.''

Damn good news for a change, Brognola thought. The breaks were rolling in, they had caught a wave, but they hadn't made shore safely yet.

"Sat phone intercepts, HUMINT, e-mail intercepts, satellite tracking," Price explained. "Wahjihab has landed in Yemen. He is on-site at the main compound. Of course, we'll need DNA analysis."

"Let's not get ahead of ourselves," Brognola said. "Phoenix just got to the back door of Target One. What about this other thing in Oman?"

"Positive confirmation by CIA operatives in Muscat. Five known terrorists, big names on our most-wanted list," Price said, "have landed and are assembled at the estate of the Wahjihab sons. They have been and are still under CIA and NSA surveillance. You know what I'm thinking, Hal?"

"What?"

"Well, again, I don't want to get ahead of the program, and depending on what happens…"

She let it trail, but Brognola knew where she was going. "Phoenix takes a little sojourn to Oman. One thing at a time. But, while we wait for the showdown, maybe you can work your sources, spin a little logistical magic?"

"Will do."

"Two minutes and counting until we have visual," Kurtzman announced.

Brognola turned, stared at the wall monitor and put a fresh cigar in his mouth.

WHENEVER IT ALL LOOKED and felt too easy, David McCarter got worried.

As the leader of Phoenix Force, he was responsible not only for the lives of his men, but also for making sure every factor on a black op was weighed, dissected, every piece of intelligence sifted through until holes were plugged.

But he knew once the bullets started to fly, all the planning in the world, all the strategic brilliance and attention to every conceivable contingency, fallout and fallback course of action didn't amount to anything next to the warrior pulling the trigger. It all boiled down to execution of the intended play, then adjusting to whatever deadly curveballs came the way of the warrior.

Simple.

In his experience, a man's skill on the battlefield was only as good as the amount of guts and determination he owned.

McCarter checked the GPS module, the CIA's sat transmission guiding them to Target Site One. Through NVD goggles, Manning driving the old Russian transport with lights out, the former SAS commando watched the black lunar landscape, searching for anything out of the ordinary.

Such as armed shadows.

Encizo, James and Hawkins were in the bed, monitoring the Predator imagery. Unless he received word otherwise that the distant ridgeline was being patrolled by militants, he had ordered radio silence.

It was grueling and slow going over bumpy, broken terrain. By day, he knew the Wadi Hadhramaut, as detailed thoroughly in sat imagery, was ripped by deep canyons, green sweeping oases in spots, mesas and mountains in other vast stretches between desert that baked under sun hot enough to irradiate gunmetal.

They'd spent hours on end in Aden hammering down the details, he briefly reflected, growing more anxious to get the team in place and let it rip. Their CIA contact gave them numbers, layout via satellite and aerial photos, intelligence gleaned from electronic intercepts, pinpointing a primitive facility for engineering the Angels of Islam.

Primitive or not, McCarter knew it had to be shut down. A grim realist, he also knew that the five of them were being asked to pull off the seemingly impossible. That, basically, as deniable expendables, they were the only ones the President of the United States could use for this dirty, even potentially suicidal mission.

The right men for the worst task imaginable. He figured they could all take a fair amount of pride that they were viewed by the Man as the best in the business of making dirty war.

The good news, he thought, the team was back together, no more CIA bulls on the rampage to deal with. Just the five of them, friends and warriors who knew one another's moves in the field before they were even putting decisive action to the test.

They could enjoy the reunion tomorrow.

McCarter told Manning to park it. If the vehicle was there when they returned...

This was no time, he knew, for any dark pessimism. If they had to, they'd either commandeer a vehicle from the al-Amin force in the wadi, or they'd leg it in all the way to Target Site Two, which McCarter had stamped as Broken Sword.

The Briton keyed his com link. "Let's go to work, mates."

CHAPTER TWENTY-SIX

The night was a green-gray ghost in Rafael Encizo's night-vision headgear, and he was poised to drop the first shadow rearing up on his advance. Why the enemy hadn't placed sentries to watch the hills for incoming and unwanted company was a mystery to Encizo and the other commandos of Phoenix Force. Arrogance? That alone killed.

Full stop, a crouch behind a boulder, and he took in the armed camp in the narrow wadi below.

They had arrived. Killzone number one.

After all the crap they'd been through on a marathon campaign with the CIA—and he was wise enough to know this was going to be no sprint to the finish line—Encizo found the Company's intel on the money.

Beretta stowed, MP-5 subgun slung across one shoulder, the multiround projectile launcher hung on the other side, Encizo stripped off his NVD goggles. Three fire barrels, dispersed around the huge tent, would provide light enough to pick out and nail the twenty-two militants down there, and the adjustment of his grim vision was made in seconds flat.

Quiet and careful with his footing, he padded down the tight gully, subgun fanning the area, a left-right-front swivel on the move. His advance had been marked earlier on the sat imagery; his path would lead him to his firepoint in a small depression, eighty meters and change out from the enemy.

Three Jeeps with mounted .50-caliber machine guns in the beds, he saw, two Russian troop transports like their own ride here comprised the motor pool, north of the tent. That was part of his assignment, making certain no one fled the wadi by vehicle. Supposedly, the al-Amin contingent in Yemen was composed of a little Afghani, some Syrian, Pakistanis, Yemenis, this and that from other Arab states, but they were all known terror operatives. Six shadows were milling around the fire barrels. AKs and a few RPG launchers, which meant the bulk of the fanatics were inside the tent.

Task number one, he knew, was to blow them out of the wadi. The fact that al-Amin militants could claim this part of Yemen, dig a cave into a mountainside in full view and even the knowledge of the Yemenis, told Encizo the conspiracy stretched to either the military powers in-country, the intelligence branch, whatever the political clout, or all three.

Not his problem to solve.

In time, whatever collaborators lurked in the shadows would be flushed out and dealt swift justice. So much, he thought, for all that big cooperation between the Yemenis and U.S. Special Forces. But that, he knew, was how too many Arabs in command of this part of the world were playing the game. It was all transparent enough to him on the surface, Arabs talking tough about fighting terrorism, appeasing the West, while dumping money into *madrassas,* shipping weapons and explosives to Palestinians, recruiting killers and such. And he had been around long enough to know that even his own side—beyond fighting the scourge of terrorism and keeping America safe—was over here for one thing only.

Oil.

His task, and that of his comrades, was point-blank simple.

Kill the bastards. He would gladly leave the politics and the bullshit diplomacy to someone else.

Encizo claimed his roost and unslung the projectile launcher. As he checked his chronometer, McCarter quietly patched through. ‘‘Hannibal to Rocket Man.’’

‘‘Rocket Man here,’’ Encizo replied.

‘‘Positioned?’’

‘‘Affirmative.’’

McCarter went down the line. Hawkins, the team's M-60 gunner and Manning, should by now, Encizo knew, have claimed their perch in the gully that spined the west face of the wadi. All of them were togged in blacksuit and were next to invisible. He heard them all confirm they were in position. James was with McCarter to Encizo's immediate left and parallel north, in front of the motor pool.

"Rocket Man, this is Hannibal. Fire at will."

"I copy."

And Encizo lifted his weapon, caressed the trigger and sent the first 40 mm charge winging toward the tent.

HAWKINS HELD OFF cutting loose with the M-60, as outlined in the strategy, until the explosions ripped through the tent. No problem taking orders from Big Mac he thought, a man he knew, respected and trusted with his life.

Sixty meters out, Manning to his left and ready with his MP-5, the Texan watched as the wadi lit up with blossoming clouds of fire and smoke.

The show was on, the curtain up, and Hawkins was keyed up to get down there and start wasting what he knew were some of the most vicious and dangerous terrorists on Earth.

The expected chaos burst through the camp, armed shadows on the run, firing AKs at shadows. They were spinning and tumbling to the ground heartbeats later as Hawkins joined the others in clamping the vise of doom. Encizo did quite the number on the tent, Hawkins thought, admiring the demolition duty for a moment. The thrill of reunion was on the shelf, but the ex-Army Ranger was damn glad anyway to be back and in business with his buddies, the right people, doing it the right way, no spook hotshots in charge. The tent was all but vaporized to flaming shreds. With the main compound seven miles north, he thought, a mountain barrier hopefully shielded all the noise of blasts and rattling weapons.

No point in worrying about anything beyond this slaughter task, he knew.

The enemy was hemmed in, Hawkins knew, McCarter and James at a firepoint north, edged right up against the motor pool, probably already wading into it, subguns burping and hosing down enemy gunners.

Hawkins and Manning left the nylon satchels with the team's C-4, sat link and other high-tech goodies behind, rolled out and started picking out the damned wherever they cried, stood their ground or bolted.

No chance for the enemy—they were completely taken down by the shock factor and brutal, overwhelming force.

Hawkins raked three shouting fanatics with thundering steel-jacketed 7.62 mm NATO rounds, blowing them back into the smoky ruins where they had staggered from, shell-shocked and hacking.

A dark figure came racing around the corner of the firewall. For a second, Hawkins glimpsed the bearded face, a twisted mask of both fear and hate. He recognized Ali Zabiri from the CIA's wanted list, confirmed by the Farm.

Zabiri, formerly of al-Qaeda infamy and now a top jackal in al-Amin, held on, screaming something in Arabic, triggering wild bursts, jerking around. Hawkins hit him hard, shell casings twirling around his grim mask, the M-60 driving the doomed militant back, the AK-47 spitting fire and lead that he heard whistle past his ears. A few more rounds into Zabiri, and the fanatic was kicked to the ground.

Just then another subgun-wielding shadow raced into the killzone trilling a war cry that died on his lips as a grisly fate reached out to give him all the hell on earth he could possibly conceive of in his worst nightmare. It turned out in the next instant that the gunner would have been better off just getting dropped by Hawkins. As the barrel hit the ground, ashes and fire gushed out, a small geyser of flames that ignited headcloth.

He tossed his subgun away, shrieking, slapping at his head and face before Hawkins spared a mercy burst he could be sure that bastard would never have shown anybody else.

Hawkins and Manning moved on, firing and mowing down the enemy at will.

IT WAS JUST the sort of problem McCarter had feared, but anticipated.

A turbaned fighter was running up the far side of the motor pool, a tac radio in hand. He went to ground, and McCarter knew that if he sounded the alarm they'd have a major problem.

"Cal!"

"I saw him!"

McCarter charged for a point of intercept, two Jeeps north, while James vectored to a point to come up on the terrorist's rear. There was no time to do anything but bull into the play. As McCarter wheeled around the nose of the jeep, autofire broke out, bullets snapping past his scalp, tattooing the fender. He lurched back, the fanatic busy, he had glimpsed, juggling the tac radio and his weapon. Reprieve? McCarter wondered. No time to debate the matter.

Taking a deep breath, the Briton went for it. He heard the familiar burp of James's HK, but the Phoenix Force leader was back out in the open, an eye blink behind the ex-SEAL, holding back on the trigger of his own subgun. The double hosing of subgun fire seemed to lift the enemy gunner off his feet six inches or so, a sudden trampoline leap that found the radio and weapon flying away.

James had the radio in hand, checking transmitting light, listening for a response from the other end. The ex-SEAL shook his head, tossed it away, then combat instinct kicked in and he threw himself to the side. James cycloned into a pivot, firing his HK as he hurled himself for cover between the jeep and the transport. McCarter had already caught sight of the shadow boiling up from behind James, but he needed a split second for the ex-SEAL to clear his line of fire. The cry of pain from the terrorist, dark spurts erupting from his chest, hardly brought any relief to McCarter as he hit the shadow with a long burst, kicking him back.

Running, McCarter shouted, "Cal!"

"I'm all right."

James was back on his feet, and McCarter, feeding a fresh clip to his subgun, found a few armed al-Amin thugs darting around, firing as they ran.

There, then gone, falling and crunching up near the fiery ruins of their tent as Encizo, Manning and Hawkins mopped up.

McCarter needed a walk-through to check for live ones. The idea was to have this wrapped within two to three minutes. On the time clock, anything, he knew, from there on could happen.

He checked the carnage, the air ripe with cooked flesh and spilled blood. He found Encizo and Manning taking reads on their IR handhelds.

"I'm clear," Manning said, scanning the firestorm, then the wall of rock to the west.

"Rafe?"

"Looks good."

McCarter took the sensor from his belt, thumbed the button, turning on the screen. He had left two mini-motion detectors behind in their transport, one in the bed and the other fixed under the dashboard. His screen was clear.

The Briton glanced at the transport truck, looked north. The path of least resistance to the main camp was an arrow-straight ride that would bring them up to the fenceline of the installation. It would also leave them exposed to any sentries perched on the ridgeline, and they could easily roll into an ambush in the mouth of the gorge. The other route, the one he had mapped out with help from the CIA, was longer, harder. They would have to drive east, then veer northwest, snake a path through a tortuous maze of wadis. Farther out, but they would be able to come in on the enemy's blind side up to a point.

What would the late Colonel Joe or Chino have done in a situation like this? McCarter wondered.

The hard way, then—go east.

CHAPTER TWENTY-SEVEN

Nawir Wahjihab felt truly blessed by God. It was a moment to savor, give thanks. Surely he was being guided along, he knew, carried by the Almighty on a divine journey toward victory.

It was a glorious sight to behold, and despite the setbacks, the long boat ride to Morocco, the flight in the Learjet to the Saudi border, the drive here, he knew that annihilation of the Great Satan was within his grasp.

Surrounded by his four top lieutenants in charge of operations in Yemen, he gazed at the steel cylinder on the table. The Russian, Girmil, was babbling on about the aerosol converter, various component parts he had labored to piece together, whining how he needed this and that if he was to continue. If he didn't so desperately need the five Russians, Wahjihab would have unslung the AK-47 and shot them dead right there in the bowels of the cave. He waved a hand.

''Enough! Will it fly?''

The Russian hesitated, glancing at his four comrades. "Yes."

"That is all I need to know. How soon can you deliver me more?"

Girmil looked and sounded nearly frantic. "Deliver more? We need certain equipment."

Wahjihab shut his eyes, ran a hand over his scowl. "Write a list. I will get it for you."

"I need to ask you something."

"What?"

"How much longer do you intend to keep us prisoners here in this cave?"

That was a good question. He didn't have a ready answer. There were arrangements to make, seeing that the drone was safely hauled out of Yemen, and that was his top priority. He had contacts in Saudi Arabia who had assured him they could smuggle this Angel of Islam safely into America. He believed, and trusted they could do exactly that. He was no longer dealing with treacherous infidels and criminal waste like the Frenchman.

"As long as it takes."

The Russian looked set to protest, but thought better of it.

"You have provisions, not much, granted, down here," Wahjihab told them all, aware he needed to keep them happy somehow, softening his tone. Disgruntled workers could become sloppy. "Whatever you need, food, drink, cigarettes, I provide everything. I have videos, magazines brought to you. You are being amply compensated for your work. But I understand.''

''You do?'' Girmil said, sounding as if he didn't understand a damn thing.

''Very well. Let us say three more months, four at the very most. I will get you what you require to make at least three more drones. When that is finished, I will see that all of you receive a very handsome bonus on top of your fee. I will guarantee you safe passage to a country of your choosing where you may finish out your lives in peace and safety and whatever pleasures you demand. Can you hold on that much longer?''

Girmil nodded. The money talk, the belief that their time here as slave labor under armed guard was winding down apparently calmed whatever his storm of anxiety. ''Do you think maybe we can get out of this cave and breathe some fresh air for a while?''

''No,'' Wahjihab told them as gently as possible. He wished he could do more by way of creature comforts for them, allow them to walk around the camp, stretch their legs. But with American satellites, the infidel military and CIA crawling all over most of Yemen—but kept back from this area by his Yemeni officers and intelligence operatives engineering various ruses to steer them to ''suspected terrorist havens'' elsewhere—he couldn't risk having them discovered, an assault on the compound now. At least not until their work was finished and he was far away from any such catastrophe.

Yes, he admitted to himself, their quarters, like the entire facility, were primitive, literally a caveman existence. The hermetically sealed glass partition was edged up against the far wall, a small decon chamber, workbenches, crates strewed about the bowl-shaped depression. As originally planned, there was no exit, no way in or out except the main entrance, which could always be observed from the main compound, two sentries always standing guard at the mouth around the clock. ''Why don't you rest now? You have earned it.''

Girmil grumbled something, fell in with his comrades, but they moved off to their cots in the far corner.

Wahjihab turned to his warriors, pointed his AK-47 at the drone. ''Akhmed, see that this is packed up and secured immediately. Take it to my truck. Abu, set up the camera in the command post. The rest of you, remain here and keep a very close eye on the Russians.''

Wahjihab left them to their chores, swiftly moved up the rocky slope that would take him out of the cave to fresh air.

Mentally he began rehearsing the message he would deliver to al-Jazeera, another call to arms for all the faithful of Islam. Like the one taped session, months back, he would cover his face with a black hood, but announce to the infidels that he was the Sword of Islam speaking, wording the message in vague terms how the judgment of God would soon consume them.

Pleased, working on the script in his thoughts, he found two of his warriors running down the cave. A voice, edged with panic, sought him out, informing him repeated attempts had been made to contact the backup contingent to the south. With all the narrow escapes, aware he was being hunted by CIA killers wherever he walked, he wasn't taking any chances of getting cornered here, gunned down in Yemen.

Wahjihab froze in midstride, his mind racing, his men looking to him to take charge, when most of his thoughts were centered on immediate flight to the Saudi border. "Send a patrol there. Go!"

Something was wrong, but he had anticipated discovery of the compound by the infidels. He retraced his path, shouted at his men, "Faster! I want the drone out of here and on my truck in five minutes!"

They were going to be hit. By whom or how many, he didn't know. Or was he just paranoid? No sense in finding out if he was right or wrong about that.

He only knew he needed to get on his way, with the drone, within the next few minutes.

"WE'VE GOT PROBLEMS, mates. Looks like the hornet's nest is stirred. Go in, go hard, good luck. Everybody's on their own. Copy that, then go."

Gary Manning took in the flurry of activity, sensed the compound was on alert, armed figures scurrying all over the grounds, inside the fencing, near the front gate. McCarter's words rang through his ears, but the Briton was gone with James to hit the cave. Silently he wished them godspeed and good luck.

The nerve-racking drive through the darkest gorges he could have ever imagined, the Predator and GPS guiding them in, then a klick and change on foot, followed by a two-hundred-yard crawl, just to get to the fencing on the east side, and he was drenched in sweat, riding a rocket of pure adrenaline now.

They were there. Do it.

Manning knew there was no choice at that point, the small wire cutters snipping through the mesh fencing.

"Gary."

He glanced at Encizo, who pointed with the projectile launcher. "That crate on the cart. They're bailing. I'm thinking they have something they want out of here in a big hurry."

Manning heard the voices, raised in what sounded like alarm, across the compound, near the big Russian-made heavy machine gun. Five armed fanatics were busy hefting a large crate, sliding it into the bed of a transport truck. Another shadow was flying up on their back sides, barking out the orders, urging them on, arms flailing. Another group of six or seven looked ready to climb into another transport truck near the labor detail.

The installation, he quickly observed, wasn't much. One guard tower, a shadow up there now, but watching the commotion near the transport trucks. A massive tunnel-boring machine, a scattering of Jeeps, APCs, two tanks to his two o'clock, he figured a sixty-yard dash to cover and really start pouring it on. The squat command center, two saucer-shaped dishes on the roof, doubled as troop quarters, or so went the CIA intel. Right then, Manning saw at least a dozen armed enemy troops marching out of the structure. Figure a fly-by-night facility, ready to pack it up and run, which made sense to Manning. How the U.S. Special Forces had managed to not catch one word about this clandestine operation up until a few days ago escaped him. Beyond whatever they did or didn't do here was moot, but he could be sure some heads would get lopped off behind the shadows where the conspirators hid.

"Rafe, T.J., I'm going for the command center. Take those two trucks out after you give the bunch coming out of the C and C a blast into their futures. I'm going to blow the building, in case someone's in there on the horn. I'll give you the heads-up when I'm ready, but keep your distance. Get as close as you can when we breach, whatever cover you can take but fire at will."

Manning squeezed through the section of fencing

he'd cut away, wondering if and when the enemy would notice they were coming to take them out.

WAHJIHAB NEARLY SCREAMED in outrage when the first of two explosions rocked the night. They were under attack, no question, and he nearly puked, when he glanced toward the warriors who had been filing out of the C and C. They had been curious, he supposed, but whatever they were wondering went with them to Paradise as they were lost inside a fireball.

Wahjihab had come too far, so close now, to stand around and get killed. Let the others become martyrs, since God would surely take them home to Paradise if they held their ground, even went down to a warrior, just as long as they made certain he could live on to fulfill the dream of jihad.

His men, he saw, were darting all around the truck now, searching out their attackers, not a shot yet fired by any of them. Enraged, he had to run up to them, scream in their faces, demanding to know if the crate was securely in the bed.

The response was feeble, at best, Abed Salid clearly frightened but blurting out that the crate was on board, the Yemeni looking at his fearless leader, confused.

"Go!" Wahjihab bellowed at them, spraying a wild burst of autofire over their heads to get them moving.

He hurried toward the cab, the guard tower a smoking pall, he noticed, when two more explosions thundered across the compound. The group he had sent to find out why the others weren't responding to their radio transmissions was torn between shooting across the compound and piling into the transport truck, and the blast shredded their numbers. Frantic, gathering speed, he searched the area to the east, where his warriors seemed to be directing their fire now. Two shadows were charging, getting dangerously closer by the second, leapfrogging from the generator to the tunnel-boring machine, fully covered and able to pick targets at random.

He urged his warriors to take the battle to the invaders—there were only two of them, after all, what were they waiting for?—while silently imploring God to bless him with speedy and safe passage out of there.

The machine-gun nest, he saw, was blown apart. It was more than he could stomach, wondering if he would make it out of there, then told himself to be strong, keep that faith he had so often told other Muslims to cling to in times of peril, many of whom were already dead and gone to Paradise.

Wahjihab flung open the door, found the keys in the ignition.

MCCARTER, SPLITTING off from James, both of them directly above the cave entrance, hit the sentries with a burst of subgun fire up their spines, flinging them away, a double nosedive in the dirt.

The war for Broken Sword was on, McCarter hating like hell to give the word that everybody was hung out there, on his own with nothing but guts, skill and trust and faith in whoever was by his side. The plan to go in quiet and mine the installation with C-4 while the two of them penetrated the cave was out the window.

Plan B?

No such thing, he knew.

On the plus side, the Briton knew that by hitting Target One first they had shaved the enemy numbers down to under thirty, provided the CIA's head count held.

And assuming no al-Amin radioman called in some reinforcements they might all stand a chance of nailing it down, call in their backup, gunships on standby, HAZMAT specialists ready to secure the cave.

McCarter hustled down the incline, took up post beside the entrance, the sounds of explosions tearing up the main compound telling him, if nothing else, that Encizo, Manning and Hawkins were in and going for the jugular.

The Briton heard voices shouting in both Arabic and Russian, figured the echo carried back there thirty, fifty yards. How many would they find? Six, ten? Intel from the CIA's mysterious source indicated the way in wasn't mined or booby-trapped.

They'd see about that.

As far as he was concerned, the Russian microbiologists, having sold their souls to the Devil, were meat on the hook.

He nodded at James, the compound on fire, shadows going down in a stretch of no-man's-land, one truck lurching ahead in flight, then swept into the cave.

CHAPTER TWENTY-EIGHT

"Fire in the hole! Acknowledge!"

"We're clear and covered but we're a little busy, Gary!" Manning heard Encizo shout over the com link, the racket of weapons fire competing for the transmission. "Do it!"

Manning was already in flight, MP-5 a roving dial, a brief stutter drilling a shadow to his ten o'clock, a smoking shadow that shimmied out of the haze of the little Cuban's opening round but now catching a 3-round send-off to the chest.

A few terrorists, firing assault rifles on the back-pedal, vanished into the smoke, claiming refuge inside the C and C.

If they wanted Paradise, he thought, they could have it.

There was withering autofire from near the flaming garbage heap of the transport truck, Encizo and Hawkins dropping a blanket of lead and 40 mm rounds that eighty-sixed that al-Amin problem.

Manning dropped to cover behind the tunnel-boring machine, saw his teammates shielded by a T-72, his hellbox on, and hit the button.

Twenty-five pounds of exploding C-4, he thought, hitting the ground, covering his head, had a way of getting people's attention.

WAHJIHAB WAS RACING by the C and C, grinding gears, gaining speed, when the explosion sent wreckage blasting through the windows, the windshield obliterated and spraying glass in his face, a gust of superheated wind sucking the air out of his lungs.

He was tumbling, his head banging off the roof, something hot and sharp lancing into his eye, blinding him, a scream bubbling from his lips.

MANNING RODE OUT the blast, aware that the transport truck with its deadly payload was racing for the fence, Encizo confirming it over the com link. He was up and moving, ready to rejoin his teammates even as the sky burned and rained down the rubble.

He had some idea, considering what they were creating here, of what was in the bed.

An Angel of Islam.

Hawkins and Manning fell in beside Encizo, who was already going after the downed vehicle, a smoking wreck dumped on its side by the tremendous blast, the Stony Man trio searching the carnage around them, dodging rubble as best they could.

"Gary, that truck's in bad shape," Encizo said. "I

smell gas. If that truck contains a cylinder and the seals are broken, and Ebola is spewing out, it might be spread through the air if the tank goes up."

"Hold it, Rafe!"

The door on the driver's side was thrust open. The muzzle of an AK-47 poked out first, followed by a bloody mask of feral hate. The gunner was gagging on either blood or terror, the weapon swinging toward the Stony Man warriors. Encizo and his teammates opened up with weapons, firing together. Their triburst, directed at the face and head, decapitated the terrorist.

There was a cloud of blood and gore, then the body plunged out of sight.

MCCARTER HUGGED the wall, opposite James, their subguns up, the shouting, just beyond what he was told was a rise that led down into the arena-shaped work area, growing to shrill panic. It was a babble of Russian, Arabic and English, coming closer, out of the light down there.

"No standoff," the Briton told James. "Take them out. Armed or not."

James nodded.

The Phoenix Force leader and the ex-SEAL cut the distance quickly, fifteen feet from the edge of the rise when they appeared, heads first, then a shoving match ensued between white coats and gunmen.

"Drop your weapons! We are walking out of here! We have the Russians!"

McCarter took it in for all of one second. Five hostages, all in white smocks, and what appeared four gunmen, hanging back, using the Russians as human armor. The shouter railed on in English for another heartbeat, assuming or knowing they were Westerners, then McCarter and James fired, holding back on their triggers, the bodies doing a jerky dance before dropping to the ground.

The Briton moved ahead to check the work area, but the silence beyond the litter of bodies told him it was all clear down there.

They were all alone with the dead.

AS THE ELDER SON, Abdullah Wahjihab knew that someday he would inherit the bulk of the money, the power and the responsibility of the jihad.

He figured he was due, after all, as overseer of much of the finances that kept the dream alive.

The kingdom then would one day belong to him. Naturally he would have to share a good portion with his brother, but the young man had always looked to him with respect, asking advice, guidance.

No problem, then, claiming the lion's share.

Respect.

His brother would understand.

He followed his father's explicit instructions not to contact him over the sat phone until the jet had safely landed near the Saudi border. There, they would be met by the Saudi cell, driven to the compound.

He felt the eyes of his younger brother and the five holy men watching him, all of them sitting comfortably in the well, sipping tea, the air-conditioning a nice chilly breeze. Perhaps they were wondering, he thought, why he was smiling. If their faith was weak—and he believed he had put to rest all their questions the night before—it would be shored up in a matter of hours, once they saw the fruits of his father's labor.

He stared out the window of their German custom-made limousine, wincing behind his sunglasses as he adjusted his eyes to the fierce glare baking the desert wasteland beyond the airfield.

He could sense they were about to begin firing off another round of questioning, forcing him to calm their nerves, hand out the blanket reassurances, when he saw the dust cloud rising in the distance, out in the desert, to the west.

He peered, watching, wondering if the shimmering heat was playing tricks on his eyes, when the oversize white van materialized, gaining speed. It seemed to be charging on some intercept course directly for them, bounding once over a break in the land, back on line.

"What is it?"

His younger brother, edging up beside him, staring out the window, at the vehicle.

"I am not sure."

He watched the van, feeling the sweat break out on his brow even though the air in the limo was a comfortable sixty-five degrees.

There was something about the manner in which that van, now racing onto the runway, pricked his anxiety. It was almost as if it had been out there, in the desert, waiting for their arrival.

The limo stopped, and he felt the first icy chill of creeping fear, something warning him they needed to back up and get as far away from that van as possible.

He was pounding on the glass partition that separated them from his armed chauffeur when he saw five armed men burst out of the van. They were running directly for the limo, the shouts and screams of the five holy men and his brother piercing his ears for a brief moment, then bullets began blasting in the windows.

THE LONG NIGHT HAD BLED into another day of slaughter, but McCarter was feeling no weariness, no anxiety, much less having any qualms about what they were now doing.

Confirmation made of the targets, and logistics already worked out between the CIA and the Farm, and they had parachuted from a C-130 right before dawn to the waiting Company van, waiting for the word to move in from the CIA surveillance team.

The sons of Wahjihab had been under surveillance

for months, but McCarter wasn't interested in the basic facts. The CIA tail had alerted the Briton they had just arrived at the old man's private airfield.

All they needed to know.

He had been tired of sweating it out in the van anyway, anxious to greet the terror party.

They went in, full-bore hosing of the limo, five MP-5 subguns riddling the vehicle, stem to stern, windows, door panels absorbing the barrage, the limo shuddering. The driver's window erupted in flying glass, slivers, dappled with red, winking in sunlight, but McCarter fired on. The pilot stepped into the hatchway of the executive jet, his shout of alarm snaring McCarter's attention that way, but he found Encizo and James turned their fire on him, blowing him back into the cabin.

The luxury ride, McCarter knew, had just become their hearse.

One clip burned through, and McCarter, marching with his commandos up to the side of the limo, slapped home another magazine, opened up again for two heartbeats, then gave the word to cease fire.

He could hear the wheezing from inside, one of them choking on his own blood, a punctured lung most likely. Aware their own time was up, McCarter took his tac radio and raised Grimaldi. Stony Man's ace relayed he was on the way to the evac site, a four-minute or so ride across the desert, then the Huey gunship would scoop them up. A CIA base in the

United Arab Emirates was their next temporary layover stop.

McCarter listened as the gasping for air grew louder, moving up to the limo, subgun out and aimed through the shattered window.

They were twitching, a mass of scarlet slumped in the well, a few glazed eyes staring sightlessly upward. He looked around the well, found the elder son clutching his chest, a pitiful look of utter despair and confusion on his face.

McCarter primed a frag grenade, told his men to fall back to the van and dumped the steel egg into the vehicle.

EPILOGUE

"It would appear congratulations are in order. For somebody, that is."

Hal Brognola found the shadow man sitting alone on the bench in the Arlington park off Wilson Boulevard, puffing on a cigarette. There was another fat white package next to him.

The big Fed wasn't sure how to take the man again, wondering what he wanted, how much he knew, but he was greatly relieved the Stony Man warriors were still breathing, and soon to be on their way back to the Farm. His anxiety, or so he hoped, was over for the moment.

It was a dead-of-night rendezvous, the shadow man reaching out earlier, a cutout of a cutout informing Brognola the mystery spook wanted a few words.

Why not? Brognola had figured. There was a lot of cleanup that needed attention in the coming days in Wonderland.

Brognola took a seat.

The shadow man patted the envelope. ''A little something for you.''

''When do you call in all these favors?''

''No markers. Relax. Enjoy victory. I'm sure you know that this war on terrorism is far from over. Funny how things work out, though. Seems Wahjihad and sons are out of the picture, five mullahs down below, wondering why they're in Hell when they thought God promised them Paradise for killing innocent people in the name of jihad. This thing, it's going to go on for years, maybe until the end of time, maybe one of them gets a nuke, or another Angel of Islam comes around, floating down Ebola over one of our cities.

''Go on, take that package. There's still a lot of work to do. What happened in Yemen and Oman and down in Mexico... I'm thinking, well, I'm thinking doomsday was just put off a little while longer.''

Brognola looked away, afraid the shadow man was all too right.

THE

Destroyer®

BLOODY TOURISTS

With the tiny Caribbean tourist trap of Union Island looking to declare its independence from the U.S., president-elect Greg Grom launches a "Free Union Island" movement, touring Dixieland to rally support. And amongst all the honky-tonks and hee-haws, some weird stuff is happening. Ordinary beer-swilling, foot-stomping yahoos are running amok, brawling like beasts on a rampage. Remo Williams is pretty sure Greg is slipping something into the local brew, but the why is another matter for him to solve.

Available in January 2004 at your favorite retail outlet.

Or order your copy now by sending your name, address, zip or postal code, along with a check or money order (please do not send cash) for $6.50 for each book ordered ($7.99 in Canada), plus 75¢ postage and handling ($1.00 in Canada), payable to Gold Eagle Books, to:

In the U.S.
Gold Eagle Books
3010 Walden Avenue
P.O. Box 9077
Buffalo, NY 14269-9077

In Canada
Gold Eagle Books
P.O. Box 636
Fort Erie, Ontario
L2A 5X3

Please specify book title with your order.
Canadian residents add applicable federal and provincial taxes.

GDEST134